The Revelation Room

Mark Tilbury

Praise For Mark Tilbury's The Abattoir of Dreams.

"This was a gritty and twisted read with so much heart and now if you'll excuse me I'll be on Amazon buying Tilbury's other books."
Amy Sullivan @Novelgossip

"Dark and cruel but incredibly compelling. I can see this one ending up in my top 10 books of the year and it will probably haunt me for a while yet."
Dee Light @Noveldeelights

"This is a master piece of writing with nothing like it around. Very violent and descriptive and extremely addictive."
Susan Hampson @BooksFromDuskTillDawn

"Mind-blowing, heartbreaking, thrilling! A gripping story that makes you feel confused and cold and utterly shaken with every succeeding detail of the dark secrets of the past unravelling."
Caroline Vincet @BitsAboutBooks

"This is a gripping and heart-breaking book that is impossible to put down. What could have been a book that was too dark and emotional for some readers has been successfully interlaced with happy heart-warming scenes to make it a brilliant book that will stay with the reader for some time, maybe forever."
Jill Burkinshaw @BooksnAll

Dedicated to George Adam Simmons, my Grandson.

Chapter One

Geoff Whittle stood in a tree twenty feet above the ground and stared at death. Death stared back at him in the guise of an automatic rifle with sunlight glinting off the barrel. A man wearing bright yellow overalls levelled the weapon at Geoff's head. Geoff propped his long-range camera in the fork of two branches, wrapped his arms around the trunk for support, and tried to make contact with God for the first time since his dog had got run over when he was a kid.

A short fat man accompanying the shooter asked, 'Who are you?'

Geoff searched his mind for lies. Terror shut down his imagination. The man with the rifle had shoulder-length brown hair and a goatee beard. He also had a nasty twitch in one eye.

Fat Man said, 'Shoot him.'

Geoff's insides turned to dust. 'No. Please don't—'

'Shoot him, Tweezer.'

'Is that wise, Father?'

'What do you mean?'

'What if he's a cop?'

Fat Man hesitated for a moment, and then said, 'He's an agent of the Devil. Shoot him.'

And so Tweezer did. The bullet ripped through Geoff's left shoulder. He felt a roar of intense burning pain. His legs buckled. The tree seemed to rock back and forth as if caught in a strong wind.

'Shoot him again.'

This time the bullet tore a hole in his right knee. He lost his tenuous grip on the tree and tumbled head first to the ground.

He instinctively put his hands out to soften the blow. Both wrists snapped on impact. His right shoulder dislocated. He screamed as the pain sent shock waves through his body. Something cracked in his spine. Instant numbness rolled down his legs and into both feet.

'Is he dead, Father?'

A few moments silence, broken only by a bird singing its song – perhaps of death – high in the tree. Sunlight burned his eyes. Two blurred shapes above him. The rifle pointing at him.

'He lives,' Fat Man said. 'Satan's own defies mortality.'

'Shall I finish him?'

'Not yet. We need to find out who he is. Where he's from. Fetch Bubba. Get him to take our guest down into the Revelation Room.'

Tweezer was about to head off when Fat Man stopped him. 'Haven't you forgotten something?'

'No, Father. You asked—'

'You think it wise to leave me unarmed?'

A nervous laugh. Tweezer handed over the gun. 'Sorry, Father.'

'And be quick. We don't know who else might be lurking about. Get word to Marcus on the tower and tell him to be vigilant. Any sign of the police, and we go into lockdown.'

'Yes, Father.'

Fat Man nudged Geoff's side with the end of the rifle. 'What brings you to Penghilly's Farm?'

Geoff opened his mouth and issued a gurgle. The sun scorched his face. 'My… back… is… broken….'

'How unfortunate. Perhaps it will stop you scaling trees in future and spying on innocent people.'

'I…can't…feel…my…legs….'

'That speaks more of demonic possession than injury. You don't fool me with your pitying sounds. My eyes see deeper than the colour of cowardice.'

A huge shadow rolled across the ground. It glided over Geoff, and took him away to a beautiful, dark, painless place.

Awake again. Being carried down concrete steps on the shoulders of a tall thin man. Through a room with bright lights, and what looked like hundreds of cannabis plants. Perhaps a hallucination?

Tweezer unlocked a door at the end of the room. 'Put him on the floor by the wall, Bubba.'

Bubba deposited Geoff on the dusty concrete floor.

'Sit him up, facing the wall.'

Bubba did. Geoff flopped forward, head almost resting in his lap.

'You can go now, Bubba.'

The big man walked from the room without a single word or a backward glance.

Tweezer leaned the rifle up against the wall. 'If you want my advice, you'll answer Father Ebb's questions honestly.'

Or what? You'll hurt me?

Ebb appeared a few minutes later. 'All quiet?'

'Yes, Father.'

'Have you taken leave of your senses, Tweezer?'

'No, Father.'

'Then please explain why the prisoner is being attended to without a rifle?'

Tweezer scurried to the wall and retrieved the weapon. 'Sorry, Father.'

'Slackness costs lives.'

'Yes, Father.'

'I shall pray for you, Tweezer. Pray that you and your senses shall one day be reunited.'

Tweezer shuffled awkwardly. 'Yes, Father.'

Ebb turned his attention to Geoff. 'Who are you?'

Geoff didn't answer. He prayed that death would come quickly.

Ebb walked to one side of him and held a mobile phone in front of his face. 'This yours?'

Geoff bit down on his lip hard enough to draw blood.

Ebb snatched the phone away. 'Must be. It was in your pocket. Along with a Ford Fiesta car key and a front door key.'

Then why are you asking?

'Pay-as-you-go phone. No contacts. No details. No wallet. No ID. What does that tell you Tweezer?'

'Tells me he's up to something.'

'We need to search the tree. See if he's secreted anything up there.'

'Shall I go now, Father?'

'Yes. And tell Sister Alice I require her presence down in the Revelation Room.'

'As you wish, Father.'

Ebb paced up and down. 'They say God moves in mysterious ways, but Satan makes the Lord look positively straightforward, doesn't he?'

'If... you... say... so....'

'Do you know who I am?'

'No.'

'What is your business here?'

'Nothing.'

A lengthy silence. And then Ebb said, 'Pleading ignorance will get you nowhere. I've got all the time in the world, Mr Tree Man.'

Geoff begged his mind to help; it was otherwise engaged, dealing with the pain tearing through his upper body.

Footsteps walked across the room. And then a woman's voice. 'Who is he, Father?'

'Satan's very own, Sister Alice. Satan's very own.'

'What does he want?'

'What Satan always wants. To disrupt God's plan. To interrupt His work.'

'What are we going to do with him?'

'Find out the true nature of his mission, Sister. Find out who sent him.'

'Maybe we should just kill him.'

'Not until I know who he is.'

'Brother Tweezer said he was up a tree overlooking the courtyard.'

'Indeed. Tweezer's searching the tree as we speak. The Imposter had a camera. Taking pictures of the farm.'

'Why would Satan want pictures?'

'That's for the Imposter to tell.'

'What if he won't talk?'

'He will.'

The confidence of this last statement sent a chill through Geoff's body.

'What if he dies before we have the information, Father?'

'God won't allow that.'

'If you're sure, Father.'

'Are you questioning my wisdom, Sister Alice?'

'No, Father. It's just… well… the unpredictability of the mortal body.'

'I'm well aware of the fallibility of the human body. But this one has a demon lurking within it.'

'Is it wise to do battle with a demon, Father?'

'Is it wise to turn a blind eye?'

'No, Father.'

'Anyway, I didn't summon you here to question the validity of my purpose. I want you to shave the Imposter of all its facial hair.'

'Why?'

'So as we can search for the mark of the beast.'

'Okay.'

'And see if you can stop the bleeding.'

'Yes, Father.'

'He can have some water. Enough to nourish him. Just in case….'

'As you wish, Father.'

'Make sure he remains facing the wall. I don't want him to be stimulated in any way.'

'I understand.'

'Right. I think we're finished here for now. When you come back to tend to him, do not engage in conversation with him.

Suppress any feelings of pity. This is a wild animal. Remain vigilant at all times.'

'Don't worry, Father. I won't let my guard slip for a second.'

Geoff heard them leave the room. The door close. The key turn in the lock. He wanted to scream. Bang his head against the wall. Die before Ebb had the chance to torture him. He thought about home. His wife, Anne, and his only son, Ben. How they would cope if he died.

Not If. When.

He'd parked Ben's car about a mile away from the farm on a housing estate. An old yellow Fiesta. Not as noticeable as his own BMW. Far better for trailing cult members.

Fat lot of good that's done you.

He forced himself to sit up. He looked at his useless legs. His torn trousers. The only blessing was he couldn't feel a thing below his waist. Not even the piss that stained his crotch. His breath came in ragged gasps. His heart galloped across his chest. One final glimmer of hope. A watch phone. A freebie from the owner of A1 Security. Geoff thought it more of a gimmick than practical, and the battery life was minimal, but it was all he had.

He held his right arm in front of his face. His shoulder shook with the exertion of this simple movement. Tears blurred his vision. Two watch faces. Two straps. He squeezed his eyes shut, wiped them with the back of his hand, looked again. One watch. He pressed a button on the side of the screen and turned it on. Low battery. One bar. He brought up a menu, selected Ben's number and hit dial.

He didn't even know if he would stay conscious long enough to make this call.

Chapter Two

Tiny pearls of sweat glistened on Ben Whittle's forehead as he carried Old Joe into Feelham Pentecostal Church in a brown canvas holdall. The bag had rubbed a sore patch on the outside of his right knee during the two-mile walk to the church. If Ben didn't know better, he would have sworn Old Joe was putting on weight. He walked through the hall, trainers screeching on the parquet flooring. There was a cacophony of shouts and jibes coming from the table tennis area where a dozen kids jostled for exclusive rights to the table. Andy, an older boy of eighteen, attempted to organise them into a cohesive group. He waved his arms in the air like a conductor trying to coax melody from chaos.

Pastor Tom White looked at Ben and rolled his eyes.

Ben raised a hand. 'How's it going, Tom?'

'Don't ask. It's like trying to take charge of a pack of puppies.'

Even in the mid-July heat, Pastor Tom was wearing his customary tweed jacket, brown corduroy trousers and trilby hat. A tall man with size thirteen feet and arthritic hands, Ben thought Tom looked as if he was some kind of crude puppet that didn't quite make it into the cast of Thunderbirds.

Tom had set the church up five years ago in a disused prefab concrete shell that had once housed Feelham Girl Guides. From the outside, with its pebble-dashed grey walls and barred windows, the building looked better suited to housing prisoners of war than worshippers. But as Pastor Tom was fond of saying, 'it's what's on the inside that counts'.

There was a poster taped to the wall behind the stage proclaiming *The Power of God*. To the side of the poster, a large wooden cross bore testament to the true nature of the church.

7

'I'll just pop Old Joe out back first, then I'll be right with you.'

'Get yourself a drink, lad. You look frazzled.'

Ben walked through an open doorway into a back room which served as both a restroom and refreshment hub. He put the bag on a pine table and tried to shake pins and needles out of his arm.

Maddie White, Pastor Tom's daughter, peered through a serving hatch that separated the restroom from the small kitchenette where she was busy filling plastic beakers with orange squash. 'Hi, Ben. How's it going?'

'Not too bad. I walked for a change. I'm so unfit.'

Maddie wiped her hands on a tea towel. 'You look all right.'

Ben's heart glowed radioactive. 'I might look a lot better if I exercised more than just my fingers on a computer keyboard.'

Maddie laughed and tucked a strand of loose hair behind her ear. She joined Ben in the rest room. Dressed in bright yellow dungarees, a white tee-shirt, and red and white spotted canvas shoes, she looked like summer to Ben.

Maddie tapped the canvas bag. 'How's Old Joe?'

'Lemme out,' a muffled voice demanded from inside the bag.

Maddie grinned. 'Poor thing. He must be roasted in there.'

'Don't encourage him.'

Too late. 'Come on, it's dark in here. I'm claustrophobic. How would you like to be stuffed inside a body bag?'

'You'll be stuffed all right if you don't stop moaning.'

'Aw, let him out, poor thing.'

Ben unzipped the bag to reveal Old Joe, a ventriloquist dummy which he used to entertain the kids with before the Bible readings. Old Joe only had one eye. It stared permanently to the left courtesy of a broken mechanism. His brown serge suit had fallen victim to moth attacks, but he was a tramp, and tramps didn't have their suits dry cleaned, did they?

Maddie leaned over and spoke as if addressing a baby in a crib. 'Hey, Old Joe, how are you?'

'Okay, for someone zipped up in a body bag.'

'You look very handsome.'

'That's the kinda girl I like.'

Some of Maddie's blonde hair tumbled forward. 'He's so sweet.'

'Don't say that. You'll make his head swell.'

'She can say what she likes. It's her prer-og-ative.'

Maddie faced Ben. 'You're so good with him. He really sounds like he's talking.'

'I am talking,' Old Joe said.

Maddie smiled. 'I can't even see your lips moving.'

'He's the dummy. I'm the smart one,' Old Joe said.

Ben wagged a finger. 'That's enough of your cheek.'

'Get me out of here. I'm stiff as a board.'

Ben shook his head. 'No.'

'You're heartless. Isn't he heartless, Maddie?'

'Heart of stone.'

'I'll zip the bag up if you keep whining,' Ben promised.

'See if I care.'

Ben zipped up the bag.

'Hey. Come on. I was kidding.'

Ben grinned. It was one of the many ways Pastor Tom had taught Ben to conceal lip movement. 'Sleight of lip,' Tom called it.

Maddie straightened up. 'Aw, let him out. He's adorable.'

'Don't encourage him.'

'How would you like to be dressed in a suit in this weather?' Old Joe asked. 'You need to buy me a swimming costume.'

'I need to buy you a gag.'

'I love him,' Maddie said.

'Marry me,' Old Joe pleaded.

'If you buy me a diamond ring.'

'I'll buy you three.'

'And where are you going to get the money to buy diamonds?' Ben asked. 'You're just a tatty old tramp.'

'I'll hustle.'

Maddie laughed. Sunshine poured into her eyes. 'Would you like a drink?'

'Scotch on the rocks.'

Ben wagged a finger at the bag. 'Not you, Hobo.'

'I'm as dry as a desert.'

Ben pretended to ignore him. 'I wouldn't mind a glass of orange, thanks.'

Maddie fetched his drink from the kitchenette. 'Busy at work?'

Her hand brushed against his as she handed him the plastic beaker. It felt like velvet. 'A bit. Dad's working on a case at the moment.'

'What's the case? Or is it sworn to secrecy?'

'It's just a missing girl. She's joined a cult. Dad's tracked them down to a farm out in the sticks somewhere. He's got the place under surveillance. He's trying to get photos of the girl to take back to her parents. Just to confirm she's there.'

'Sounds dangerous.'

'He'll be all right.'

'Those cults creep me out. I remember reading about that one in America. Waco. They all died in a fire when the FBI stormed it. Killed themselves. Seventy-odd men, women and children. Terrible.'

'That's America for you. This lot probably worship the moon and drink chicken blood.'

'I'll ask my dad to pray for them.'

Ben wondered if Maddie could also get Pastor Tom to ask God to grant his father the virtue of patience while he was about it. 'Thanks.'

Maddie looked at her watch. 'Better get cracking; it's nearly eight.'

Ben drained his drink. 'Wish me luck.'

'Good luck. I'll come and watch the table tennis tournament as soon as I've finished doing the rolls.'

Ben was about to walk back to the hall when his mobile rang. He fished it out of his jeans. His father's watch-phone number. He pressed to accept the call. 'Dad?'

A breathless rasping noise gurgled through the earpiece.

'Dad?'

The rasping noise turned into a whine and then a deep growl.

'Dad? Is that you?'

A long drawn out wheeze. 'I…'

'What's wrong? Where are you?'

'I'm…'

'Have you had an accident?'

'Dying…'

Ben's stomach lurched. Goosebumps hatched all over his body. 'What's happened?'

'No… time… they're… coming…'

Ben looked behind him. 'Who's coming?'

His father gasped. It sounded as if he was trying to suck in breath through gravel.

'I'll call the police. Where are you?'

His father coughed and wheezed. 'No… cops…'

'Dad?'

'No… cops… he'll… kill… me….'

'Where are you?'

The phone went dead. Ben shook it as if trying to revive his father's voice. He pressed it back to his ear. 'Dad? Can you hear me?'

Maddie put a hand on Ben's arm. 'What is it?'

Ben gawked at the phone. He tried to gather his thoughts, but it was like trying to gather feathers on a windy hilltop. 'It's my dad.'

'What's wrong? Has he had an accident?'

Ben struggled for words. 'Oh, Jesus, Maddie, he sounded in a bad way. Like he couldn't breathe.'

'Ring him back.'

Ben tried. 'No answer.' He tossed his phone on the table and paced around the room. 'What am I supposed to do now?'

'Call the police.'

'He told me not to. He was adamant about that.'

'Perhaps he's had an accident. He might be concussed,' Maddie tried.

Ben shook his head. 'But he would've just told me to call an ambulance.'

'Do you think it's got anything to do with this cult?'

Ben remembered Maddie's earlier reference to Waco and shuddered. 'God knows. But he rang me on his watch-phone. That means he's either broken his other phone or someone's taken it off him.'

'Try him again.'

Ben did. Again, no answer. The watch-phone didn't have a messaging facility. It was a straight dial-in and dial-out device. He tossed his phone back on the table and slumped in a chair. 'Shit.'

Maddie reached down and put her hand on Ben's. Normally, this action would have written a love letter and posted it straight to Ben's heart. Instead, he flinched, stood up, and started pacing around the room again.

'Try to calm down, Ben. Do you know where this farm is?'

Ben shook his head. 'I don't have a clue. He never tells me anything. He goes off for days on end sometimes. One time he got beat up and had to go to casualty. He never said a word about who did it or why. It's just the way he is.'

Pastor Tom appeared in the doorway, his red and black checked shirt patched with sweat. 'When you're ready, big guy? They're all raring to go.'

Maddie walked over to her father. 'Ben can't help tonight.'

Tom looked at Ben, eyebrows raised. 'What's wrong, son?'

Maddie answered for him. 'Ben's got a problem at home.'

'Oh?'

'You'll have to do the table tennis tournament on your own.'

Pastor Tom frowned. 'Don't worry about the tournament. I'll get Andy to see to that. I'll be right back.'

Chapter Three

Ben told Pastor Tom about the phone call and the case that his father was working on.

For once, those clear blue eyes looked troubled. 'Maybe you should just call the police, anyway.'

Maddie tightened her ponytail. 'You heard what Ben said; his father told him not to.'

Tom didn't look convinced. 'But they're professionals. They'll have the proper experience to deal with this.'

Ben shook his head. 'I can't risk that.'

'Perhaps your dad's not thinking straight,' Tom said. 'He might be disorientated. Wandering around dazed somewhere.'

'I reckon the cult's got him,' Ben said.

Tom took off his hat, pulled a handkerchief from his breast pocket and mopped his brow. 'Has this cult got a name?'

Waco popped into Ben's mind. 'I don't know.'

'And you have no idea where it might be?'

Ben shook his head. 'It'll probably be in Oxfordshire somewhere. He doesn't like to rack up too many miles.'

Tom put his hat back on. 'That's a start.'

'That narrows it down to the whole county,' Maddie said. 'Should be simple.'

'I'm not saying it is simple,' Tom said. 'But when there's a mountain to climb, you have no choice but to start at the foot of it.'

Ben didn't feel equipped to climb Salisbury Hill, let alone a mountain. 'And what am I supposed to do if by some miracle I find this cult? Abseil down the roof and burst through the window like the SAS?'

'You'd be surprised what you can do when the Lord challenges you.'

'My mother will go into meltdown.'

'Let's just try to deal with one thing at a time,' Tom said. 'Do you have an address for the folks that hired your dad?'

'It'll be written in the appointments book. But they won't know where the cult is, will they? That's why they hired us.'

'They must have given your dad some information to work with.'

The air was hot and heavy. Now he knew how Old Joe felt being zipped up in his 'body bag'. Why did this have to happen? Youth club was supposed to be the highlight of his week. He'd spent the last few nights practising new jokes with Old Joe. Now the joke was on him. He couldn't get over how weak and scared his father had sounded. How could he be reduced to such a quivering wreck? His father, the chin-up, back-straight ex-policeman who'd set up Whittle Investigations after taking early retirement from the force.

'Ben?' Maddie prompted.

'I can't think straight. My head's all over the place.'

Tom fiddled with the rim of his hat. 'It's your choice, son. You either call the police, or you can try to work something out yourself.'

Ben groaned. 'I can barely manage my hair, let alone a rescue mission.'

'You're stronger than you think, son.'

'And what am I supposed to tell my mother?'

Tom formed a steeple with his fingers. 'Explain to her as best you can what has happened.'

'Have you met my mother? She frets over what to cook for dinner.'

'So reassure her.'

Ben laughed. 'If I tell her I'm going to rescue my father from a cult, she'll ring the undertakers to arrange both of our funerals.'

Tom touched Ben's hand. 'I shall pray for your mother in her hour of need.'

Ben didn't believe in God; not as a single entity sitting up in Heaven listening to prayers and dishing out salvation. But he thanked Pastor Tom, anyway. Whatever the rights and wrongs of religion, Tom's intentions were good. As for his mother, she might need tying to a chair and shooting with a horse tranquilliser dart. 'You don't know my mother.'

'The Lord does, son. The Lord knows your mother better than she knows herself. Would you like me to come home with you?'

Ben took a deep breath. He needed to get his head straight. 'I don't want to put you to any trouble.'

'It's no trouble.'

'She's going to fall to bits, Tom.'

'Then it's your job to put her back together again. People have an amazing capacity to cope. Incredible resilience. I didn't think I would ever get over my wife's brutal murder. I rejected everything. I even lost my faith for a while. But guess what?'

Ben shook his head and set off firecrackers in his neck.

'I got through it. I picked myself up. I had a two-year old little girl who needed me. Bit by bit, I put the jigsaw back together again. And you can do the same, son. You just need to trust the process of life.'

'I'm not as strong as you, Tom.'

'Nonsense. Life makes you strong. The tests that the Lord gives us are all designed to strengthen us. After Susan died, I blamed God. Shoved the lot of it at His door. Why was I being punished? I was in Rwanda trying to help. Trying to make a difference. I'd dedicated my life to teaching the disadvantaged, giving hope to the poor, so why did He take Susan? She wasn't even thirty years old.'

'I'm sorry, Tom, I didn't mean to—'

'I didn't think I was cut out to raise a little girl on my own. Come back to England and start again from scratch. We were all set to live our lives out in Rwanda. We had plans. Simple plans for a simple life. But the thing is, Ben, I found the strength, because God gave me the strength. Slowly but surely, my faith returned. I started teaching again. I raised Maddie as best as I could. I lived again. And you will find the strength, too.'

Ben wanted to believe him, but it was hard to have faith when you'd spent most of your childhood at the mercy of bullies just because you had a stammer and a mop of hair that resembled a bird's nest.

'The Lord trusts you, son. The Lord has faith in you. Susan's death, as terrible as it was, as heart-breaking as it was, was God's way of putting me to the test and giving me the strength and courage to succeed.'

'And what happens if I don't want to accept the test?'

'That's your choice, son. It's what we call freewill.'

'Come on, Ben,' Maddie said. 'You can do this.'

Ben looked into her beautiful green eyes. He wanted to thump his chest and declare himself ready for battle, but he was just plain old Ben Whittle. He still slept with the light on at twenty-two years of age, for God's sake.

Tom wedged his hat back on his head. 'Come on, son. Let's get you and Old Joe home.'

Ben stood up. He felt like a condemned man about to walk to the gallows. He picked up the canvas holdall. For once, Old Joe was quiet.

Chapter Four

Ben led Tom and Maddie into the front room where his mother was watching *Coronation Street*.

Anne Whittle looked from one to the other like a dormouse contemplating cats. 'Is something wrong?'

Ben's stomach churned. 'We need to talk to you.'

'Why? What is it?'

'Let's go inside.'

They followed Anne along the hallway and into the front room. She muted the telly. 'Well?'

'Sit down, Mum.'

'I'd rather stand, if it's all very well with you.'

Ben looked at Pastor Tom.

'It's your husband,' Tom said.

'Geoff? What about him?'

'We think something may have happened to him.'

Anne frowned. 'What in tuppence is that supposed to mean?'

Tom removed his trilby. 'We don't know, Mrs Whittle. He phoned Ben asking for help.'

Anne's hands flitted around her face like nervous birds looking for somewhere to roost. 'Help? Why? Where is he?'

'He may have been abducted,' Tom said.

'Who the hell by?'

'You know the missing girl he was looking for?' Ben said. 'The one that joined a cult?'

Anne nodded.

'We reckon the cult's got him.'

Anne looked at her son as if he'd just told her his father had been abducted by aliens. 'I knew something was wrong. I told

Aunt Mary he hadn't phoned all day. He always phones. Even when he's busy.' And then, as an afterthought. 'Of course, she made her usual snide remarks about him probably having an affair.'

'I'm sorry, Mum.'

Anne walked over to a mahogany coffee table and picked up her mobile phone. 'I knew something was wrong. We always get fish and chips on a Friday.'

Ben watched her fiddle with the phone. 'What are you doing?'

'We have to call the police.'

'We can't.'

'Why in heaven's name not?'

'Because Dad said not to,' Ben said. 'And he meant it.'

Anne's mouth opened and closed like a gate flapping in the wind.

'Sit down, Mum. It's been a huge shock to all of us.'

Anne sat on the edge of the sofa. She plucked at her lips as if trying to pluck a reason from her mouth. 'I don't understand.'

Maddie offered to put the kettle on.

Pastor Tom agreed. 'Good idea.'

Anne's bottom lip trembled. 'Can't you just go and get him?'

Ben wanted to hug her. Promise everything would be all right. But he couldn't. Not when he didn't believe it himself. 'We don't know where the cult is.'

'So how are you going to help him if you don't even know where he is?'

Ben needed painkillers. His knee throbbed, thanks to a fracture sustained in childhood. The damned thing always flared up when he was exhausted. Like a constant nagging reminder of his humiliation.

A tear trickled down Anne's cheek. 'Well?'

Ben remembered the awful sounds accompanying his father's call. 'I don't know yet, Mum. That's what we need to figure out.'

'And you think you will?'

Ben sighed. 'I'm going to try.'

Pastor Tom looked at Anne. 'Would you like something stronger than tea?'

'I don't drink alcohol.'

Maddie called out from the kitchen and asked where the teapot was. Ben joined her, grateful for the distraction. He took a teapot from a wall cabinet and handed it to her.

'How do you like your tea?'

Ben rubbed the back of his neck. 'My knee's throbbing. I'll just have a glass of water and some paracetamol.'

'Your mum took the news quite well, considering.'

Ben swallowed three painkillers. 'It's going to be a long night.'

'I'll stay over if you want,' Maddie offered.

'You don't have to do that.'

'I could help your mum.'

'She'll be all right. She's got sleeping tablets.'

'I'm not doing much until Sunday service.'

'I—'

Maddie put the teapot on a tray. 'I want to.'

A hand squeezed Ben's heart. 'The milk's in the fridge, and there's a sugar bowl up in that cupboard.'

'Well? Do you want me to stay?'

'What about your dad?'

'He'll be fine. Perhaps we could do some brainstorming later? See if we can come up with a plan of action?'

Ben didn't feel he had much of a brain left to storm. 'If you're sure.'

'I wouldn't offer if I wasn't. You go on through. I'll see to this.'

They sat around the dining table in silent contemplation. Pastor Tom sipped his tea and smiled at Anne. 'You have a lovely home.'

Anne ignored the compliment. 'I always knew something like this would happen. I always said to Aunt Mary that he'd end up getting hurt.'

Ben thought you were bound to be vindicated one day if you always erred on the side of pessimism.

Like you, a voice whispered in his head.

Anne banged her teacup down on the saucer. 'It's beyond me why he always has to do dangerous jobs. First the police force, and now this stupid detective work. It's just asking for trouble.'

Ben massaged his knee. Why did painkillers take so long to get into the system?

Anne blew her nose in a tissue and tucked it in the sleeve of her cardigan. 'Do you remember that time he fell through that shed roof?'

Ben did. How could he forget? His father had spent a week in hospital with a broken ankle, and then three months recuperating at home with a foul temper to accompany his injuries.

Anne kept looking out of the window as if her husband might pull up at any moment with a bag of fish and chips and a guilty grin.

'He was trying to get pictures of some floozy in a bedroom, if I remember.'

Ben's knee gnawed at his nerves. 'It was a bloke.'

Maddie handed Anne a cup of tea. 'If it's all right with you, Mrs Whittle—'

'Anne. Please call me Anne.'

'If it's all right with you, Anne, I could stop over for a while. Just to help out.'

Anne took a sip of tea, and then said, 'I think we should just call the police and let them deal with it.'

Ben begged God for some of that strength Pastor Tom talked about. 'I've already told you. Dad doesn't want us to call the police. He wouldn't say so without good reason.'

'What if he's fallen through another roof? Banged his head?'

Pastor Tom finished his tea and turned to Maddie. 'It might be better if we went home. Let these folks have some space.'

'I want Maddie to stay,' Ben said.

Tom didn't look convinced. 'Anne?'

'It makes no difference to me whether she stays. I just want my husband back.'

Tom stood up. 'I've got to make tracks. You call me tomorrow, Madeline.'

Maddie nodded.

'I want you back for Sunday service.'

'Of course.'

Ben showed Pastor Tom out. 'I appreciate this, Tom.'

'Take care of your mother, son. She's in shock.'

Ben didn't have a clue how a useless geek like him was supposed to look after his mother *and* rescue his father. 'We're all in shock, Tom.'

'God bless you, son. I shall pray for you.'

Ben closed the door and returned to the front room. His head felt like a block of concrete. Someone was trying to dig up that concrete with a pneumatic drill. Maddie was sitting beside his mother on the sofa, comforting her.

'We'll find him, Mum.'

Anne stood up and walked over to the window. She looked left and right several times, putting Ben in mind of a dog waiting for its master to come home. She turned back to face Ben. 'When did he phone you?'

Ben looked at his watch. 'About an hour ago.'

'Have you tried to ring him back?'

'Yes. There was no answer.'

'Try him now.'

Ben did. Same result. He'd also tried his father's main phone and the cheap pay-as-you-go that his father took on surveillance operations. No answer on those either.

Anne plucked a fresh tissue from a box of Kleenex on the coffee table and dabbed her eyes. 'So what are you going to do now?'

'Try to find him.'

'And what if this cult captures you as well?'

Ben shuddered. 'Why don't you take some sleeping tablets. Get a good night's rest, Mum?'

'Perhaps I will. You wake me up straight away if there's any news.'

Ben didn't think there would be any need to wake her. Not unless Tom's prayers summoned a miracle. 'Of course.'

Anne shuffled out of the dining room as if her mind and body were disconnected from one another.

Ben closed the door behind her. 'She'll be out for the count soon.'

'She's lovely.'

'She can be. Do you want a proper drink? There's vodka in the cabinet.'

'I'll stick to tea, thanks. Do you want one?'

'Can I have a coffee? Strong and black. Three sugars.'

They sat at the dining table drinking coffee. Ben told Maddie how Pastor Tom had helped him after he'd fallen from a conker tree and fractured his knee. 'I spent most of that summer with your dad. That's when he introduced me to Old Joe.'

Maddie looked surprised. 'I don't remember you.'

'You were always out. Your dad reckoned you were a boy in disguise.'

Maddie smiled. 'I was a bit of a tomboy.'

'Back then you wanted to be an explorer.'

'Cool.'

'And an astronaut.'

'Funny what we want to do when we're kids. All those silly dreams and big expectations.'

'I just wanted to be normal,' Ben said. 'Normal and left alone.'

Maddie frowned. 'Why?'

'I used to get picked on.'

'By who?'

'Just other kids at school. I had a bad stammer. They used to call me Stutter-buck.'

'Kids can be so cruel.'

Ben shrugged. 'It's all in the past. It doesn't really matter now. Old Joe belonged to your granddad.'

'Granddad John?'

Ben nodded.

Maddie took a sip of coffee. 'Granddad John was great. We used to visit him in Sunnyside Nursing Home. He could still do these amazing card tricks. He was pushing eighty, and he had a girlfriend. Betsy. She had this great big puff of white hair and the kindest eyes you could ever imagine.'

Ben smiled. 'Cool.'

'Granddad John died two years ago. Betsy went a few months after. It was so sad.'

'At least they're together again now.'

'Nana June might have something to say about that! Anyway, why did dad give you Old Joe?'

'To help me overcome my stammer. At the time it was bad, especially when I was under pressure. The more I tried, the worse it got. But your dad taught me the art of ventriloquism. How to control my thoughts. It was weird at first because it was like magic when I spoke through Old Joe. It didn't take me half an hour to say a simple sentence. Then, bit by bit, I spoke properly without using Old Joe.'

Maddie grinned. 'Wow! That's fantastic.'

'Not that I'm much cop at it. Even Old Joe reckons I'm rubbish.'

'Don't put yourself down. You're brilliant with him.'

'It's all down to your dad, Maddie. He's a great man.'

'I know.'

'I can't ever repay him.'

'You already have.'

'How?'

'By turning out to be such a good person.'

Ben blushed. 'I wish.'

'You've got a lot going for you.'

'Like what? A dead-end job and a missing father?'

Maddie didn't respond. 'You said there's an appointments book?'

'In the office.'

He led Maddie through the kitchen and into a small eight-feet-square room that had started life as a brick-built coal shed. He switched on the light. A shiny black desk with a computer and a printer dominated one wall. Next to this, a filing cabinet. Ben unlocked it and took out a black leather-bound book. He put the book on the desk and leafed through it.

He stopped about halfway and tapped the page. 'Here we go. Barnaby and Annabelle Hunt, Britannia Bungalow, The Street, Upper Feelham. Girl's name is Emily Hunt. Missing for two years. Demanding money from her parents. Aged nineteen. There's a phone number.'

'You need to pay them a visit first thing tomorrow and find out what they know about this cult.'

'And then what?'

'We take it from there.'

Ben closed the book. He felt like a bird with one wing trying to take off in a high wind.

Chapter Five

Ben stood on the front doorstep of Britannia Bungalow and introduced himself to Annabelle Hunt.

'Is everything all right? Has something happened to Emily?' The woman's eyes looked as if they were already in mourning for her daughter.

'No. Emily's fine as far as I know. Can I come in?'

She stepped aside and ushered Ben along a narrow hallway into the front room. Her husband, Barnaby, glanced up from his newspaper. 'Who's this?'

'This is Ben. Mr Whittle's son.'

Barnaby looked back at his newspaper. 'Who the blazes is Mr Whittle when he's at home?'

'The private investigator that's looking for Emily.'

Barnaby's cheeks flared red. 'What's happened now? That blasted girl's been nothing but trouble since the day she was born.'

'Considering you were away playing silly war games for most of Emily's childhood, you're not in any position to refer to it.'

'Pie-crust. History seems to have rewritten your memory, woman.'

Behind the kitchen door, the Hunts' Yorkshire terrier, Ritzy, yapped as though taking part in the argument.

'It's you that's rewritten history. Your brain must have a piece of shrapnel lodged in it.'

'Shrapnel, be damned.'

Annabelle sighed. 'Ignore him, Ben. He's given to occasional bouts of decency if you stay in his company for long enough.'

'And my wife is given to occasional bouts of honesty.'

Annabelle rolled her eyes.

'And before you ask, I've already coughed up a king's ransom for no good reason. I'm not parting with a penny more.'

'No one's asking you to. If you'd just give Mr Whittle a chance to speak.'

Barnaby put down his paper and looked at Ben as if he were a fly that needed swatting. 'If you're not after more money, young man, what do you want?'

Ben looked at the floor. The spirals in the red and gold Axminster carpet threatened to hypnotise him. To make matters worse, he'd not slept a wink all night. He'd let Maddie have his bed. The sofa had offered no solace to his aching, restless body. 'My father's gone missing.'

Barnaby's cheeks were now flame-grilled. 'What do you mean, "missing"?'

Ben explained the phone call.

Barnaby seemed in no mood to offer sympathy. 'All he had to do was find her and take a few pictures. Talk about incompetence.'

Ben apologised.

Barnaby wasn't listening. 'Imagine if we behaved like that in the army? We'd all be serving under the shadow of the swastika by now.'

Annabelle stepped in and dismissed her husband. 'Don't be so dramatic. We'd all be serving under the swastika if the Yanks hadn't joined the war. As you well know.'

Barnaby stood his ground. 'Our freedom has nothing to do with the Americans. As I recall, all they did was drop an atomic bomb on the Japs.'

Annabelle tilted her head up. 'If you insist on mixing fact with fiction and being so damned rude, go to your study and sulk. Or better still, take Ritzy for a walk. The air will do you good.'

'What bloody air? I'm more likely to get poisoned with all the lorries that go thundering through here these days.'

'If only.'

Barnaby walked into the kitchen and banged the door shut behind him.

'I'm so sorry about him,' Annabelle said. 'He's spent most of his life shouting down subordinates in the army. He doesn't know how to speak with a civil tongue.'

'It's all right.'

'It's not. And I apologise for his behaviour. Please take a seat.'

Ben sat down on a floral two-seater sofa.

'What are you going to do about your father?'

'Try to find him. I was hoping you might know where this cult is based?'

'I haven't got the faintest idea. That's why we hired your father.'

'Do you know anything at all about them?'

Annabelle shook her head. 'Not very much. She got mixed up with this busker chap in Oxford. From that day on she behaved differently.'

'In what way?'

'She became more and more withdrawn. Impatient. Angry, even. It was terrible. She hated our way of life. She turned on her father, which I suppose you could interpret as standing up to him.'

'Do you know this busker's name?'

'I should do. I heard it every minute of the day before Emily left home. His name is Marcus.'

'What about a surname?'

'She never mentioned it. It was all Marcus-this and Marcus-that. I assumed it was a passing phase. Rebelling against her upbringing. She even called Barnaby a capitalist pig or something like that.'

'Oh.'

'Serves him right. He's always tried to treat her like one of his recruits.'

Ben felt sympathy for Emily. His father and Barnaby Hunt sounded like kindred spirits. He also felt sorry for Annabelle Hunt. Her carefully made-up face and neatly permed grey hair gave her the appearance of a woman in control; her twitching hands and bitten nails suggested otherwise. 'How old is Emily?'

'Nineteen last birthday.'

'When did you last see her?'

'Not this Christmas, but the one before. She came home and gave me a present.' Annabelle held out her hand and showed Ben a cheap looking bangle dangling from her skinny wrist. 'She stayed about an hour. She told me she loved me, and then she left.'

'And she's not been back?'

Annabelle sniffed. 'No. Barnaby was his usual blustery self, following her out into the street and making a show of us. Shouting at the poor girl. Asking her when she was going to get a job. Get a wash. Behave like a civilised human being. He called her an "aimless hippy".'

'Our records show that Emily was demanding money.'

'Yes. She sent a letter about three months ago asking for money for the Rapture.'

'The Rapture?'

'Some religious nonsense. It's got something to do with the end of time. A spaceship is supposed to be coming down from Heaven to pick up the good and the great, or some such thing.'

'A spaceship?'

'It's utter hogwash. The cult is trying to extort money from its members. If you ask me, they've all been brainwashed.'

Ben saw an opening. 'The money Emily asked for? Where are you supposed to send it?'

Annabelle pulled at the sleeve of her cardigan. 'I haven't got to. They will send someone to pick it up.'

'Was there a postmark on the envelope?' Ben asked.

'No. It was hand-delivered. Do you want to see it?'

Ben nodded. 'If that's all right.'

'She asks for quite a considerable sum of money. Two hundred thousand pounds.'

Ben abandoned discretion. 'Bloody hell! How much?'

'I'll go and fetch it.'

Annabelle returned a few minutes later with the letter. She handed it to Ben. 'I gave her everything, Mr Whittle. All of me. You look too young to have children, but one day you'll understand. You'll understand that there is no greater love than the one you have for your child.'

Ben took the letter from the envelope and read:

Dear Mother,

It's been a while. Hope you are well. I would ask about Father, but I expect him to be floating on his usual bed of cholesterol. It's been hectic here. We've been working hard making preparations for the Rapture. For our glorious union with the Lord Jesus Christ.

I know Father will dismiss this letter. But I speak the truth. The universal truth of Jesus Christ. I shall pray for Father that he might see the error of his ways. I know that he can't see what he is. That is one consequence of bigotry. The Lord will judge him accordingly.

We are The Chosen. We are to meet with the Lord on The Final Day of Reckoning. To help us achieve this glorious dream, we need a vast sum of money to construct a spaceship. All members of The Sons and Daughters of Salvation are being asked to contribute the sum of two hundred thousand pounds. Please don't tell me you cannot afford this, because I know that you can, with plenty left over to indulge your extravagant lifestyle.

Please look upon this as my inheritance. What is due. I shall spend it wisely, for there is no greater purpose than serving the Lord. We shall be resurrected as was Jesus after the Crucifixion. The Lord is our salvation. He, and He alone is our keeper.

A motorcycle courier will collect the money from you on a date which will be specified in my next letter. You are to hand it to him in Daddy's brown leather briefcase. Please don't think about having him followed.

Your loving daughter,
Emily.

Ben put the letter on the coffee table. 'Have you had any more contact with your daughter since this letter?'

'Nothing.'

'When did the letter arrive?'

'Easter. We called your father soon after that.'

Ben recapped. 'So all you know is that your daughter met a busker in Oxford called Marcus and then she went off and joined this cult?'

'That's about the size of it.'

'What were you going to do if my father located Emily?'

'Barnaby was talking about going and getting her back. Forcibly, if need be. He claims to know *people*.'

'Have you got a photograph of Emily that I could borrow?'

'I've got nothing up to date. Your father took the last school one. Emily hated having her picture taken. I'll see what I can find.'

Annabelle returned five minutes later with a six by four photo taken on a beach. 'Our last family holiday together.'

Ben took the photo. Emily's brown eyes looked blank. Her dark hair was scraped back from her forehead and tied in a ponytail. 'How old is she here, Mrs Hunt?'

'Coming up to sixteen.'

Ben wrote his mobile number on the back of a business card and handed it to Annabelle. 'I've got to get going. I'd be grateful if you'd contact me if your daughter gets in touch again.'

Annabelle took the card and promised that she would. She showed him out. 'Good luck, Mr Whittle.'

Ben thought it would take a lot more than luck to resolve this mess.

Chapter Six

Ben returned home to find Maddie and his mother looking through an old photo album. His mother was still wearing her pale blue dressing gown. Her hair looked as if it were trying to flee her scalp.

Maddie looked up and smiled. 'How'd it go?'

Ben sat at the dining table. 'Not too bad.'

Anne looked at her son with bloodshot eyes. 'Did you find out where this cult is?'

'Not yet.'

'What did the parents say?' Maddie asked.

Ben touched the teapot. Cold. 'Just that the girl started seeing a guy in Oxford. A busker. He got her involved in the cult.'

'That's a fat lot of help,' Anne said.

Ben sighed. 'Maybe you ought to stay with Aunt Mary for a while.'

'And what should I tell her? That Geoff's been taken hostage by a load of maniacs in a cult? And then spend the next God knows how long listening to her telling me I married the wrong man. She reckons everyone should marry a bank manager like she has. Sitting there all smug with her mock-Georgian house and mock-me manners.'

'Can't you tell her that Dad's away on a case?'

'She won't believe me. She'll be suspicious. And then she'll think he's having an affair. Or worse still that we've split up.'

Maddie turned to Anne. 'I could stay here with you.'

'What about your duties at the church? Your dad said he wanted you home tomorrow.'

'Lighting a few candles and saying a few prayers? I'm sure he can cope. He managed youth club by himself last night.'

'A couple of hours is one thing,' Anne said. 'You can't just uproot and—'

'It'll be all right,' Maddie assured her. 'It's about time he learned to stand on his own two feet.'

'You'll need clothes,' Ben said.

Maddie grinned. 'So take me home. We can have a chat with my dad, and then I can pack my stuff.'

***

Pastor Tom listened as Ben recounted his visit to the Hunts' bungalow and described the contents of Emily's letter.

'So when Ben goes off to find this busker, Anne will be on her own,' Maddie said.

'And does Ben's mother want you staying with her?'

Maddie pouted. 'Of course she does.'

'You've not forced this upon her?'

'No.'

'She'll be glad of the company,' Ben added. 'In all honesty, I dread to think what she'll be like on her own.'

Tom nodded. 'She'll feel like she's lost half her heart. But you've got to be careful. You need to give her time—'

'We don't exactly have time, do we?' Maddie interrupted.

'All right. Go ahead if you think it's for the best.'

'I *know* it's for the best.'

'I suppose I could get Rhonda to help out at the church.'

'Rhonda will love that.'

'Rhonda?' Ben asked.

Maddie smiled. 'Rhonda comes to every service. Monday, Wednesday, Saturday and Sunday. She's sweet on Dad.'

Tom looked away. 'Don't be daft.'

Maddie ploughed on. 'She walks over three miles to get to church, come rain or shine. That's either dedication or love.'

Ben understood Rhonda; he would walk barefoot across mountains to spend time with Maddie. 'Are you sure you're all right with this, Tom?'

'Your father is missing, son. Only a mean-spirited person would deny help to someone in need.'

'So I can pack, then?' Maddie said.

'Go on.'

Ben watched Maddie bounce out of the room. She looked like sunshine in her bright yellow dungarees. He thanked Tom.

'What are you going to do if you find this busker, son?'

Ben felt something pass through him. Something spiritual he couldn't define. Peace? Love? Goodness? 'I thought I could follow him. See if he can lead me to the cult.'

Tom was quiet for a while, and then said, 'You could try to join the cult, son. Get inside. Help your dad that way.'

'That's what I was thinking. But to be honest, Tom, the thought of going anywhere near that bunch of lunatics terrifies me.'

'The only thing to fear is fear itself. Try to remember that.'

'What if they smell a rat?'

'Trust in yourself and trust in the Lord.'

'I work in an office at home. I sometimes put missing posters on lampposts. Go to the stationery store. I'm hardly James Bond.'

'You're much stronger than you think, Ben.'

'My dad doesn't even trust me.'

'Really? So who did he call in his hour of need?'

'He's got my number on speed-dial. That watch-phone's not up to much except in an emergency.'

'Nonsense. He called you because he trusts you.'

'That's why he's always telling me to buck my ideas up, is it?'

'It's a thin line between criticism and motivation.'

'I don't even know what to say if I do find this busker.'

'Tell him what he wants to hear. Tell him you want to turn your back on society.'

'Not a bad idea as it goes!'

'The letter said Emily wanted money for the Rapture. Do you know what the Rapture is, son?'

Ben shook his head. 'Seems like a load of nonsense just to get money to finance the cult.'

'The Rapture can be a dangerous concept in the wrong hands. Waco being a classic example of that. The time of the Rapture is known as Tribulation. What it boils down to is a rebellion against Satan. There will be great battles between good and evil. Some of those with faith will be chosen to be saved and taken to Heaven.'

'In a spaceship?'

Tom nodded. 'Jesus will return to earth to judge those left. He will rule for a thousand years. Then Jesus will defeat Satan and banish evil forever. The world will be destroyed and a new Heaven and earth will be created.'

It all sounded like hogwash to Ben. 'Do you believe that's true?'

'I don't know, son. Anything's possible.'

'Do you think there really is such a thing as Heaven and Hell?'

'Absolutely, son.'

'What if I mess up, Tom? What then?'

'The Lord trusts you, son. Remember that.'

Maddie returned to the kitchen and plonked a large leather suitcase on the floor. 'I think I've got it all.'

Tom grinned. 'You're staying a while, then?'

'A girl needs clothes.'

'Are you sure you don't want to pop the kitchen sink in there while you're at it?'

Maddie collapsed on top of her suitcase. 'Pick me up off the floor. I'm hysterical.'

'Go on. Get outta here.'

As they were about to leave, Tom looked at Ben. He didn't speak. It was as if he was trying to convey a message through telepathy. A message of love and understanding. Ben wanted to tell Tom how much he loved him. Admired him. Respected him. But somehow he knew he didn't need words to convey those things. Acknowledgement was written in Tom's eyes in clear blue ink.

Chapter Seven

Edward Ebb sat at the head of a large pine table in the kitchen and addressed his three most trusted followers. 'Are we all agreed that the Imposter is an agent of the Devil?'

The group, all dressed in obligatory yellow overalls, confirmed their belief that the Imposter was indeed in the employ of Satan. Sister Alice went further. 'I believe he is in the grip of demonic possession.'

Ebb wiped something off the front of his white suit jacket. 'Indeed, Sister. That much is apparent by the way he froths and spits and curses.'

Brother Marcus didn't seem quite so sure as the others. 'It could be that he's in pain.'

Ebb shook his head. 'Don't be deceived by his illusionary manner. The only thing causing him pain is God's presence.'

'He fell a long way,' Marcus added. 'And he's been shot.'

'And your point is?'

Marcus looked away. 'Just saying.'

Ebb turned his attention to Tweezer. 'Have you anything to add?'

'The long range camera I found in the tree indicates a spy. I'll take the film to Boots on Monday and get it developed.'

'Could be he's a reporter,' Marcus said.

Ebb's eyes gleamed like hot coals. 'He's a reporter all right. Satan's. I want him bound to a chair with rope before I go anywhere near him again.'

Marcus took a sip of water and placed his glass on the table. 'Is there any need if he's paralysed?'

'Paralysis has no bearing on his potential threat. I've seen demons leap through naked flames and into pits of acid.'

Sister Alice crossed herself.

Ebb asked her if she'd found anything whilst shaving him.

'No, Father.'

'The mark of the beast will be somewhere upon him. Did you shave his pubic area?'

'No.'

'It might be prudent to do so.'

It was Alice's turn to look sceptical. 'I don't know, Father. He's very hard to manoeuvre, what with him being all dead weight.'

'Brother Tweezer can help you.'

'Thank you, Father.'

Ebb was quiet for a moment, and then said to Tweezer, 'I want you to go back up in that tree.'

'Why?'

'To see if there's anything you missed the first time.'

'But there wasn't anything else. Just the camera.'

'How high did you go?'

Tweezer's right eye twitched. It looked as if he was winking at Ebb. 'To where he fell from, Father.'

'I want you to climb right to the top. Leave no stone unturned.'

'Shouldn't that be leaf?' Marcus mumbled.

'But why, Father?' Tweezer said. 'I've had a good look.'

Ebb felt like poking out that twitching eye with a chicken bone. He didn't like tics; they were an indication of possession. 'Because he may have secreted other evidence up there. Carved hidden messages into the bark.'

Tweezer made the mistake of asking what sort of messages.

'If I knew that, I wouldn't be damn well asking you to go up there, would I?'

'No, Father.'

'Does the bible not say *Seek and ye shall find*?'

'Yes, Father.'

'It doesn't say *sit on thy fat backside and the answer shall bite you on the beak*, does it?'

Marcus laughed.

Ebb rounded on him. 'Something funny, Brother Marcus?'

Marcus reconstructed his face into a mask of sobriety. 'No, Father.'

Ebb turned back to Tweezer. 'And when you're finished, I want you to look for his car.'

'I've already looked.'

'Where?'

'Along the track.'

'Are you trying to test my patience?'

'No, Father.'

'Do you think the Imposter is going to park along the track whilst he carries out surveillance?' Ebb didn't wait for an answer. 'Of course he isn't. He's going to secrete the car out of sight somewhere.'

'But he could have put it anywhere,' Tweezer argued. 'I don't even know what it looks like.'

'It's a Ford Fiesta,' Ebb said. 'It's embossed on the key.'

'All right. I'll have a scout about and see what I can find.'

'Thank you. And just bear in mind whilst you're having a "scout about", I don't want to see you back here until you locate it. Is that clear?'

'Yes, Father.'

Sister Alice ran a hand through her short spiky hair. 'Can I make a suggestion?'

Ebb nodded.

'Why don't we try a different approach with the Imposter?'

'Such as?'

'Pain relief.'

'What the bloody hell for?' Ebb squawked, forgetting Rule 47: No Swearing. 'Perhaps we should go the whole hog and turn the Revelation Room into a five-star hotel suite, complete with sauna and Jacuzzi?'

'I didn't mean—'

'Are you forgetting what we're dealing with here, Sister Alice?'

'No, Father. I just thought pain relief might offer him an incentive to talk.'

'We have a strict rule about medication, Sister Alice. As you well know. We must never interfere with God's will.'

'I know, Father. But this isn't interfering with God's will, is it? It's trying to coax answers out of the Devil's own. There's a difference.'

After a few moments' deliberation, Ebb said, 'I don't know. It might be a trap.'

'A trap, Father?'

Ebb nodded. A bead of sweat dripped onto his top lip. He licked it off. 'Remember that he is more than capable of planting ideas into an unguarded mind.'

'But a few paracetamol isn't going to hurt,' Alice protested. 'It might tempt him.'

Ebb shook his head. 'No. We're not breaking the rules on medication for anyone. Especially the Imposter. The Lord does not permit the use of drugs, just as he forbids drinking alcohol and eating meat. Next thing, you'll be suggesting we offer the swine a hog roast and a glass of wine.'

Alice gave up. 'As you wish, Father.'

Ebb did. He stood up. 'It's clear that the Imposter wants to strike fear and confusion at the heart of The Sons and Daughters of Salvation. Satan's agents come in many guises. Animals. Birds. Fish. That is why we have a strict rule to never eat the flesh of these creatures. We don't want to ingest evil, do we?'

No one did.

'Mark my words, half the evil in this world is spread by Burger King and McDonald's.'

'Amen to that,' Alice said.

'Gluttony and greed dominates every single high street in the world. Abstinence makes the heart stronger. The spirit unburdened. The mind pure.'

'Makes me bloody hungry,' Marcus muttered.

'Did you say something, Brother Marcus?'

'Just said I'm peckish, Father.'

'Is that so?'

'Yes, Father.'

'Would you like to go into the Revelation Room for a while?'

Marcus straightened up. 'No, Father.'

'Realign your thoughts?'

'No, Father.'

'Keep the Imposter company?'

'No. I—'

'Then keep your mouth shut whilst I'm speaking.'

Marcus bowed his head. 'Yes, Father.'

Ebb paced up and down. He stopped at a large white ceramic sink and poured himself a plastic tumbler of water. He drained it in one and mopped his head with a cotton handkerchief.

'Are you all right, Father?' Sister Alice asked.

Ebb didn't answer. He dropped the tumbler in the sink. He closed his eyes and held onto the sink for support. There was a humming noise in the back of his head, like the steady thrum of an electrical substation. A storm was coming. He could sense it the same way as animals could. An instinct. A secret vibration. Call it what you will, it was strong, and very rarely wrong.

Alice went to his side and held his free hand. 'Father?'

He tried to smile. Tried to reassure his favourite member that things were okay. He'd be fine in a moment or two. But the humming grew louder.

'Father?'

The words echoed around the base of his skull like thunder. 'A storm is coming, Sister.'

'Is it the Imposter?'

'The Imposter is the foreteller of evil.'

Alice crossed herself.

Ebb's eyelids fluttered. His breathing came in rapid pants. 'Can you smell the flowers?'

Alice sniffed the air. 'I—'

'I can smell paradise.'

'Amen,' Alice said. The sentiment didn't touch her eyes.

'I can taste Heaven.'

'What does it taste of, Father?'

'Raspberries,' Ebb answered, as a wave rolled across the top of his brain. 'Raspberries and honeycomb.'

'Do you want to sit back down, Father?'

Ebb shook his head. A mistake. The wave turned into a tsunami and almost capsized him. He gasped for air. 'Steady me, Sister.'

Alice held onto his arm and rubbed his shoulder.

Something stirred in the pit of Ebb's stomach. He rocked from side to side. 'We are blessed. Truly blessed. We must give thanks to the Lord. For he is within me as I speak.'

Tweezer stood up. He looked as awkward as a vegetarian in a slaughterhouse. 'Father?'

Ebb took a deep breath and puffed out his chest. 'The Imposter is a sign.'

'A sign, Father?'

Ebb didn't hear him. His heart was suddenly filled with love. Church bells chimed in his ears. Tears leaked down his cheeks. 'Jesus speaks.'

'What does He say, Father?' Alice asked.

Ebb's right arm trembled. 'The Imposter has been sent to learn of our preparations for the Rapture. We must remain vigilant. We must fight his wicked ways with every ounce of strength in our bodies. This is a sign that the Rapture will soon be upon us. We must....'

'Father?' Alice prompted.

Ebb suddenly collapsed, the right side of his body gripped by a violent epileptic seizure.

Chapter Eight

Ben and Maddie stepped off the bus in Oxford High Street at nine-fifteen on Tuesday morning. After two fruitless trips to the city on his own, Maddie had agreed to accompany Ben whilst his mother helped Pastor Tom at the church. She'd perked up slightly when Tom had asked her if she was any good at flower arranging. It was only a month ago that Anne had completed a course to study the subject. No tip-off from Maddie!

After three hours of searching, the nearest they'd come to finding a busker was a preacher on a soap box banging a tambourine to emphasise his words. Ben sat on a bench which was just a narrow tilted strip of wood designed to offer no comfort.

'They make them like this to stop people sleeping on them,' Maddie said.

'They're all heart.'

Maddie sat down beside him. 'They'll make it a criminal offence to be homeless next. Shoot vagrants on sight for daring to litter their precious city.'

'Chop off the hands of beggars to stop them begging.'

'Chop off the feet of tramps to stop them tramping.'

'This country sucks.'

'Like a kid's straw in a milkshake,' Maddie agreed. 'Did you see that Big Issue guy outside Debenhams?'

'The big dude with the shaved head?'

Maddie nodded. 'I wonder if he's seen our busker?'

'He looks as if he might have eaten him.'

'Swallowed him whole,' Maddie agreed. 'Shall we ask him?'

'Do you reckon we ought to buy a Big Issue?'

'We could give him a tenner. It might help to jog his memory.'

Big Issue guy was still standing outside Debenhams. He offered Ben a magazine, and a smile that looked capable of mincing beef.

'I was wondering if you could help me,' Ben said. 'I'm looking for someone.'

Big Issue squinted at Ben. 'Are you a copper?'

'Me? God, no.'

'We're looking for my sister,' Maddie said. 'Show him the picture.'

Ben took Emily's picture from the back pocket of his jeans and handed it over. 'It's not up to date. She's nineteen now.'

Big Issue handed the picture back to Ben. 'I ain't seen her. When did she go missing?'

Ben tucked the picture back in his pocket. 'Two years ago.'

'Kids vanish all the time. The street just sucks them up. Paedophiles and pimps everywhere.'

Maddie hooked her thumbs in the side of her bright red dungarees. 'She may have run off with a busker. A guy called Marcus.'

'Name don't ring any bells. Thousands of kids end up with some twat who offers them the world and then takes them straight to Hell.'

Ben sighed. 'That's reassuring.'

'That's the way it is.'

Ben turned to Maddie. 'Come on, let's go.'

Maddie ignored him. 'She's nineteen. You have a think about that.'

'I lost three toes in Afghanistan and got discharged from the army without so much as a thank you. You think about that.'

'I'm sorry to hear that.'

'Serve your country, and what do you get? Treated like shit.'

Maddie touched his arm. 'I'm sorry.'

'I've seen people with arms and legs blown off. No one gives a tin-shit. Welcome to the world.'

Maddie and Ben started to walk away.

Big Issue called after them. 'There *is* this one guy. I don't know his name. He comes in a few days a week. Usually on a Wednesday and Friday. Sometimes more. He's young. Good-looking, I suppose, if you like that sort of thing. Wears a shitty looking pinstripe suit and a straw hat.'

Maddie turned around. 'And he busks?'

'Busks. Deals. Yaps to all the girlies. Fancies himself. A right regular arsehole.'

Maddie smiled a smile to open hearts. It caused a knot in Ben's stomach. 'Where does he busk?'

Big Issue pointed across the street towards Boots. 'Over there, sometimes. Sometimes he stands outside the Methodist church.'

Maddie nodded. 'Thanks so much for that. What's your name?'

'I've got many names, love. Most of 'em ain't very nice. But you can call me Gary.'

Maddie shook Gary's hand. 'I'm Maddie. This is Ben. Have you got a mobile, Gary?'

'Yeah. But I ain't got no credit.'

'If I give you some money for credit, could you give me a ring the next time you see this busker?'

'I suppose.'

Maddie plucked a *Big Issue* out of Gary's hand and wrote her mobile number on the back. She handed it back to him.

Gary grinned. 'I hope you're going to pay for the *Big Issue*.'

Maddie turned to Ben. 'Give him twenty pounds.'

'What for?'

'Ten for his phone, and ten for the magazine.'

'But—'

'But nothing, skinflint. It's my sister that's missing.'

'Do the right thing, dude,' Gary said. 'You might need help one day.'

Ben fished his wallet out and handed over the cash. Anyone with half a brain knew the money would end up in an off-licence till.

Maddie smiled. 'There. That didn't hurt too much, did it?'

More than you'll ever know, Ben thought.

Maddie turned back to Gary. 'We'll be kicking around in Oxford for the rest of the day. Would you call us if you see him?'

Gary promised that he would.

Ben thought the promise might as well be written in steam.

'After today, it'll take us about an hour to get here. So call us straight away,' Maddie said.

Gary nodded. 'Okay.'

As they walked away, Maddie turned to Ben. 'That's a start.'

'He won't call.'

'He might.'

'Twenty quid's a lot of money to pin to a donkey with might for a tail.'

Maddie ignored him. 'Let's get something to eat. I'm starving.'

Ben wasn't. His stomach was too knotted to be hungry. They went to McDonald's, where he spent most of the time lost in thought and twirling cold fries between his fingers.

Maddie finished her meal and wiped her mouth with a serviette. 'Let's give it until four. If we've heard nothing by then, we'll head off home.'

'I suppose.'

'At least Gary can keep an eye out for him.'

'If he doesn't spend the money on booze.'

'We'll just have to trust him, won't we? Come on, let's do another sweep of the streets and then sit down by the Methodist church Gary mentioned.'

Ben thought if Gary had mentioned a busker in a hot-air balloon, Maddie would have spent the rest of the day looking up at the sky.

By the time they sat down outside the Methodist church an hour later, Ben's feet felt as if they'd been fed through a shredder. 'What time's the next bus home?'

'Twenty past four or ten to five.'

He glanced at his watch. Another two hours. 'Even if we do find this busker, and I manage to join this stupid cult, it will be way too late for my dad. I mean, it's Tuesday now. He already sounded as if he was at death's door on Friday night.'

Maddie smiled. The patient smile of a parent with an inattentive child. 'You have to keep believing, ben.'

'In what? Miracles?'

'Believing things will turn out all right.'

'And what am I supposed to say to this busker? Hey, mate, do you belong to a cult?'

'Just chat to him. See how the land lies. Convince him you're searching for answers. Tell him you hate modern living. Play it by ear.'

Ben's stomach churned. 'I'm no good at pretending.'

Maddie took his hand. 'You have to trust yourself, Ben. Take one step at a time.'

'And then trip myself up.'

Maddie let go of his hand. 'If you're so worried about it, why don't we do it together?'

'Do what?'

'Join the cult.'

'I couldn't ask you to do that.'

'You're not asking. I'm offering.'

'What about my mother? Who will look after her?'

'We'll think of something.'

'Like what?'

'I could get my dad to ask Rhonda.'

'Rhonda doesn't even know my mum.'

'Rhonda's got a big personality. She'd cope. Trust me.'

'My mother has two modes: nervous and hysterical.'

'Your mother's bearing up well, considering.'

'That's more to do with happy pills than anything else.'

'If you don't want me to help, then fine,' Maddie said. 'I won't force you. It was just an idea.'

'And what about your dad? How's he going to feel if you put your neck on the line?'

'He'll understand.'

Ben stamped his foot to shoo away a pigeon that was paying close attention to his trainers. 'I don't know. Maybe we should just go home.'

Maddie plucked a strand of hair off her forehead. 'And then what?'

Ben didn't have a clue. Infiltrating the cult was a marvellous idea if this was a movie and he was an all-action hero. He stood more chance of flying to the moon on a broomstick.

Maddie's phone beeped. Private number. She answered it. 'Gary?'

Ben groaned. What did *he* want? More money? A date with Maddie? A medal?

Maddie smiled. 'Thanks, Gary. Take care.' She turned to Ben. 'Come on, let's go. The busker's outside Marks and Sparks.'

Ben's stomach tightened. 'Shouldn't we work out what to say first?'

'No. We don't want to sound like we've got a script. It's better to just go with the flow.'

'Like a drowning man in a river?'

'Very funny.'

The busker was singing *All You Need is Love*. Badly. A few girls stood around him. He had the bluest eyes Ben had ever seen. Deeper blue than Pastor Tom's, but with the same sparkle. There was a straw hat perched on his head. His skin was either tanned or unwashed.

'He looks like a gypsy,' Ben said.

'Nothing wrong with gypsies. Have you got any change?'

Ben fished out a few coins and handed them over. Maddie stepped forward and threw the money into a small plastic bowl. She turned back towards Ben. 'Your generosity knows no bounds.'

'I've already shelled out twenty quid.'

The busker finished his song to a smattering of applause from the girls. He bowed and smiled at Maddie.

Maddie smiled back. 'That was cool.'

He tuned his guitar. 'Thanks.'

Ben imagined John Lennon spinning in his grave.

'Do you do requests?'

'Depends.'

'On what?'

Busker tweaked a string and raised the guitar up close to his ear. 'Whether I know it or not.'

Maddie twirled her ponytail. '*Living on a Prayer*? Bon Jovi?'

'Don't know it.'

'*Girls Just Wanna have Fun*?'

Busker grinned. 'Is that right? I could do *Pretty Woman* if you like.'

Ben almost groaned out loud.

Maddie put her hands on her hips. 'I'm Maddie.'

Busker seemed deep in contemplation for a few moments. And then: 'I'm Marcus. What's Maddie short for? Madam?'

Maddie smiled and moved a few steps closer. 'Cheeky! It's short for Madeline.'

Ben gawked at Marcus as if the man had just revealed himself as Jesus Christ Himself.

'You should learn to play the mandolin, Madeline.'

Maddie smiled. 'So what do you do, Marcus? Are you a student?'

'Do I look like a parasite?'

'I take it you don't like students, then?'

Marcus strummed his guitar with a single downward sweep of his hand. 'Have you seen this city?'

'Nice buildings.'

'Inhabited by rats.'

Maddie wiggled her hips and sang the chorus of *We Built This City*.

'Do you want to join my band?'

'I thought you were a one-man-band?'

'There's always room to expand. Especially with a pretty girl.'

'Flattery will get you everywhere.'

'Aren't you going to introduce me to your boyfriend?'

'This is Ben.'

Marcus looked at Ben as if he was trying to read his mind. 'Do you sing? Or are you the dancing bear?'

Ben tried to look nonchalant. The man was a charmer. A magnet for girls like Emily Hunt.

Maddie asked Marcus if he was from Oxford.

'Nope. You?'

'No. We're hiking across the country. Trying to get out of the rat race.'

'Good for you.'

Maddie hooked her thumbs in the side of her dungarees. 'I had a job in a bakery. Up at four every morning. Too knackered to think most of the time. I jacked it in after Christmas. Me and Ben just hit the road.'

'Where's all your stuff?'

Maddie frowned. 'Stuff?'

'Clothes? Belongings? Sausages and beans to cook on the campfire?'

Maddie took a deep breath. 'Our backpacks got stolen in Newbury. Cleaned us out, more or less. We've been sleeping rough.'

'That's tough.'

'You can't trust anyone these days. If I could get my hands on them....'

'What are you going to do?'

Maddie shrugged. 'Go home, I suppose. Back to living with mummy and daddy. To be honest, I'd rather drink ditch water.'

'Don't get on with your folks, then?'

'You could say that.'

'Let me guess: middle class. Dinner parties. Designer furniture.'

Maddie laughed. 'You don't know them, do you?'

'I don't need to. There are thousands of them all across the country. I suppose they think you're wasting your life, wasting your education, and wasting their precious time trying to induct you into their hall of shame.'

'Wow. You must have second sight.'

'Nah. Just see things clearer than most.'

'They want me to be a teacher.'

'A propagandist of the capitalist state?'

'I wouldn't go that far.'

Marcus strummed an A-minor chord a few times. He then accompanied it with a reasonable rendition of John Lennon's *Working Class Hero*. At the end of the song, Maddie clapped. A little too enthusiastically for Ben's liking.

'That was good,' Maddie said.

'The best songs always tell the truth. The similarities between Lennon and Jesus Christ are startling. Both were outspoken and controversial. Both driven by a need to heal people. Both wanted peace. And both were murdered in their prime.'

Ben thought the comparison was ridiculous. 'Lennon was a bit before my time.'

Marcus looked at him as if he'd just threatened violence. 'Jesus was a bit before my time, but that doesn't mean I can't learn from his teachings.'

'I'm not suggesting we can't learn—'

Marcus flapped a hand as if swatting a fly. He looked at Maddie. 'So what do your parents do? When they're not entertaining guests with caviar and lobster, that is.'

'My dad's a headmaster at a private school. My mum works for a charity.'

'I bet she goes to Africa once every few years to feel their pain and suffering.'

'She does work with Oxfam.'

Marcus turned to Ben. 'What about you, Ben? What are you running away from?'

'I'm not running away from anything. I don't get on with my old man.'

'Bit of a control freak?'

Ben noticed both of his front teeth were chipped and yellowed. It put a welcome dent in the guy's good looks. 'You could say that.'

'And what does he do to justify his existence?'

Ben rummaged in his imagination for an answer. 'He works in a bank.'

Marcus snorted. 'Don't get me started on bankers. They're nothing short of legalised criminals.'

'I couldn't agree more,' Ben lied.

Marcus launched into a scathing attack on everything from bankers' bonuses to the IMF. 'Still, I suppose he's all right to tap for a few quid?'

Ben shrugged. 'I suppose.'

'What bank does he work for?'

'Barclays.'

Maddie jumped in and rescued Ben. 'Do you know if there's anywhere we can stay?'

Marcus didn't.

'We're not fussy, are we, Ben?'

'No.' *Just stupid and way out of our depth.*

'What do you do when you're not busking, Marcus?' Maddie asked.

'I give my life to the Lord.'

'Seriously?'

Marcus clenched his plectrum between those stained teeth. 'Seriously.'

'You don't look like a vicar.'

'You don't have to belong to a corrupt organisation like the church to give yourself to the Lord.'

Maddie tapped her chest. 'It's what's on the inside that counts, right?'

'Exactly.'

'Follow your heart.'

Marcus put down his guitar and took a pouch of tobacco from his crumpled jacket pocket. He rolled a cigarette. 'I'm not promising anything, because it's not up to me, but I belong to a religious group. We're called The Sons and Daughters of Salvation.'

'Wow,' Maddie said. 'That's a grand title.'

Marcus grinned. 'It is a bit of a mouthful. I could ask if they need an extra pair of hands. We give our lives to the Lord. That doesn't mean to say we spend all our time down on our knees worshipping the sun. Quite the opposite. We oppose convention.'

'Do you have any particular faith?'

'No. We believe in the truth. I can't explain what we do in a few short sentences. It's a lifestyle based around God's will. Do you believe in God, Maddie?'

'Yes.'

'What about you, Ben?'

Ben nodded. He was afraid to open his mouth in case the truth came jumping out and scuppered their plan.

Marcus turned back to Maddie. 'Would you be willing to put your trust in the Lord?'

'Yes.'

'Like I said, it's not up to me. I'll have a word with the boss. If you meet me back here tomorrow at three, I'll let you know what he says.'

'Are you sure?' Maddie said. 'We don't want to put you to any trouble.'

'It's cool.'

As they walked away, Maddie reached out and grabbed Ben's hand. 'That went better than I thought it would.'

Ben didn't answer. He couldn't help thinking he'd just looked into a vast black hole and glimpsed the spectre of his own death.

Chapter Nine

By the time Ben and Maddie arrived at the Pentecostal church, Anne had returned home. Pastor Tom was sweeping the hall, jacket unbuttoned, trilby jammed on his head. 'How'd it go?'

'Good,' Maddie said.

Ben asked how his mother was.

Tom leaned the broom up against a chair. 'She's bearing up, son. It did her good to come and help. Took her mind off things for a while. So what happened in Oxford?'

Maddie recounted the day's events, including the cover story she'd given Marcus relating to her background. 'So we're going back tomorrow to see what his boss has to say.'

'You're *both* going back tomorrow?' Tom said. 'I thought you was taking care of Ben's mother?'

'Ben can't do this on his own. You could ask Rhonda to help out with Ben's mum?' Maddie said.

'Rhonda's already helping out here. What am I supposed to do, split the poor woman in two?'

Maddie laughed. 'Jesus fed the five thousand with a loaf of bread.'

'Five loaves and two fish,' Tom corrected. 'And just in case you haven't noticed, I'm not Jesus.'

'Anne would love Rhonda.'

'I'm not sure, Madeline. It's a big ask.'

'Rhonda won't mind. She's so sweet on you she gains weight just looking at you.'

'You've got too much of an imagination, young lady. Anyway, I need all the help I can get. If I lose both you and Rhonda, how am I supposed to get the church hall painted out? And I wanted to sort out the garden. I can't do it all on my own.'

'You can get some of the kids from youth club involved.'

'I want the hall painted, not destroyed.'

'They'd enjoy it. Kids can go a long way on fizzy drinks. Rhonda and Anne could help out with the church services.'

Tom turned to Ben. 'What about you, son? Is this what you want?'

'I don't want to put you to any trouble, Tom.'

'It's just a matter of delegating the work,' Maddie interrupted.

'Perhaps you'd be good enough to go to the kitchen and pour us all a nice glass of lemonade. There's a fresh bottle in the fridge.'

Maddie pouted. 'So you can both talk about me?'

'No. So we can all have a nice cold drink. I'm parched.'

Maddie flounced off to the kitchen. When she was out of sight, Tom shook his head. 'She's got her mother's stubborn streak. Sometimes that's a good thing, but sometimes it can be a hindrance. All I'm asking is that you both take a step back and try to see the wood for the trees.'

'I don't want her to come with me if it's going to cause trouble, Tom.'

'Madeline gets a bee in her bonnet, next thing you know, she's got a working hive.'

Ben smiled.

Pastor Tom didn't. 'Trouble is, son, bees can sting.'

'Like I said, I don't want her—'

Tom held up a hand. 'I've always let her have free rein to make her own decisions. Even when she was little. Children need space to grow. To make their own mistakes because they will be stronger for it. But there's a whole world of difference between allowing a child to grow and allowing a child to walk in front of a ten-tonne truck. Do you see what I mean, son?'

Ben did. He'd spent most of his life trying to avoid ten-tonne trucks.

'If she ends up going with you, all I ask is that you take care of her as best you can. That girl is the most precious thing in the world to me.'

Ben looked at the floor. His best had never been good enough. Not for his father. Not for Whittle Investigations. Not for his playground tormentors. Stutter-buck hadn't even been able to put a proper sentence together without getting all tangled up in vowels and consonants. So how was he supposed to take care of Maddie?

Ben spat out the words lodged in his throat. 'I d-don't think I can do this, Tom.'

'Don't put yourself down, son. I can still remember that kid who jumped out of the conker tree.'

'Fell,' Ben corrected. How could he ever forget the day that Stutter-buck took flight after spending the best part of two hours trapped in that conker tree?

'What was it you said that day?'

Ben tugged his earlobe. 'I can't remember.'

'You said you wished you were dead. Do you remember?'

He remembered only too well. The humiliation. The searing pain in his right knee. Pastor Tom bending over him.

'You said that you couldn't see any point in carrying on? But there's always a point, son. Even when we don't see the point of the point if you catch my drift?'

Ben wanted to reach out and hug Pastor Tom. Something he'd never been able to do with his own father. 'I suppose.'

'But I watched that kid grow.'

'Like a beanstalk.'

'I watched him lose that stammer. I watched him battle. Word by word. Do you remember how we talked about climbing a mountain that summer?'

'Yes.'

'How I said that it's important not to look up. You remember why it's important not to look up?'

'Because it always looks higher than it is.'

'Too right, it does. Same thing as if you look down from the top. It looks a mighty long way to fall. Do you remember how I said you need to find footholds to help you up the mountain?'

Ben did. He remembered almost every minute of that summer eight years ago. Pastor Tom had called the weather schizophrenic. One minute it was pouring with rain, the next, scorching sunshine. Tom had told Ben how the weather always played havoc with his joints, but it hadn't stopped him teaching Ben how to work Old Joe's mechanism with his misshapen hands gripping the levers.

'You climbed that mountain, son. You stood on the summit and you planted your flag right in God's face.'

Ben didn't think he'd reached a summit. He worked in an office and made Airfix models in his spare time. His social life consisted solely of youth club. Two stars for being a good boy, a big fat zero for enterprise.

'You deserve a medal for what you've achieved.'

'I bet you say that to all the kids,' Ben said, in his best Old Joe voice.

Tom's eyes sparkled beneath the shadow of his trilby. 'I know you're sweet on Madeline, son. That's why I know you'll do your best to look out for her.'

A blush crept up Ben's neck. 'Maddie's a good friend.'

Tom smiled. 'When I was in Rwanda, I met the most wonderful people you could ever wish to meet. They had nothing. Decimated by war, poverty and disease. But do you know the one thing they all had in abundance?'

'Each other?'

'They had hope, son. And hope is the rope that will get you up the mountain.'

Maddie returned with two glasses of lemonade and handed one to each man. 'We've made real headway today.'

Tom drained half his drink in one draught. 'And now you need to stand back and take stock. It's one thing agreeing to join a cult, quite another getting mixed up in one. They're dangerous.'

Maddie put her hands on her hips. 'We won't get very far *without* getting mixed up with them.'

'This isn't a game, Madeline.'

'Neither was Rwanda. But it didn't stop you and Mum staying out there, did it?'

'That's differ—'

'What was it you always told me? Face evil. Confront it. Never turn a blind eye. Wasn't that what you said?'

'Yes, but—'

'Who said it's wrong to turn a blind eye and just walk away?'

Tom put his glass down. The warmth vanished from his eyes. 'I said those things, Madeline, because they're true.'

'So what's the problem with me wanting to help Ben, then?'

'Nothing at all. I just don't want you rushing headlong into something you can't control. You need to have a proper plan of action.'

'I know that. I'm not stupid.'

'You're not immune to getting hurt.'

'I survived the attack on the village in Rwanda.'

'God can't always be there to look out for you, Madeline.'

Maddie looked at Ben. 'You'll look after me, won't you?'

Ben held up a hand. 'Please don't fight.'

Maddie's eyes flashed in the sunlight. 'We're not fighting.'

'I don't want you to come,' Ben lied.

'Tough. I'm coming with you whether you like it or not.'

'Then I won't go.'

Maddie gawked at him. 'So you're going to give up just like that? Just because—'

Ben stamped his foot and then felt instantly childish. 'I don't want to cause trouble. I've had enough trouble with my own family. This isn't your problem.'

Tom turned to Ben. 'It's all right, son. If Madeline wants to go, then she goes with my blessing. All I ask is that we sit down together and work out a proper plan.'

Maddie nodded. 'Okay by me.'

Ben wasn't so sure. 'And if it all goes wrong?'

Maddie grinned. 'I've got a black belt in Tae kwon do.'

'That won't be much use against a gun.'

'Then we'll just have to outsmart them. I could twist Marcus around my little finger if I wanted to.'

Ben remembered his father's desperate call. 'It'll take more than that.'

Maddie tilted her chin up. 'I know this cult isn't a few hippies sitting around a campfire smoking a peace pipe. I'm well aware of the dangers. I just want to help you, Ben.'

Ben opened his mouth to protest, but arguing with Maddie was like arguing with the wind about which way it was blowing.

'Come on. Let's go to the kitchen and thrash out a plan of action,' Tom said.

Maddie agreed. 'I'm up for that.'

Tom poured fresh lemonade for the three of them. They sat huddled around the small kitchen table like conspirators plotting the downfall of an adversary. Tom plonked his glass down and wiped his mouth. 'Does this cult have a name, son?'

'The Sons and Daughters of Salvation.'

Tom whistled. 'That's quite a mouthful.' He pulled out his iPhone and googled the name. He scrolled through the search results. 'Zilch. Are you sure that's the right name?'

'I didn't expect them to be famous,' Maddie said.

Tom put his phone back in his jacket pocket. 'So what have you told Marcus?'

'We were hiking across the country,' Maddie said. 'Someone stole our stuff.'

'And he seemed okay with that?'

'Why wouldn't he be?'

'Because liars are good at spotting liars, Madeline. They're experts at it.'

'He seemed fine,' Maddie assured him. 'I told him my dad was a headmaster at a private school. I said I had posh parents who didn't understand me.'

'What are you going to do if he tries to look up this private school on the internet? At the very least, you'll need the name of a real one.'

'I'll tell them I don't have a clue. I'm not interested in what he does.'

Tom formed a steeple with his fingers. 'Be careful. From what you've told me, it's likely they'll try to extort money from your fictional family.'

Maddie didn't seem too concerned. 'We won't be there long enough.'

Tom looked at Ben. 'What about you? What did you tell Marcus?'

'I told him my dad was a bank manager.'

Tom was quiet for a few moments, and then said, 'If you do join this cult, make sure you hide a phone somewhere. That way you'll have something to fall back on if you need help.'

Ben wondered if his father had any spare watch-phones kicking about in the house.

'Put the phone somewhere no one else will look. Maybe an outbuilding or something. Be smart.'

Maddie grinned. 'A smartphone.'

Tom grinned back. 'A smartphone for a smart alec.'

'Hey, that's a boy's name.'

'If the cap fits.'

'Much better than your trilby.'

'Seriously, guys, first sign of any trouble, and you get out of there. Run naked if you have to.'

'Across hot coals,' Maddie promised.

'Be vigilant. Be careful.'

A big part of Ben wished that Marcus's leader would say no. That way, no one could ever accuse him of not trying.

'I shall pray for you both tonight,' Tom said. He looked at Ben. 'And I shall pray for your father.'

Ben thought his father might already be with Pastor Tom's God, eating roast beef and mashed potatoes.

Tom pursed his lips. 'Go to your mother, Ben. Tell her what's happening. Reassure her.'

Ben thought it would be easier to reassure a polar bear that the ice cap was still in good shape. 'I'll try.'

Chapter Ten

Edward Ebb looked at the Imposter and shook his head. He didn't look in good shape. He kept whinging and whining that he'd broken his spine, but Ebb doubted the validity of the claim. He'd kicked and thrashed well enough when Ebb had poked a red-hot needle into the wound in his shoulder.

Ebb conceded the Imposter may well have suffered serious injuries, but he didn't care. He wasn't a doctor. It was of no consequence. But he needed to tread carefully because Satan was at his most potent when lying dormant.

Tweezer had made a good job of securing his upper body to the back of a kitchen chair with rope. His arms were pinned to his sides. Lumps of congealed vomit spilled onto his chin. His bald head gleamed with sweat beneath the overhead lights.

Ebb unscrewed the cap of a bottle of Evian spring water. 'Are you thirsty?'

The Imposter croaked something unintelligible.

'What's the matter? Afraid it might be holy water?'

'No.'

'Who are you?'

He studied Ebb with devious eyes. Full of pity. Full of deceit. Full of hate. 'I'm… a… bird-watcher…'

Ebb laughed. 'A bird-watcher? So how come you had a long-range camera in the tree with you?'

'I was—'

'We've had the film developed. Guess what?'

His nose started to bleed again. 'What?'

Ebb resisted an urge to poke out an eye. 'There wasn't one picture of a bird on that film. Not one. But there were plenty of pictures of my courtyard.'

'I—'

'Who sent you?'

He looked away. The way liars always did when backed into a corner.

'Did a demon send you?'

'No.' The word came out in a bubble of blood.

'Would you like a drink?'

The Imposter nodded.

'Then tell me who sent you?'

'No one. I—'

Ebb turned the bottle upside down and tipped half the contents onto the dusty concrete floor. He then righted the bottle and took a swig. Wiped his mouth. 'That's so good. Nice and cold. Straight from the fridge.'

The Imposter licked his cracked lips with a lizard tongue.

Ebb screwed the cap back on the bottle. 'I'll let you have some if you tell me who you are.'

His eyes narrowed. He looked like a fox with the scent of chicken in its snout.

Don't trust him, Pixie-pea.

Ebb jumped and turned around. There were three skeletons pinned to wooden crosses on the far wall. The middle one had a pink wig lodged on its skull and sunglasses covering its eye sockets. Ebb addressed it cautiously. 'Don't you worry about that. I've got his cards marked.'

Never trust a man with a beard, Pixie-pea.

Ebb gawked at the skeleton. 'He hasn't got a beard. Sister Alice shaved it off to look for the mark of the beast.'

'Don't split hairs, Pixie-pea. You know full well he normally wears face fuzz.'

'Leave me alone. I'm busy.'

The skeleton appeared to grin at him. He didn't like that grin. It smacked of smugness and arrogance. He turned back to face the Imposter. 'Tell me who you are and I'll let you have a drink.'

'A… bird-watcher….'

Ebb threw the bottle at him. It bounced off his forehead and landed on the floor next to his chair. The Imposter wriggled like a maggot on a fishhook. At one point, he almost tipped himself over.

'Sit still. I shan't pick you up if you tip yourself over.'

He stared at Ebb with those deceitful eyes. 'Please. I'm… in… agony….'

Ebb snorted. 'And I'm a busy man. All you need to do is tell me who you are and who sent you, and this will be over and done with.'

Done and dusted, Pixie-pea.

Ebb ignored the voice. 'Wouldn't you like that?'

The Imposter nodded his head and winced. Ebb noticed that two of his front teeth were missing. 'Would you like Sister Alice to splint that leg and wash your wounds?'

He nodded.

'So tell me who you are?'

The Imposter exercised his right to remain silent.

Ebb reached into the pocket of his white ceremonial robe and pulled out a small glass vial. He held it up in front of his quarry. 'Do you know what this is?'

'No.'

'It's holy water. Do you know what holy water is?'

'Yes.'

'Good. So you'll understand it burns the skin of evildoers?'

His eyes widened. 'Please… don't… do… this…'

Ebb uncapped the bottle. There was a tiny dropper attached to the lid. He drew some of the liquid into the dropper and stepped closer. Close enough to smell his rank body. The stench of bodily waste was almost too much to bear.

He wheezed and rasped like a knackered engine trying to whirr into life. 'Geoff… my name's… Geoff….'

Ebb stepped back, looking for signs of deception. 'Geoff who?'

He sucked in air through clenched teeth. He gasped five or six times, as if he were about to deliver a baby demon, and then shook his head.

Ebb tried to summon patience. It was wearing as thin as the Imposter's hair. 'Geoff who?'

He looked away.

The demon was toying with him. Teasing him. Trying to provoke him. Ebb refused to rise to it. 'I don't particularly care what your name is. I want you to tell me who sent you.'

'I'm a bird-watcher.'

'Did Satan send you?'

'No.'

'Does Satan reside in you?'

A long drawn out wheeze, and then: 'No.'

'I expect nothing other than denial from a terrorist.'

The Imposter's eyes rolled back in his head. Further indication he was harbouring a demon. 'I'm not—'

Ebb raised a hand and stepped back. 'I fear no evil. I shall not stand in the shadow of evil. I am the light, and I am the resurrection.'

'I'm... Geoff....' The words sounded as if they'd been raked over hot coals. The hot coals of Hell.

'Show yourself, Satan.'

'I'm... not... Satan....'

'Denial is always the first port of call for Satan's seafarers.' He stepped forward again and held out the dropper. 'The holy water shall determine your validity.'

He stared at Ebb with those treacherous eyes.

'Do you fear the holy water, Satan?'

Satan did. He'd written his confession in a thousand lines upon the Imposter's face. And well he might fear the holy water. Just as he'd been right to fear the hot needle that Ebb had thrust into his wounded shoulder. Like all cowards, Satan was not as good at taking pain as he was at dishing it out.

Ebb dripped a few drops of holy water onto the Imposter's right hand.

The coward did not stand on ceremony. He bucked and writhed and tipped himself sideways onto the cold concrete floor. His head hit the ground with a nasty thud, reminiscent of when Ebb had hit his mother over the head with a shovel many years ago.

'Come forth, Satan. Come forth and show yourself.'

Satan seemed content thrashing about on the floor inside the Imposter's body. Ebb had intended to drop some acid onto the weasel's other hand, but he didn't want to risk his own safety by getting too close. A wounded animal was a dangerous animal.

'Come forth, Satan. Come into the light and face the truth.'

Satan's rage frothed and bubbled on the Imposter's lips. Ebb wouldn't have been at all surprised to see ectoplasm forming a cocoon around him. He retreated to a safer distance and screwed the cap back onto the bottle.

'I shall send Sister Alice and Brother Tweezer to attend to you later.'

The Imposter didn't look very grateful. He wriggled and moaned and scraped his head on the rough concrete floor as if trying to burrow his way out of the Revelation Room.

Ebb was in no mood to pander to whims. He walked out of the Revelation Room and locked the door behind him. As soon as he understood Satan's purpose here, the Imposter could go straight to Hell courtesy of death by a thousand cuts.

Chapter Eleven

Ben and Maddie found Marcus standing outside Marks and Spencer talking to a scruffy looking youth in baggy jeans and a tee-shirt with the word 'Dope' printed on the front. Marcus handed the kid something. They touched knuckles.

In spite of the heat, Marcus was wearing a long trench coat that reached right down to his knees. As the youth walked away, he squinted at Ben with bloodshot eyes. He grinned at Maddie. 'Hey, good to see you.'

Maddie accepted Marcus's outstretched hand and shook it. 'Good to see you, too.'

Marcus tipped back his straw hat. 'I'll cut straight to the chase. I've had a word with our illustrious leader, and he says he's willing to give you guys a go.'

Maddie punched the air. 'That's brilliant news.'

Ben felt sick.

Marcus let go of Maddie's hand and grinned. 'It sure is.'

'We spent last night in an alleyway,' Maddie said. 'I got woke up about a hundred times by a bloody tomcat.'

'Edward doesn't like cats.'

'Nor do I, now,' Maddie said.

'He says they're devious. He's got a dog. Max. An Alsatian. Do you like dogs?'

'I don't mind them.'

'Ben?'

'They're all right,' Ben lied. Aunt Mary had owned an Alsatian when he was about six or seven. It was the nearest thing he'd seen to a bona fide monster. He remembered being terrified of it every time they visited.

'You might get a chance to walk it.'

Ben shuddered. 'Cool.'

'There's loads of land at the farm. I hope you're fit. Anyway, we'd better get going. Edward's waiting for us.'

They followed Marcus through a series of alleyways and shortcuts to a wide tree-lined street. An assortment of large detached houses sat back from the road. Some of them had vacancies signs hanging in the front windows.

Marcus pointed to a red Land Rover 90 parked a hundred yards up the road. 'There's Edward.'

Ben's stomach flipped over.

'Make sure you address him as *Father*. And only speak to him when he speaks to you. Okay?'

Maddie nodded.

'Be respectful at all times.'

Ben's feet felt as if they were wading through treacle. Everything seemed to move in slow motion. The air was thick and heavy. Maddie grabbed his hand. She squeezed it once and then let go. Ben wiped his palms on the front of his jeans.

As they got within a few feet of the Land Rover, a short, bald, overweight man dressed in a white cotton shirt and matching trousers stepped out onto the pavement. He dabbed his forehead with a red handkerchief. 'This must be Ben and Maddie?'

Marcus touched the rim of his hat. 'Yes, Father.'

Ebb stuffed the handkerchief into his pocket and held out his hand to Ben. 'I'm Edward Ebb. Delighted to meet you, Ben.'

Ben shook Ebb's hand and told the biggest lie he'd ever told in his life: 'Pleased to meet you.'

'Father,' Marcus prompted.

'Father.'

Ebb turned to Maddie and shook her hand. 'You have lovely eyes, Madeline.'

'Thank you.'

Creep, Ben thought.

'Marcus tells me you've both been sleeping rough.'

Maddie nodded. 'Yes, Father.'

Ebb pursed his lips and studied Maddie. 'You'll be pleased to know those days are behind you now.'

'Thank you, Father.'

'You're welcome, Madeline. Before we get going, I must ask you both to put on a blindfold.'

Ben's hesitated. 'Why?'

Ebb smiled; it reminded Ben of sugar-coated doughnuts for some inexplicable reason. 'It's nothing personal, Ben. Far from it. Just a security measure.'

'I don't get it.'

Ebb sighed. 'There are those who seek to destroy us. I know that sounds hard to believe in the twenty-first century. You'd think that such bigotry was dead and buried along with the dinosaurs. But bigotry is our greatest enemy. One we have to fight at all costs.'

'Amen,' Marcus chirped.

'Should anyone leave us, we like to be assured that our location remains a secret.'

My father found you easily enough, Ben thought. *And so did we.*

'What you don't know, you can't tell,' Maddie said.

'Precisely, Madeline. We try to go about our business and avoid confrontation. We're just a peace-loving group of people trying to do what is right in a morally bankrupt world.'

'Amen,' Marcus chirped again.

Ebb pursed his lips and gazed off into the distance. 'From the minute you leave the cradle, the bigots have got their claws into you. I hope in the coming months you will come to recognise the hypocrisy that dominates the so-called free world. See it for what it is and rise up against it.'

A shiver rippled through Ben's body.

'If you both want to jump in the back, Marcus will sort out the blindfolds for you once you are comfortable.'

Marcus held the door open as Ben and Maddie clambered inside. He then walked to the front of the vehicle and returned with two balaclavas. Neither had eyeholes. Just a small slit in the middle to accommodate the nose.

Ben tried not to panic as his world was plunged into darkness. Marcus leaned across him and buckled his seatbelt. He could smell stale tobacco and garlic on Marcus's breath. He imagined those rotting front teeth sinking into his flesh like a vampire's.

'How does that feel?' Marcus asked him.

'I can't breathe.'

'You'll be fine once we get rolling,' Ebb promised. 'I'll open the window.'

Marcus slammed the door and went to Maddie's side. Ben listened in disbelief as Maddie told Marcus that she couldn't wait to get going.

Ebb started the engine. 'Is everyone set?'

'Yes, Father,' Maddie said.

Marcus jumped in the passenger seat and closed the door.

Ebb asked Ben if he was ready for the journey.

Ben wanted to rip the balaclava off his head and run away as fast as his knackered knee would allow him.

'Brother Benjamin?' Ebb prompted.

'Yes. Father. I'm fine.'

Chapter Twelve

The journey lasted almost an hour. It seemed like a week to Ben. Every muscle in his body ached and his head pounded.

Ebb switched off the engine. 'Okay, folks, you can take the balaclavas off now.'

Ben ripped the thing from his head and threw it on the floor. He screwed up his face as bright sunlight invaded his eyes.

Ebb turned around. 'Home sweet home.'

Maddie touched Ben's arm. 'Are you okay?'

Ben resisted an urge to reply with sarcasm. 'I guess.'

Marcus held the door open for Maddie and helped her out of the Land Rover.

Ben climbed out onto the parched earth of a farm courtyard. He stamped his feet to encourage life into his legs. A stone outbuilding and two derelict barns surrounded the courtyard. There was a tall thin guy wearing bright yellow overalls working in one of the barns.

Ebb paraded up and down in front of Ben and Maddie like a sergeant major greeting raw recruits. 'Welcome to The Sons and Daughters of Salvation. First things first; I'd like to introduce you to one or two house rules.'

Maddie looked about her. 'Wow. A farm.'

Marcus warned her not to speak unless spoken to.

Maddie plucked a strand of hair out of her eyes. 'Sorry.'

Ebb strutted about like a peacock. 'Sorry is not a word I accept, Madeline. Sorry implies that you have disobeyed me. However, on this occasion, I will let it go because you are still new. A little excited, perhaps?'

'Yes, Father.'

Ebb smiled.

A smile cooked in oil, Ben thought.

'The Sons and Daughters of Salvation are dedicated to serving the Lord Jesus Christ. We like to think that it offers our members a level of depth and meaning that cannot be found in the outside world.'

Ben looked around the courtyard. Was his father being held captive in one of the barns?

He's dead. Dead and buried and rotting away in the cold earth.

Ebb brushed something from the front of his shirt. 'As Brother Marcus has already said, you are only permitted to speak when I address you. Is that clear?'

'Yes, Father,' Maddie said.

Ebb looked at Ben with coal-black eyes. 'Benjamin?'

My name's Ben, not *fucking Benjamin.* 'Yes, Father.'

Maddie pointed to a brick-built tower standing fifty feet above the courtyard. 'What's that?'

'For the last time, stop speaking out of turn, Madeline,' Ebb said. 'If you have questions, Brother Tweezer will be more than happy to answer them later.'

Ben looked at the tower. There appeared to be someone standing at the top. A distant blob decked in yellow.

Ebb continued. 'Now, listen up, because this is important: every member of The Sons and Daughters of Salvation is considered an equal. We wear the same clothes. We eat the same food. We speak the same language. Anyone who gets ideas above their station will be punished. Is that clear?'

'Yes,' Maddie said.

Ben nodded.

Ebb drew himself up to his full height of just over five and a half feet. 'It is not sufficient to simply nod your head.'

'Sorry.'

Sweat trickled down Ebb's face and glistened on his top lip. 'You'll learn, Benjamin. You'll learn soon enough. It's still early days. We're bound to encounter teething problems. As long as you understand the chain of command. Myself, then Brother Tweezer, then Brother Marcus and Sister Alice. You may go to any of the aforementioned with grievances, and they will bring those grievances to me. Do you understand?'

Ben and Maddie answered in unison. 'Yes, Father.'

'But positive people don't carry grievances. Positive people get on with the job in hand. Positive people serve the Lord without fear or favour. I want you to both empty your pockets and place the contents on the ground in front of you.'

Ben suddenly remembered the pay-as-you-go phone he'd bought from Tesco the night before. Pastor Tom had told him to hide it somewhere safe in case of emergencies. What was he supposed to do now? Pretend he didn't have it? Hurl it into the bushes surrounding the courtyard?

After a few moments, Ebb asked, 'Have you got a problem, Benjamin?'

Ben shook his head.

'I don't hear you, my friend. I asked if you've got a problem?'

Ben's head was alive with the damned things. 'No, Father.'

'Then why are you standing there as if you've been struck dumb? I asked you to empty your pockets.'

Ben looked at the baked earth. The baked earth offered no solutions. He took the phone from his pocket and laid it on the ground, along with some loose change and a Snickers wrapper.

Ebb smiled. 'Do you have a sweet tooth, Benjamin?'

'Sometimes. When I need energy.'

'Address the Father properly,' Marcus shouted.

Ben bowed his head. 'Sorry. Father.'

'The Lord shall give you all the energy you need, Benjamin. He shall shine his light upon you and fill you with His energy.'

'Yes, Father.'

Ben watched Maddie empty the front pouch of her dungarees. A pack of chewing gum. A comb. Some lipstick. A screwed up fiver. A keying with a Snoopy fob.

'Thank you, Madeline. Now I'd like you both to strip down to your underwear.'

'Here?' Maddie moaned.

'It's a warm day.'

'But I burn in the sun.'

'You won't be in the sun long enough to burn,' Ebb snapped.

Whilst they stripped, Marcus scooped up their belongings and stuffed them into the pocket of his trench coat. He then walked over to one of the barns.

Ben stood in his boxers. The sun beat down on his exposed body. The earth scorched his feet. Out of the corner of his right eye he could see Maddie looking at him. He stared ahead, flushed with embarrassment. He hated his body. He looked like a skeleton with a stoop.

Marcus returned with a large black refuse sack. He pulled out two pairs of bright yellow overalls and handed one each to Ben and Maddie. 'Put these on.'

The overalls were baggy around the middle and two inches short on the legs. Ben was just relieved to be covered up.

Marcus put Ben and Maddie's clothes in the bin liner and knotted it at the top.

'Get Bubba to burn them,' Ebb said. 'When he's done that, tell him to come to the kitchen.'

'Yes, Father.' Marcus walked towards the barn where the tall, thin guy was working.

Ben watched Marcus walked towards the barn where the tall, thin guy was working. Now all he had left in the world was a hideous pair of bright yellow overalls and a thumping headache. This was going so much better than he could have imagined. All he needed now was Ebb's dog to rip him to shreds, and his day would be complete.

Ebb stood in front of Maddie. 'Yours look made to measure, Madeline.'

'Thank you, Father.'

Ebb inclined his head and moved in front of Ben. 'Yours seem to have come up short, Benjamin.'

'Yes, Father.'

'Brother Gerald was about your height. I'll see if Sister Alice can find you a pair of his.'

Ben wondered where Brother Gerald was now. *Dead? Murdered? Buried in a field?*

'I trust you don't mind hand-me-downs?'

Ben saw something flash in those coal-black eyes. Something akin to a shadow in a window. 'No, Father.'

Ebb smiled. 'Perhaps some of his enthusiasm might rub off on you. They say energy can be stored within material objects.'

Marcus returned from the barn. 'All good, Father.'

Ebb rubbed his hands together. 'Let's get inside and meet the others.'

They followed the two men out of the courtyard and along a narrow path overgrown with weeds and moss. Brambles and tall hedgerows flanked the path.

Ben trod on a stone and then stubbed his toe on the path. 'Can't I have my trainers back?'

'We don't wear shoes,' Ebb said.

Ben looked at Ebb's sandals. What the hell was that on his feet, then? Illusions?

'Shoes inhibit direction,' Ebb added. 'We must be in direct contact with Mother Earth at all times.'

Ben wondered what happened in winter. Did everyone have to walk around barefoot and end up with frostbite?

They walked up to a large detached farmhouse with dirty, cream-coloured rendering and rotted window frames. There was a brass wolf's-head knocker fixed to the front door. Ebb banged it three times, pausing a few seconds between each one. 'The place needs a bit of work, but the Lord is our main priority.'

It needs demolishing, Ben thought.

A short, middle-aged woman with grey spiky hair answered the door. She was also dressed in the obligatory yellow overalls.

She wore a pair of half-rim spectacles with gold chains dangling from the arms.

'Good afternoon, Sister Alice.'

'Good afternoon, Father.'

'I'd like you to meet Benjamin and Madeline. They'll be joining us.'

Alice smiled. 'Pleased to meet you both.'

Ben didn't like the look of Alice any better than he liked the look of Ebb and Marcus. It was as if they all wore masks over their true identity. Beneath the masks, he imagined maggots crawling amongst rotting flesh.

Alice stood aside. They walked into a hallway with filthy cream walls and a bare oak floor. 'I trust you are well, Father?'

Ebb closed the door. 'Very well, Sister Alice. Thank you.'

Alice led them along the hallway and into a massive kitchen. One end of the kitchen was given to functionality, with a large ceramic sink and a range of dark-oak cupboards and base units. Ben thought it made his local fried-chicken outlet look obsessed with hygiene. A huge pine farmhouse table, that looked capable of hosting the Last Supper, dominated the centre of the room.

Alice fetched a teapot from the worktop next to the sink and plonked it down on the table. 'I've just made it.'

Ebb told Ben and Maddie to sit at the table. He then turned to Marcus. 'After you've changed, I want you to relieve Brother Tweezer up the tower. I'd like him to come and meet Madeline and Benjamin.'

Marcus stood up. He inclined his head like a butler and then walked out of the room. Ben noticed a strange look in Marcus's eyes. A blank look that suggested he wasn't in control of his own mind.

Alice poured tea for everyone. Ben didn't want tea. Especially black tea without sugar. To make matters worse, he burnt his top lip when he took a sip.

Ebb grinned. A greasy grin that smeared oil on his chops. 'I'm sorry if it's not to your usual taste, but I'm afraid we don't use artificial flavourings.'

Dinner will be a riot, then, Ben thought.

Ebb's smile evaporated. 'But you'll soon acclimatise. In fact, I can guarantee you will come to hate artificial flavours as your taste buds return to their normal state.'

Ben doubted it. Salt and ketchup had got him through some of his mother's worst culinary disasters. He stared at his mug of tea and wondered how the hell Ebb considered milk to be artificial.

Ebb pursed his lips. 'Most of the allergies and illnesses in the western world are caused by poor diet and a tendency towards gluttony.'

Ben tried to marry Ebb's words with the man's waistline. Ebb seemed unaware of the contradictions.

'Here at The Sons and Daughters of Salvation, we only take what we need, and need what we take.'

Alice bowed her head. 'Amen.'

'Indulgence is a sin.'

Alice agreed. The glasses perched on the end of her nose made her look like an old school mistress.

Ebb blew steam from his mug and took a sip of tea. 'The indulgences of the free world are banned here. Your system will soon learn to dismiss them.'

Alice crossed herself. 'Praise Jesus.'

Ebb turned his attention to Ben. 'What's your poison, Benjamin?'

'Huh?'

'Stand up, Benjamin.'

Ben stood. His knee begged for an ice pack. One–nil to the tormentors of Stutter-buck.

Ebb studied Ben for a few seconds. And then said, 'Please refrain from such banal responses. "Huh" is not an answer.'

'Sorry.'

'Sorry, Father,' Alice corrected.

Ebb put his mug on the table. 'What's your indulgence, Benjamin? Alcohol? Cream? Pork?'

'I like sugar in my tea,' Ben blurted.

Ebb regarded him as if he'd just admitted to liking murder. 'Sugar is the Devil's dust.'

'Amen,' Alice agreed.

'The Devil sprinkles it like fairy dust. But what are his motives?'

Sweat trickled down Ben's back. The coarse material of the overalls rubbed against his skin. He wanted to tell Ebb he suffered from eczema. That his mother had to rub cream into his back sometimes. That the itching drove him mad when it flared up. But Ebb would only attribute the eczema to his western indulgences and tell him that a radical change of diet would soon clear up his skin.

Ebb continued. 'His motives are simple. He wants to weigh us down. He wants to turn us into slugs, slithering in the slime of our own excesses.'

Alice bowed her head. 'We shall not succumb.'

Ebb banged the table. The loose flesh around his chin rippled. 'We must resist temptation.'

'I can do without sugar,' Ben said, afraid that he was about to be carted away and flogged to within an inch of his waistline.

Ebb held up a hand. 'The Devil serves behind the counter of every single outlet in every single town. It is our duty to stand against him.'

Alice crossed herself. 'We shall not be tempted, Father.'

'From the bakery to the burger bar, he peddles his filth.'

'We see him, Father.'

'Indeed we do, Sister Alice. He is mustard gas on a succulent beef sandwich.'

Alice pushed her glasses up her nose and sniffed. She didn't seem to have a response to Ebb's somewhat cryptic statement.

Ebb continued on less confusing ground. 'But we will flush him out. Flush him out and send him to burn in the pits of Hell for all eternity.'

Alice seemed more comfortable with this. 'Amen.'

Ebb dabbed his face with a sodden handkerchief. 'Sit down, Benjamin.'

As Ben sat down, his knee cracked and almost spilled him to the floor.

Ebb studied him. 'Are you all right, Pixie-pea?'

'Yes, Father,' Ben lied. 'I'm fine.'

Ebb turned to Alice. 'Gather the troops. It's time to introduce everyone. Brother Bubba's in the barn. I told Brother Marcus to tell him to come in before he relieved Tweezer up the tower, but he can be inclined to grow moss on his brain. Give him a nudge.'

'Yes, Father. Right away.'

Chapter Thirteen

Dressed in bright yellow overalls, The Sons and Daughters of Salvation filed into the kitchen one at a time and sat at the huge pine table. Ben looked at the two women sitting either side of Sister Alice. Neither bore any resemblance to the photograph of Emily Hunt.

With everyone settled, Ebb stood at the head of the table and clasped his hands in front of him. 'Thank you, one and all, for coming. I'd like to take this opportunity to introduce you to Benjamin and Madeline. They will be joining us for the journey.'

There was a smattering of greetings and polite smiles.

Ebb smiled at Ben. 'Stand up and tell the group about yourself.'

Ben held onto the table for support. Every muscle in his body ached. 'I'm Ben,' he managed, as all cohesive thought abandoned his head. What was he supposed to say now? *I'm here to rescue my father, if you haven't killed him already?*

An uneasy silence fell across the room, broken by the ticking of a china clock on the wall above the sink.

Ebb cocked his head to one side. 'Tell the group why you're here, Benjamin.'

Ben saw that shadow lurking in Ebb's eyes again. 'I want to do something positive. I don't like what the world has become.'

Ebb clapped his hands together. 'Amen to that.'

'Amen,' the group agreed.

Encouraged, Ben added that he wanted to lead a positive life and make a real difference to the world.

'How do you propose to make a difference?' Ebb asked.

'By doing the right thing, Father.'

'You can only do the right thing by opening your heart to Jesus, Benjamin. Are you willing to open your heart to Jesus?'

'Yes, Father.'

Ebb nodded, like a triumphant gladiator acknowledging the roar of the crowd. 'Sit down, Benjamin. It's clear that your intentions are good. We shall see later whether they are genuine.'

A chill passed through Ben's heart.

Ebb turned to Maddie. 'Please introduce yourself to the group.'

Maddie stood up and treated everyone to a smile that never failed to make Ben's heart turn cartwheels. 'My name is Maddie – Madeline – and I'm twenty years old. I just want to be given an opportunity. A chance to do something good. A chance to belong to something that means more than just following the latest trends. I want to be with people who can see further than the end of their iPhones. Live in a world that cares. Cares about poverty. About making a real difference to people's lives. I'm sick of listening to politicians ranting on about saving the planet and then dropping bombs on it. I want to be with people who care about the same things as me. People who believe in the power of love instead of the power of the bullet....'

Ben gawked at Maddie as she trailed off.

Ebb applauded. 'Amen, Madeline. Amen.'

The rest of the group obliged Maddie with a smattering of applause.

Maddie looked around the table. 'Thank you.'

Ebb grinned, revealing a row of small, even teeth. 'That was a wonderful introductory speech, Madeline. Please be seated.'

As Maddie sat down, a stocky guy dressed in the obligatory yellow overalls entered the kitchen. He had shoulder-length brown hair and a goatee beard. He sat down next to Ebb.

Ebb clasped his hands together. 'Ah, Brother Tweezer. Thank you for joining us.'

Tweezer inclined his head. 'Glad to be here, Father.'

Ben couldn't see one flicker of emotion in Tweezer's dark eyes.

'I'd like you to meet Brother Tweezer,' Ebb said. 'My right-hand man.'

A shiver rolled up Ben's spine.

'Brother Tweezer, if you'd be so good as to tell our guests about yourself.'

Tweezer stood up. 'Pleased to meet you both. My name's Tweezer. I'm forty years old. And before you say it, I know, I only look half that age.'

Polite laughter. Ben wondered if someone was standing just out of view with a cue-card.

Tweezer held his hands out, palms up. 'Let me tell you, brothers and sisters, the Father saved me. I was a sinner, folks. A sinner of the worst kind. For I killed a man.'

As if on cue, the group mumbled thanks to the Lord for saving a mortal sinner like Brother Tweezer. Except Bubba, who studied the table.

Tweezer looked at the ceiling. 'I'm not proud of what I did. Far from it. I'm ashamed.'

Ebb nodded. 'We feel your shame, Brother Tweezer. We share your shame.'

Tweezer rattled on. 'The motorcycle gang I belonged to gave me a false identity and made me worship a false god.'

Ebb pumped a fist in the air. 'We condemn all false gods to the pits of Hell.'

'After I killed him, I stood over that poor dead soul and wept like a child. Wept at the senselessness of it all. Feud after feud. The hatred. The disregard for life. Have you ever hated someone?' Tweezer asked Ben.

Ben remembered the other kids at school. 'Maybe.'

Tweezer looked at Maddie.

'No.'

'Then you are lucky. I was cursed by a cruel and vindictive mind. My ego was like a raging bull.'

'Hatred is a sin,' Ebb cried.

'Hatred is a sin,' the group chanted.

'Did that man deserve to die? Of course he didn't. But my mind was so distorted with hatred, I believed my actions were justified. He took my woman. Violated my property. He deserved to be skinned alive. Beating him to death with a hammer was too good for that low-down dog. But after my anger was spent, I fell to my knees and wept tears upon his dead body. Tears of shame and remorse.'

'The sin of vengeance,' Ebb shouted.

Tweezer agreed. Bubbles of spit formed at the corners of his mouth. He looked off into the distance. 'Forgive me, Father, for I have sinned.'

Ebb closed his eyes. 'The Lord has forgiven you, Brother Tweezer.'

'Thank you, Father. I am humbled by the Lord's love.'

Ebb raised a hand. 'Praise be.'

'If I could go back right now and tell that reckless angry fool to put down his hammer and walk away from violence, then I would. As God is my judge, I would.'

Ebb touched Tweezer's arm. 'The Lord knows you would, Brother. The Lord hears you.'

Tweezer took a deep breath and wiped his mouth with the back of his hand. 'Sometimes we have to go to the lowest place, folks. We need to feel the flames of Hell burning our backsides before we wake up and reach out to Jesus.'

'Satan is the salesman of the broken dream, Pixie-pea,' Ebb babbled.

'I sold my soul, Father. Made that man strip naked. And then I beat him to death.'

Ebb made the sign of the cross. 'The Devil coerced you, Brother.'

'But Jesus saved me. Jesus told me to walk away and reject the ways of Satan.'

'Jesus loves you,' Ebb shouted.

Tweezer agreed. 'No more gangs. No more violence. No more retribution. I walked away from a life of sex, drugs and violence.

One step at a time, I learned to walk again. I slept beneath the stars, knowing that Jesus was watching over me and guiding me towards my destiny.'

Ebb raised his hands. 'Praise Jesus.'

'And that journey ended right here at Penghilly's Farm. I must have walked a thousand miles.'

'The Lord mapped your path, Brother Tweezer.'

'A beautiful journey,' Tweezer concluded.

'The Lord showed mercy to a wretched soul like you, Brother. He does not refuse those who seek to change. Those who seek to obey His ways.'

'I am blessed, Father. I thank Jesus for bringing me here. For giving me the chance to serve the Lord and lead a valid and worthwhile life.'

'Thank you, Brother Tweezer. You may be seated.'

The group applauded as Tweezer sat down. Tweezer held his hands up in *a gee-shucks-it-was-nothing* gesture.

Ebb gestured to the tall guy who'd been working in the barn. 'This is Bubba.'

There was a sadness in Bubba's pale blue eyes. His thinning grey hair was combed back, and his face looked like tanned leather. He reminded Ben of a loyal dog who'd been on the receiving end of a boot too many times.

Ebb made the sign of the cross. 'Bubba doesn't speak. But I can tell you, without fear of contradiction, he is a loyal and valued member of The Sons and Daughters of Salvation.'

Bubba bowed his head and looked at the table.

Ben wondered why he didn't speak.

Ebb turned to the middle-aged woman with the short, spiky grey hair and half-rimmed glasses. 'If you'd be kind enough to introduce yourself to Benjamin and Madeline, Sister Alice.'

Alice stood up. 'I'm Sister Alice and I'm fifty-nine years old. My journey started soon after I lost my husband seven years ago. Roger was my life. My rock. My anchor. His death ripped my heart in two.'

Ebb bowed his head. 'We share your loss, Sister Alice.'

'Thank you, Father. Before Roger drowned in a boating accident, I had the best of everything. Clothes. Shoes. Finest food. Opera. Theatre.'

'The sin of opulence.'

'Yes, Father. The sin of opulence, of which I am truly ashamed. After Roger's death, I drank heavily. Gin. Wine. Vodka. Anything that would help. Antidepressants. Painkillers. Within two years, I was a wreck. Most mornings I couldn't even be bothered to get out of bed. My head felt like a swamp. My body was bloated. My eyes were puffy. I let my hair go. I looked how I felt and felt how I looked. But in some strange way, there was a comfort in my misery.'

'It takes courage to live with loss,' Ebb said.

Alice looked at Ebb. 'But everything changed the day Father Edward came to my door spreading the word of Jesus.'

'Jesus showed me the way to your door, Sister Alice.'

'You saved me, Father.'

'I was a mere conduit, sister. It was Jesus Christ Himself who came unto me and told me of your need.'

'I owe my life to you, Father. You and Jesus.'

'Jesus does not turn a blind eye to those who have lost their way. He is the light. He is the resurrection.'

'Praise Jesus,' Alice shouted.

Ebb stood up and closed his eyes. He took several deep breaths and raised his hands above him. 'Jesus is among us now.'

A communal gasp rippled through the kitchen.

Ebb swayed from side to side. 'Jesus is proud of you, Sister Alice. He tells me you have surpassed all expectations.'

Sister Alice's lips trembled. Tears spilled from her eyes. She clutched her hands to her chest. 'Thank you, Lord.'

'But there is much work to be done. Jesus wants every single one of us ready for an arduous and challenging journey. We must not fear the path we tread. We must stand up to Satan and defeat him at every turn.'

'Praise Jesus,' the group chanted.

Ebb pursed his lips. 'Jesus tells me that Satan will come to us in many forms. He will hide among us and seek to destroy us. We must repel him. Be resolute. Ready to act against him at all times. We must beware the Imposter.'

'Beware the Imposter,' Sister Alice echoed.

Ebb strutted up and down the kitchen, head cocked to one side, as though deep in conversation. He stopped at the head of the table and rested his hands on the edge. He looked at each member in turn. 'Jesus trusts us. Jesus loves us. Jesus is in our hearts. Praise Jesus.'

'Praise Jesus,' the group chanted.

'Jesus must leave us now, but He wants you all to be assured that you are blessed with His everlasting love. Praise Jesus.'

'Praise Jesus.'

Ebb told Sister Alice to sit down. He then turned to a thin woman with long dark hair and pale blue eyes. 'Sister Dixie? If you'd be so kind.'

The woman stood up. 'My name is Dixie. I'm twenty-six years old. Jesus saved me from a life of debauchery and abuse.'

'Jesus feels your pain, Sister Dixie,' Ebb said.

Dixie looked around the table. 'From the age of ten, my stepfather abused me. Mentally and physically. By the time I was thirteen that excuse for a man had taken my virginity. I hated him with all my heart. He raped my soul.'

Ebb shook his head. 'Suffer the little children.'

Ben didn't think the phrase meant what Ebb had intended, but he was in no mood to correct the maniac.

Dixie took a deep breath. 'I hung about with older kids. Smoking weed, nicking stuff, bunking school. Nothing too heavy. Just rebelling. Then I met Jazz. He treated me good. At first.'

Ebb sneered. 'The seeds of seduction.'

Dixie looked out the kitchen window as if her childhood was playing out among the weeds and the brambles. 'He bought me things. Nice things. Shoes. Coats. Skirts. Handbags. He called me his princess. He even bought me a ring and told me we would get married one day. We would live in a big house with a swimming pool and a Jacuzzi.'

Ebb made the sign of the cross. 'Lead us not into temptation.'

'Jazz had a flat. He asked me to move in with him just past my fifteenth birthday. I didn't need convincing. I'd have walked over hot coals to get away from home. I packed a few things in a bag, and that was that. I never went back home again. Ever. But the good times didn't last long. Within a few weeks, Jazz was knocking me about. A slap here and a slap there. I used to think I was doing something wrong. You know, like I hadn't tried hard enough. But then it escalated. He started bringing men back to the flat. He made me have sex with them.'

'The Devil's disciples,' Ebb said.

Dixie took a deep breath. 'He used to tell me I was useless. Useless in bed. Useless at giving his so-called friends a good time. Some friends! Punters, more like. I'd become a whore without even realising it. I don't remember turning sixteen. By the time I reached seventeen, my life was a conveyor belt of sex, drugs, beatings, more sex, more beatings, more drugs.'

'Jesus feels your pain, Sister Dixie.'

Dixie looked at Ebb. 'You saved me, Father. You rescued me from the clutches of evil. I owe my life to you.'

'The Lord brought me to your door, Sister. The Lord is your salvation. Thank you for sharing. You may be seated.'

Dixie smiled. A worn-out smile detached from her eyes. She sat down. 'Thank you, Father.'

Ebb stretched himself up to his full height. 'You see the evil we are up against? Satan is as slippery as an eel coated in oil. We must not let our guard down for one second. He is as elusive as the wind. As dangerous as the turning tide. One wrong move, and, BAM!' Ebb thumped the table. 'He'll be upon you like a hog in heat.'

Tweezer held his hands up. 'Lord, we ask that you protect us from evil.'

'Amen,' the group mumbled.

Ebb gestured towards a young girl with a sandy-brown crewcut. 'Sister Emily. Please introduce yourself.'

Ben's heart thudded in his chest. Even though she looked nothing like the girl in the photograph, having the same name was just too much of a coincidence.

Emily stood up and looked at Ebb. Her eyes looked red as if she'd been crying. 'My name's Emily. I'm nineteen years old. And I owe my life to The Sons and Daughters of Salvation. Before I found Jesus, I was a lost soul.'

'Praise Jesus,' Ebb chirped.

'I was a wretch, lurching through life with no purpose. I hated my life. My father was a bully. He was an officer in the army.'

The coincidences piled up in Ben's head.

'I never saw much of him when I was growing up. He was always away from home. I didn't like school. I had no proper friends. Girls were too bitchy to bother with. As for boys, they were all immature.'

'You are a paragon of virtue, Sister Emily.'

'Thank you, Father.'

'Please continue.'

'But when I found Jesus, my life had meaning. A purpose. The capitalist world has always disgusted me. The hypocrisy of a society built on greed and selfishness. Everyone treading on top of one another, with no consideration for anyone else.'

'The Lord watches. The Lord sees. The Lord knows the truth,' Ebb babbled.

Emily nodded. 'I thank the Lord Jesus Christ and The Sons and Daughters of Salvation for rescuing me from a meaningless life. For filling up my heart with joy and purpose.'

Ebb raised a hand. 'Thank you, Sister Emily. You may be seated.'

Ben watched Emily sit down. She didn't look like someone whose heart was full of joy and purpose.

Ebb instructed Bubba to stand. The guy was six feet six in his bare feet. He studied the table as if his life was mapped out in the knots and scratches.

Ebb introduced him. 'This is Bubba. Because he doesn't speak, I'll say a few words on his behalf. First things first; I think it's fair to say that Bubba was built with the farm....'

A ripple of dutiful laughter.

Ebb raised his hand. *I know. I should've been a stand-up comedian.* 'Bubba used to work for Brother Cyril right back when Penghilly's Farm was a working farm.' Ebb paused and looked at Bubba. 'Eggs and potatoes, if memory serves me?'

Bubba nodded.

Ebb continued. 'Brother Cyril was the original owner of Penghilly's Farm. Sadly, he is no longer among us. He had an accident with a tractor when we were felling trees. The Lord took him to eat at His table, folks. May God rest his soul.'

'God rest his soul,' Tweezer echoed.

'A sad day. But who are we to question the Lord's intentions? We are here to serve. But let it be known that we are all grateful for Brother Cyril's contribution to The Sons and Daughters of Salvation.'

Bubba stared at the table. He seemed to mouth something. A silent prayer, perhaps?

'Bubba has been a good and loyal servant. I felt it my duty to help him. To understand him. To take him into my care and show compassion.'

Tweezer held up a hand. 'A gracious act, Father.'

Ebb agreed. 'We are nothing without benevolence and compassion. Nothing but empty shells. Bubba has proved to be a selfless worker. An honest man who has given himself without complaint to the Lord. He speaks volumes without words. The Lord is proud of you, Brother Bubba.'

Bubba nodded and studied the table.

'Brother Cyril came in a dream and spoke of his love for you, Brother Bubba.'

Bubba chewed his bottom lip. Ben thought the big man looked on the verge of tears.

Ebb told Bubba to sit down. 'Okay, that's the introductions over. Any questions?'

There were dozens perched on Ben's tongue like birds on a telephone wire. 'No, Father.'

'What happens now?' Maddie asked.

'You will both be indoctrinated into the group.'

'How?'

Ebb waved a hand. 'All in good time, Madeline. All in good time. Sister Alice?'

'Yes, Father?'

'Show Madeline to her quarters.'

'Yes, Father.'

Maddie walked out of the room behind Sister Alice. She didn't look back at Ben. She put him in mind of a prisoner being escorted to her cell.

Ebb turned to Tweezer. 'Take Benjamin to his quarters and go through the house rules with him.'

'Yes, Father.'

Ben followed Tweezer out of the kitchen, along the hall, and up a flight of stairs to a first floor landing. So this was it. No going back now. They would either rescue his father, or they would die trying. It was as simple as that.

Chapter Fourteen

Tweezer led Ben into a ten-feet-square room with a brass plaque on the door proclaiming Brothers. Two pine bunk beds dominated one wall, with matching wardrobes opposite. Bare floorboards threatened Ben's bare feet with splinters.

Tweezer pointed at the bunk bed on the left. 'You can have the top bunk above Bubba. Brother Marcus occupies the other bottom bunk. He's tetchy about anyone sleeping above him. I've got my own room.'

Ben looked at the thin blue mattress. It looked about as comfortable as a bed of nails. There was a blue sleeping bag rolled up and placed on a lumpy pillow at the top of the bed.

Tweezer sniffed and wiped his nose on the back of his hand. 'The wardrobe on the left belongs to Marcus. He's got more clothes than the rest of us put together. You'll have to share with Bubba. You'll find underpants and vests in the drawer underneath. Socks and winter boots are in the Mud Room downstairs. They're for winter use only. All soiled laundry goes in the laundry bin in the bathroom. Emily takes care of that. You'll have all this explained to you in more detail after your inauguration.'

'Inauguration?'

'Induction into the group.'

Ben stared at the dirty cream walls. The paint was cracked and peeling in places. Sunlight filtered through the grime on a window next to his bunk.

Tweezer looked at his watch. 'Supper's at seven. There's a bathroom along the landing if you want a scrub-up first. I wouldn't bother with the shower. I could piss faster than that thing.'

Ben nodded. 'Okay.'

Tweezer stroked his beard. 'I'll give you one or two ground rules. Nothing too heavy. Just an idea of how we expect members to behave. First off, there is no talking allowed after nine at night. You may read the Bible and pray, but conversation is banned. I'd advise you to pay attention to this. Sometimes the Father will ask for chores to be carried out, but again, silence must be observed at all times.'

'What sort of chores?'

'A never-ending list. Kitchen duty. Yard duty. Cleaning. Mending. Maintenance. Helping Bubba outside with the goats and the farm work.'

'Why doesn't he speak?'

Tweezer shrugged. 'Search me. Like the Father says, he was here when the farm was built.'

'How does anyone know his name, then?'

'That's a lot of questions, Benjamin. Remember what curiosity did to the cat?'

'Sorry.'

'If you must know, I think he tried to say "Brother" at his inauguration, and could only manage Bubba.'

'I wonder what's wrong with him?'

'You're not here to wonder, Benjamin. You're here to serve the Lord Jesus Christ.'

Ben looked out the window and fought an urge to jump out of it.

Tweezer sneezed and wiped his nose. 'Bloody hay fever. I'll be glad when winter's here.'

'Antihistamines are good for hay fever. My mum suffers from hay fever.'

'We don't allow medicine. The Father says it interferes with God's will.'

'How?'

Tweezer ignored the question. 'You're not any good with plumbing by any chance?'

Apart from putting a plug in the sink, his plumbing skills were zero. 'No. Sorry.'

'Have you got any skills?'

'No.' *Unless buggering things up counted as a skill.*

'Please address me properly. I'm willing to cut you some slack, because I know this takes time. I took a while to get into the swing of things, but I can tell you from experience, it pays to learn quickly.'

Ben nodded. 'Sorry.'

'Brother Tweezer.'

'Brother Tweezer,' Ben repeated.

'Good man. Right, where were we? Ground rules. No one may leave the farm other than the Father, myself and Brother Marcus. That rule is rigid unless the Father gives special consent. To be honest, if you want my advice, forget the outside world. It's full of contamination and corruption, anyway.'

Ben wondered how Tweezer, Marcus and Ebb avoided such widespread contamination and corruption. Were they immune to it? Vaccinated against it?

Tweezer rattled on. 'The Devil stalks the streets, Benjamin. None of us are safe. Even Brother Gerald fell foul to temptation.'

Ben remembered Ebb's offer to give him Brother Gerald's overalls. 'What happened to him?'

'It was a personal matter between the Father and Brother Gerald. It was dealt with.' Tweezer's lips pressed into a thin line as if to underline the point.

Ben shuddered.

'We don't believe in hospital treatment. Medicine violates God's will.'

'Isn't that similar to what Jehovah's Witnesses believe?'

'The Sons and Daughters of Salvation may have certain similarities to other religious groups, but we are unique. It's important that you never refer to any other religious groups in the presence of the Father. Is that clear?'

'Yes, Brother Tweezer.'

'We believe that the body is a holy temple. We do not permit abuse of that temple with tobacco or alcohol. Do you smoke or drink alcohol?'

'I drink sometimes, but I don't smoke.'

'Then abstinence should come easy to you.'

'I guess.'

'Address me properly.'

'Brother Tweezer.'

'Don't be so flippant around the Father.'

'No, Brother Tweezer.'

Tweezer sneezed four times and then pinched his nose between his thumb and forefinger for a few seconds. 'Saturday is our day of rest. That's not to say you won't be called upon to perform tasks, but as a rule, you are free to rest. Our motto is work, rest and pray. A simple philosophy that has served us well.'

Ben was certainly ready to pray. With all his heart and soul to any God that would have him.

'All men are to remain celibate. Procreation will be punished by castration. It might sound a barbaric measure, but it is designed with compliance in mind. In short, Benjamin, keep it in your trousers.'

'Yes, Brother Tweezer.'

'Everything is God and God is everything. All reality is part of the whole,' Tweezer babbled. 'Man is part of God, and man never dies.'

Ben wondered who occupied all the graveyards.

'No contact is allowed with the outside world, other than to procure funds.'

Ben remembered Emily Hunt's demand for money. 'Funds?'

Tweezer ignored him. 'You must never question the Father, or those designated to act as leader in his absence. Doing so is tantamount to disagreeing with God Himself.'

Ben nodded. 'Yes, Brother Tweezer.'

'That's about it for now. The Father will fill you in on the finer details later, but that's the gist of it. Any questions?'

'No, Brother Tweezer.'

'We sound a bell for supper at seven. Attend as soon as you hear it. The Father doesn't tolerate slack behaviour.'

'Yes, Brother Tweezer.'

Tweezer walked out of the room and closed the door. Ben took a deep breath. The air was stale. It smelled of old socks and bad breath. Dust swirled in shafts of sunlight. He walked to the window and peered through the grime at a back garden overgrown with weeds and brambles. Beyond the garden, a field stretched off into the distance. The brick-built tower loomed over the courtyard like a prisoner of war guard post.

Ben tried to lift the sash window, but it was either stuck or locked. A splinter stabbed his thumb. Did The Sons and Daughters of Salvation permit the removal of splinters? Or would that be classed as interfering with God's will?

Ben pressed his nose up against the glass. He could see the shape of someone in yellow overalls standing behind the guardrail at the top of the tower. It was impossible to tell for sure who it was, but considering Ebb had told Marcus to relieve Tweezer, he didn't need a pair of binoculars to confirm who it was. Marcus was holding a rifle. Sunlight glinted off the barrel like a Devil's wink.

Ben's breath fogged up the window. He wiped it clean with his sleeve and looked out again. The rifle seemed to point at him. Ben ducked down out of view.

'What have I done?' Ben asked the empty room. One look into Edward Ebb's eyes had been enough to tell him that his father was already dead. And one look at that tower was enough to tell him he would suffer the same fate.

He sat on the floor with his back against the wall and thought about Pastor Tom and his mother. He closed his eyes and wished with all his heart he'd never come anywhere near this god-awful place.

Chapter Fifteen

Ben sat at the kitchen table sandwiched between Bubba and Tweezer. There was a plastic dinner plate and a plastic tumbler on the table in front of him, along with a plastic knife and fork. The tableware reminded Ben of a children's party. Even though he'd not eaten since early morning, his appetite refused to be tempted by the food.

Dixie and Alice sat opposite Ben, with Ebb in his rightful place at the head of the table. Emily was busy setting bowls of salad and new potatoes on the table. There was a huge plastic jug of lemon juice in the middle of the table.

Ben looked at Ebb. 'Where's Maddie?'

Tweezer nudged him in the ribs. Hard. It was a nudge that said *shut up, right now!*

Ebb stood up and clasped his hands in front of him. He was wearing a white robe tied around the middle with a black sash. He looked dressed for martial arts. 'Since you ask, Benjamin, Madeline is preparing for inauguration.'

'What do you mean, "preparing"?' Ben asked.

Tweezer rounded on him. 'Be quiet.'

Ebb waved a hand. 'She's resting.'

'I apologise for Benjamin's manners, Father.'

'He will learn, Brother Tweezer. He will learn.'

They sat in silence as Emily finished laying the table. Emily then took her seat alongside Alice and Dixie.

Ebb raised a hand and looked around the table at each member in turn. He closed his eyes and bowed his head. 'Oh merciful Lord, we give thanks for this wonderful meal which You have so generously provided. We are not worthy of Your kindness and Your bountiful provision, Lord.'

'We are not worthy,' the group chanted.

'We are Your humble servants, Lord.'

Tweezer raised his hands. 'Praise Jesus.'

'Praise Jesus,' the group agreed.

'I'm ravenous,' Ebb said. 'Pass the sweet potatoes, please, Sister Alice.'

They ate in silence. Ben noticed that most of the members looked at their food as if mesmerised by it. Next to Ben, Tweezer sniffed and champed his food. If Ben's father was at the table, he might have told Tweezer to close his mouth while he was eating. He might also have told Bubba to tuck his elbows in, and Ebb to mop a yellow streak of butter from his chin.

Ben forced food into his mouth and chewed. He hated salad at the best of times. Thoughts of Maddie dominated his mind. What did *preparing for inauguration* mean? It sounded creepy and full of menace.

Ebb finished his meal and belched. He wiped grease from his mouth with a paper napkin. 'That was a fine meal, Sister Emily.'

Sister Emily inclined her head. 'Thank you, Father. Shall I clear the table now, Father?'

'Yes. Thank you.'

Ben watched Emily clear the plates. He wanted to reach out and grab her arm, ask her if her name was Emily Hunt. The Emily Hunt. He searched her face for telltale signs of the girl he'd seen in the photograph. Nothing. Could four years change a person so much? The only thing Sister Emily shared with photo—Emily was a lack of expression.

It's because her hair's cropped, Ben thought, clutching at straws. *It makes her face appear more severe. Angry, with a hint of sorrow.*

But everything else fitted. Marcus. The cult. The names. Everything. As for Ebb, he looked more than capable of killing someone. Enjoying it, even. And Tweezer had already confessed to killing a man with a hammer.

With the table cleared, Ebb told Sister Emily to pour drinks. She dutifully obliged, filling each member's beaker from the jug of iced lemon. Ebb raised his glass. 'To our merciful Lord.'

'Our merciful Lord,' the group chimed.

Ebb drained his drink in one long draught and banged his beaker down on the table. After a few moments, he stood up and clapped his hands together like a teacher bringing a class to attention. 'I'd like to welcome our good friend, Benjamin, to The Sons and Daughters of Salvation.'

'Welcome, Benjamin,' the group chanted.

Ben wanted to scream from the top of his lungs that his name was Ben, not Benjamin. A short and simple name with no fancy frills. Just like him. He looked at the table. Next to him, Bubba appeared to mumble something.

Ebb rested his hands on the back of his chair. 'It's been an eventful day, brothers and sisters. A day to be thankful for. It's rare we get to welcome two new members into our fold. We thank You, Lord, for bringing Madeline and Benjamin to The Sons and Daughters of Salvation.'

'Praise Jesus,' Tweezer said.

Ebb smiled. 'Praise Jesus.'

Did you smile like that when you killed my father? Ben thought. *When Tweezer smashed his skull to a pulp with a hammer?*

Ebb looked at his watch. 'How the time flies. Jesus must have given it wings today.'

The group responded with polite laughter.

Ebb raised a hand. 'It's seven-thirty. Benjamin's inauguration will take place at nine prompt. I believe Sister Alice has prepared the robes?'

Alice bowed her head. 'All done, Father.'

'Thank you, Sister Alice. You are commended for doing such a wonderful job at such short notice. Sunday will be a day of rest for you.'

Alice thanked him as if he'd just offered her a cottage in the country complete with housemaids and gardeners.

Ebb dabbed his forehead with the same napkin he'd used to wipe his mouth. He turned his attention to Bubba. 'Your task is to erect the apparatus for Benjamin's inauguration in the Gathering Barn, okay?'

Bubba nodded.

Ebb pursed his lips. 'Don't let me down.'

Bubba shook his head.

Ebb clapped his hands at Bubba as though addressing a servant. 'You are relieved. Go to your duties.'

Bubba ambled from the room, shoulders stooped. His bones poked through the yellow overalls like tent poles beneath canvas. Ben's mother would have described Bubba as someone who looked as if he'd *been through the wars.*

Ebb turned to Alice. 'You and the sisters can attend to the dishes. After that, get ready.'

Alice bowed her head. 'Yes, Father.'

Ebb waited for the women to set about their duties and then sat down. 'How are you settling in, Benjamin?'

As well as a cat in a kennel. 'Fine, thank you, Father.'

'What do you think of our humble abode? Do you think you'll fit in?' Ebb asked.

'Yes, Father.'

'I'm afraid the place needs a makeover. I believe autumn is pencilled in, Brother Tweezer?'

'Yes, Father.'

'The Lord has set us a heavy workload. I'm afraid the farm has suffered as a consequence. But we do as best we can. Do you have any special skills, Benjamin?'

'No, Father.'

'Everyone has a skill. Sometimes it's just a case of digging deep to find it. I'm sure you can use a paintbrush?'

Ben hated painting. Gloss paint always gave him a sore throat and brought him out in spots. 'I don't mind painting.'

Ebb pursed his lips. 'Do you like animals?'

A vision of a snarling Alsatian popped into Ben's head. 'I don't mind them, Father.'

'Perhaps you could help Bubba with the goats. We sell their milk to a local shop. It's good for allergies.'

Ben thought Tweezer could do with some goat's milk to help with his hay fever.

'Are you a vegetarian?' Ebb asked.

'Not really.'

'That's a strange answer.'

'Yes or no,' Tweezer prompted.

'I only like chicken.'

Ebb studied him with those button brown eyes. 'We don't believe in slaughtering animals. We believe the Lord made all creatures to live a life free of persecution. We believe that we should respect the wishes of the Lord.'

'Amen,' Tweezer agreed.

'Only the ill-informed resort to killing and eating animals, Benjamin.'

Ben wondered how Ebb's philosophy squared with Jesus feeding the five thousand with fish.

'It's a savage world you have left behind, Benjamin. But you are free now. Free of the burdens of greed and barbarity.'

Ben could think of better ways to describe the world he'd left behind. Sane, for instance. 'Thank you, Father.'

'Abstinence is sustenance.'

What the hell was that supposed to mean? 'Yes, Father.'

'Less is more,' Tweezer elaborated.

Ebb glanced at Tweezer. 'Precisely, Brother Tweezer. I'm sure Benjamin understands the concept of greed well enough.'

'Yes, Father. Sorry, Father.'

Ebb turned his attention back to Ben. 'I'm told you were previously homeless, Benjamin?'

'Yes, Father.'

'Walking the streets of your own volition?'

'Yes, Father.'

'Why did you leave home?'

Ben's stomach tightened. 'I didn't get on with my parents.'

'Why?'

There was no room for errors now. 'I didn't like the way they lived. It was all for show.'

'The vulgarity of pretentiousness.'

'They were more concerned about their Persian rugs than they were about me.'

Ebb looked pleased. 'Bourgeois pigs.'

'They were constantly on at me to do this and do that. Be more like them. But I didn't want to. I just wanted to be myself.'

Ebb banged the table, making Ben jump. 'You are made in God's image, Benjamin. How dare they try to mould you in their own?'

Ben crossed his fingers beneath the table. 'I'd just had enough. Me and Maddie drew out our savings and hit the road.'

'How long have you been away from home?'

'Six months, Father.'

'I'm informed your possessions were stolen?'

'Yes, Father. We were staying at a campsite down by the river. We went to get a shower, and when we came back, everything was gone. Tents. Money. The lot.'

Ebb raised his hands. 'Don't you see what this means?'

Ben didn't.

'It was God's plan to bring you here. The Lord chose you, Benjamin. Hand-picked you. Do you believe in destiny?'

'I don't know, I—'

'Do you believe that anything is possible?'

Ben nodded. It was a damned sight easier to agree with Ebb than challenge him. A damned sight safer, too. 'Yes, Father.'

'The Lord has shown you the sin of opulence. He has shown you the vulgarity of competition. I'm told your father is a banker?'

'Yes, Father.'

'A greedy banker who rubs his hands together in glee, whilst the poor rub their hands together to stay warm.'

'A parasite,' Tweezer added.

Ebb brushed something off the front of his robe. 'A parasite, indeed. Just like the energy bosses who condemn the poor to freeze in order to furnish their yachts and private jets. Sunning their bodies in the Mediterranean sun whilst the poor have to choose between eating and heating.'

'Hypocrites,' Tweezer shouted.

Ebb took a deep breath. 'Corrupt to the core. But you have been chosen, Benjamin. Chosen to stand against them. Are you ready to accept the Lord's challenge?'

'Yes, Father.'

'The Sons and Daughters of Salvation allow no room for Satan. We believe in hard work and honest endeavour. We shall stand shoulder to shoulder and be resolute in our purpose.'

'Amen,' Tweezer agreed.

'Are you ready for that challenge, Benjamin?'

Ben looked into the black abyss of Ebb's eyes. 'Yes, Father.'

'Are you ready to commit your life to the Lord Jesus Christ?'

'Yes, Father.'

'You can have no contact with the outside world. The outside world has no place in The Sons and Daughters of Salvation.'

Ben remembered the tower and the man standing guard at the top with a rifle.

'The Sons and Daughters of Salvation is not for the faint-hearted. You are about to be inaugurated into a cause from which there will be no return. Are you ready for the journey, Benjamin?'

Ben's heart fluttered like a wild bird trapped in a cage. 'Yes, Father.'

'Brother Tweezer will prepare you for your inauguration.'

'Yes, Father.'

Chapter Sixteen

Dressed in a white gown secured around the middle with a bright yellow sash, Ben followed Tweezer down the stairs and into the kitchen. The tops of his feet were sunburnt. The coarse fabric of the robe rubbed against them as he walked. Tweezer had pre-warned Ben not to speak unless in direct response to a question from Ebb.

All the other members of the group, except for Marcus, stood around the table like nervous guests at a wedding. They were all dressed in matching white robes with yellow sashes, except for Ebb, who had a distinctive black sash with purple embroidered edges.

Ebb clapped his hands together. 'Brother Bubba is ready for us. If you'd like to follow me outside, we'll begin.'

Tweezer held onto Ben's elbow and guided him into place behind Ebb. The rest of the group fell in behind them. They walked out of the kitchen, along the hall and out of the front door. A slight breeze whispered among the trees. A plane flew overhead; Ben wished with all his heart he was on it.

Ebb led them through the courtyard and into the barn Bubba had been working in when Ben and Maddie had arrived. The barn was cool after the stifling heat of the farmhouse. Lanterns cast shadows across the walls. Bubba stood at the far end of the barn, hands on hips, back against the wall. He didn't look up or acknowledge their arrival in any way.

Ebb stopped and turned to face the group. 'Get into place, please.'

The group formed a semicircle behind Ebb, Tweezer and Ben.

Ben stared in disbelief at a full-sized wooden cross lying on the floor.

'Are the preparations complete?' Ebb asked Bubba.

Bubba nodded.

'Come and help Brother Tweezer get Benjamin onto the cross.'

Ben tried to take a step back, but Tweezer held his arm in a vice-like grip. 'We must do as the Father says.'

'I'm not—'

'Silence. You are to comply with all aspects of your inauguration.' Ebb eyes looked like splotches of oil.

Ben bit down on his tongue. His bad knee threatened to collapse and spill him onto the ground.

Bubba untied the sash securing Ben's robe. The coarse material slipped from his shoulders and formed a puddle of fabric on the floor.

Ebb stood over the cross. 'We ask You to bless our humble servant, Benjamin, Lord. We ask You in the name of Jesus Christ to forgive his wretched soul.'

Tweezer told Ben to lie down on the cross.

'Why?'

Tweezer took a deep breath. 'Do not question God's will. Lie down on the cross with your arms stretched out over the crosspiece.'

Ben grappled with reality. 'You're going to crucify me?'

Ebb smiled. 'Only metaphorically, Benjamin. We won't use a hammer and nails. Jesus Christ suffered unimaginable horror on the cross to save our wretched souls. Your suffering is not quite of comparable magnitude.'

'But why are you doing this?'

'Your inauguration is not a questions and answers session. Please refrain from being disrespectful.'

'I'm not being disrespectful. I just don't understand why I—'

Ebb held up a hand. 'That you are talking back is showing a distinct lack of respect. A flagrant disregard for the will of the Lord.'

Ben resorted to the truth. 'I've got a bad knee.'

Tweezer stepped in front of Ben and hit him across the left cheek with the back of his hand. The sound echoed through the hollow acoustics of the barn. Ben staggered back and put a hand to his cheek.

'Lie down on the cross, Benjamin,' Ebb said.

'I can't.'

Ebb turned to the rest of the group. 'Pray for Benjamin. Pray that he may find the strength to overcome his weakness.'

The group bowed their heads.

Ebb turned his attention back to Ben. Beads of sweat glistened on his forehead like tiny jewels. 'Benjamin?'

'What?'

Tweezer drew back his hand again, making ready to strike. Ebb stilled him. 'Join the rest of the group, Brother Tweezer. Pray for Benjamin.'

Tweezer lowered his hand. 'Yes, Father.'

Ebb smiled at Ben. A greasy doughnut smile dusted with sugar. 'I understand you're afraid. Fear is a natural response to the unknown. But I can tell you right now; fear is Satan's greatest ally. That heinous beast feasts upon fear.'

'I—'

'What do you fear, Benjamin?'

Being stripped naked and pinned to a cross by a bunch of mad bastards in white robes. 'I don't know, Father.'

'Precisely. You don't know. But let me tell you, Benjamin, fear turns brother against brother, sister against sister and father against son. Fear is the stampede in the burning building. Do you understand?'

Ben didn't. 'Yes, Father.'

'You only fear the cross because you don't understand why I am asking you to lie upon it.'

Ben massaged his cheek. 'Yes, Father.'

'You have nothing to fear but fear itself?'

'Yes, Father.' Ben thought It was like being reassured by a crocodile it was safe to swim in the river.

'Do you know what courage is, Benjamin?'

'Overcoming fear?' Ben tried.

'Courage is not wanting to do something, but doing it anyway. Does that sound like a fair description to you?'

'Yes, Father.'

Ebb pointed at the cross. 'This cross represents courage. Think how Jesus must have felt being nailed to His cross. Do you think He blubbed like a baby in bath water and pleaded with Pontius Pilate to let Him run off home to His mother?'

'No, Father.'

'Damn right he didn't, Pixie-pea. Jesus embraced death. He went to His cross with valour and dignity.'

Tweezer punched the air. 'Praise Jesus.'

Ebb seemed annoyed by Tweezer's interruption. And then: 'He suffered to save us, Benjamin. So don't you stand there and fear the reaper when the reaper isn't even in attendance. Lie down on your cross.'

Ben looked from Ebb to Bubba and then back again at Ebb. Surely they were all going to burst out laughing in a minute, pat him on the back and tell him this was all a silly joke in a stupid nightmare. Just like his mother used to when he was plain old Stutter-buck dreaming about the bullies who drove him up a conker tree.

Ebb held out his hands, palms up. 'Embrace this night, Benjamin. This is your time. The Night of Naked Reconciliation.'

Ben shuddered and looked at the cross. Manacles were secured to each end of the crossbeam. He hadn't noticed them before, not when his mind had been expecting nails.

'Go to your cross, Benjamin. Brother Bubba will assist you.'

Ben knelt on the floor. He allowed Bubba to help him into position. He stretched his arms out over the crossbeam. Bubba secured his wrists. He then used a leather strap to secure Ben's ankles to the bottom of the cross.

The wooden cross was hard and rigid beneath his spine. Every fibre in his body ached. At least Maddie wasn't there to witness his humiliation.

Ebb stood over him and grinned. 'That wasn't so bad, was it?'

Nope. Just normal run-of-the-mill stuff you do every day. 'No, Father.'

'Brother Tweezer?'

'Yes, Father.'

'You and Brother Bubba may raise the cross now.'

As the two men hauled the cross into an upright position, the force of gravity almost wrenched Ben's shoulders from their sockets. He cried out and twisted his head from side to side. He bit down on his tongue hard enough to draw blood. His right knee buckled and his shoulders jarred as the two men dragged the cross to the far wall. When in place, Bubba secured it to the barn's timber frame with four massive screws.

Ebb stood in front of Ben. 'It might be a little uncomfortable at first, but you will soon acclimatise.'

Ben tried to push up to relieve the pressure on his shoulders. His right knee collapsed.

'It will pay you to keep still. Wriggling like a maggot on a fish hook will do nothing other than cause stress to your joints.'

Ben tried to relax and take the tension out of his shoulders. He took several deep breaths. Bile burned his throat.

Ebb smiled like a salesman about to complete a rather good deal. 'That's better. You'll appreciate my advice as the night wears on.'

'I've got bad knees.'

'We all have our cross to bear, Benjamin. Every single one of us. You are not unique. Anyway, we're not here to discuss your knees. We're here to observe The Night of Naked Reconciliation.'

Ben turned his head to one side so he didn't have to look at Ebb's grotesque face. It was getting more and more difficult to draw breath.

Ebb raised his right hand. 'I call The Sons and Daughters of Salvation to order.'

The group shuffle forwards. All eyes were on Ben as Tweezer and Bubba joined Alice, Dixie and Emily. Only Marcus was absent, but Ben knew where he was: manning the watchtower, ready to shoot anyone who might be dumb enough to try to escape.

Ebb turned his back on Ben and addressed the group. 'Brothers and Sisters. My loyal, faithful servants. The Lord is with us. Praise the Lord.'

'Praise the Lord,' the group chanted.

'He shines His everlasting light upon you all. He recognises the invaluable contribution you have all made to The Sons and Daughters of Salvation. He wants you all to be assured that your effort and your sacrifice shall be rewarded in the Kingdom of Heaven.'

'Praise the Lord,' Tweezer shouted.

The rest of the group followed Tweezer's lead.

Ebb raised both hands in the air. 'Please join me in wishing well our humble servant, Benjamin, as he faces The Night of Naked Reconciliation. Let Jesus shine his light and love upon him as he sheds the shackles of his past. Let Jesus nurture him as he is born again into a world of sacrifice and servitude. Praise Benjamin.'

'Praise Benjamin,' the group chanted.

'We ask you, Lord, to give Benjamin the courage and the strength he needs to overcome adversity. Praise Benjamin.'

'Praise Benjamin.'

Ben noticed that Bubba made no attempt to speak. The big man stared at the ground as Ebb rambled on. It looked as if Bubba wanted the ground to open up and swallow him whole. Ben wished the ground would open up and swallow all The Sons and Daughters of Salvation.

Ebb reached into a pocket on the side of his robe and pulled out a pair of surgical gloves. He snapped them on. 'Benjamin?'

Ben shuddered. 'Yes, Father?'

'Satan is inside you.'

'No. No, he's not, Father.'

Ebb smiled. His tongue peeked from his lips like a serpent about to strike. 'He is, Benjamin. He might use his charm to hide himself, but he doesn't fool me. Not one bit. Are you aware of the tactics of terrorists?'

Ben stared at those murderous hands and shook his head.

'A popular ploy of the terrorist is to hide among civilians. Why do you think they do that?'

Ben shook his head. He couldn't care less what terrorists did.

'They do it because no one can distinguish them from innocent civilians. Cowards, jackals, ferrets and weasels. What do you think about that, Benjamin? Disgusting, right?'

Ben looked at Ebb's hands and imagined them probing his naked body, seeking Satan.

'Satan is a terrorist,' Ebb continued. 'He is a terrorist of the worst kind. He hides among all of us. The good, the great, the weak, the strong, hoping we do not find him and flush him out. But Satan is mistaken. He does not fool us.'

Tweezer joined Ebb in front of the cross. 'Satan does not fool us.'

'We have learned to look behind the bushes.'

'And under the rocks,' Tweezer added.

Ebb looked at Ben like a man doubting the pedigree of a horse. 'Where does he hide in you, Benjamin?'

Ben pushed up. The leather restraints cut into his ankles. 'He's not inside me.'

Ebb jabbed Ben in the ribs with his forefinger. 'He's in you, all right, Pixie-pea. I can smell his rancid breath on your lips.'

Ben twisted his head to one side.

Ebb turned to Tweezer. 'I fear he's already laid siege to Benjamin's tongue.'

'You're right, Father.'

Ben writhed on the cross. 'Satan's not fucking well inside me.'

'See how Satan decorates the denial of his own existence with profanity?'

Ben's bladder threatened to empty. What the hell did he say? *All right, it's a fair cop, Satan's inside me. Go get him.*

Ebb took a step back. 'Do you know what the good guys do when the terrorists hide among the civilians?'

Ben didn't have a clue.

'They attack anyway. It's better than surrendering to their cowardly tactics. To do so would allow them to multiply like cancer cells. Do you see the logic in that?'

Ben didn't see the logic in anything anymore. 'I suppose.'

'Satan hides inside you. It's my job to flush him out, Benjamin.'

'Satan's not inside me.'

Tweezer stroked his goatee. 'Do you doubt the Father's integrity?'

'No.'

Ebb laughed. 'Your pathetic attempt at compliance isn't fooling anyone, Satan.'

Tweezer agreed. 'He's inside him as sure as eggs make omelettes.'

Ebb reached into his pocket and pulled out a small glass vial. He unscrewed the cap and drew a small amount of clear liquid into a dropper attached to the lid. He moved closer to Ben.

Ben pushed up on the leather restraints securing his legs. His right knee cracked. Pain shot through his leg and speared his stomach. 'Let me go. Please. I don't want to do this.'

Ebb pointed the dropper at Ben. 'See how Satan hijacks him?' He reached up and dripped a few drops of liquid onto Ben's left wrist.

Ben screamed and thrashed from side to side as a thousand white-hot needles tattooed his skin. The pain in the rest of his body was totally eclipsed by the burning in his wrist.

Ebb stepped back and turned to the rest of the group. 'See how Satan resists the holy water?'

'Yes, Father,' the group mumbled.

Tweezer stepped up close to Ben. 'Not so bold now, are you, Satan?'

Ben screamed.

Ebb seemed unconcerned. He moved to the other side of the crossbeam. 'Satan scurries around inside him like a rat in a henhouse. But we shall flush him out. Flush him out so God's light can scorch his eyeballs.'

'Praise Jesus,' Tweezer hollered.

Ebb administered a shot of acid to Ben's right wrist.

Ben screamed and thrashed on the cross as the whole of his right arm caught fire.

Ebb stepped back and studied Ben as if he was an exhibit in a science laboratory. He screwed the cap back on the bottle and put it back in his pocket. 'It's going to be a long night.'

One of Ben's knees popped. The one Stutter-buck had fractured all those years ago when he'd jumped from the conker tree. He gasped for air. His wrists felt as if they'd been set alight with napalm. 'Fuck, fuck, fuck—'

Ebb held up a hand. 'I hear your profanity, Satan. I hear your curses. I hear your vulgarity.'

Ben vomited. Bile dribbled down his chin.

'See how Satan tries to garner pity?'

'We afford him no pity,' Tweezer said.

'F-Fuck,' Ben shouted.

Ebb shook his head. 'We pay no heed to you, Satan. We do not fear you.'

Ben wasn't aware that he'd wet himself. Or that his left shoulder had dislocated. The burning in his wrists trumped everything else at the moment.

Tweezer turned to Ebb. 'Should we light fires beneath his feet, Father?'

Ebb seemed to ponder this for a moment. 'Perhaps, Bother Tweezer. I fear we may need more radical action to rid Benjamin of his unwanted guest.'

'No,' Ben shouted.

'Satan controls him.'

Tweezer agreed. 'Satan is his puppet-master.'

Ebb wiped sweat from his forehead with the back of his hand. 'Possession is a terrible thing. But a rotten tooth has to be pulled out whether the mouth likes it or not.'

'Please don't d-d-do anything else.'

Ebb made a sign of the cross. 'Benjamin is not the first soul you have used to trick your way inside The Sons and Daughters of Salvation, Satan. Nor will he be the last. But we remain steadfast and vigilant. Resolute.'

'See how the holy water has marked him, Father?'

'Confirmation of my gravest fears, Brother Tweezer.'

Ben knew he was going to die. No one would ever find him. His mother would go to her grave never knowing what had happened to him.

Tweezer pointed at Ben. 'Leave now, Satan.'

Ebb held up a hand. 'Enough. Leave him be. Benjamin needs to prepare himself for the exorcism.'

'Yes, Father.'

'Come. We shall pray for Benjamin's soul.'

Chapter Seventeen

Maddie lay on a king-sized bed in Ebb's quarters, her wrists handcuffed to a brass head rail. Her white robe was still fastened around the middle with its yellow sash, but the bottom part had flapped open to reveal the tops of her legs. Her hands were dead. Pins and needles drip-fed her arms with a steady, throbbing tingle.

The room, a converted attic in the farmhouse, was painted brilliant white. Even in the fading light, it seemed bright and disorientating. There was a large cross fixed to the wall above the bed. Through a skylight above the bed, Maddie could see ribbons of cloud bleeding into the darkening sky. Compared to the derelict state of the rest of the building, the room seemed like paradise.

She had no sense of time. After they had left the kitchen, Sister Alice had taken her upstairs to a room with a brass plaque secured to the door. The plaque had the word Sisters inscribed on it. Sister Alice had given her the robe and told her to put it on. She'd then fetched Maddie a drink of elderflower juice. Maddie hadn't realised just how thirsty she was until she'd started drinking. She'd drained it in several long gulps.

Soon after, Maddie had felt tired enough to sleep on broken glass. Sister Alice had helped her out of the room and up another flight of stairs to Ebb's quarters. And that was all she could remember. Sister Alice must have put her on the bed and handcuffed her wrists to the head rail.

Maddie watched Ebb walk into the room. He dabbed at his head with a white handkerchief. She could see the mound of his stomach beneath his robe. So much for abstinence.

'It's a hot one today, Madeline.'

Maddie looked into those button brown eyes for signs of humanity. Nothing. Two lumps of black coal.

Ebb smiled. Flesh folded around his eyes. 'Would you like a drink? We don't want you dehydrating.'

Maddie shook her head. 'Where's Ben?'

'Please address me as Father.'

'Father.'

'In this world of inflated prices, Madeline, manners are free. Perhaps your headmaster daddy should have taken time out of his busy schedule to teach you that.'

Maddie looked at the skylight. 'I wouldn't have listened to him if he had.'

'I don't suppose you would,' Ebb agreed. 'You have spirit, Madeline. Spunk. I admire that. I'm afraid Benjamin is a wet sponge.'

'Where is he?'

'Aren't we forgetting something?'

'Sorry… Father.'

'That's better. It's quite painless, isn't it? As for Benjamin, he's well. He's getting ready for his inauguration.'

'What do you mean?'

Ebb put a finger to his lips. 'Too many questions, Madeline. All will be revealed in good time.'

'Is it too much to ask why I'm chained to this bed?'

'Yes, Madeline, it is.'

'My arms are dead.'

'A numb arm never hurt no one. Think how Jesus felt nailed to the cross. Your discomfort is not comparable.'

'I just want to know what's going to happen to me.'

Ebb sat on the edge of the bed. 'You will bare your soul, Madeline. Bare your soul to Jesus.'

Maddie's throat closed. 'How?'

'Did you used to take a peek at your Christmas presents before Christmas day? Sneak down in the middle of the night and rattle all the goodies wrapped up under the tree?'

Maddie grappled with the sudden change of direction. 'No.'

'I'll bet you did. I'll bet mummy and daddy spoiled you rotten at Christmas. Contaminated your head with all those dirty material possessions. I'd even venture as far as to say they bought you a puppy, right?'

'No.'

Ebb ignored her. 'How much is that doggy in the window? The one with the waggly tail?'

'I don't even like dogs.'

'I'll bet it was a Labrador.'

'No.'

'Complete with a roll of toilet paper wrapped around its cutie-pie Labrador body.'

'No.'

'What did you call it?'

'Nothing.'

'*Nothing*? That's not a very nice name for a puppy. What about Fido? That's a good doggy name.'

'I didn't—'

'My dog's called Max. Do you like the name Max?'

Maddie tried to shrug. Her cuffs jangled against the head rail. Hot needles injected her shoulders. If she could just wrap her legs around Ebb's neck and twist. Her legs were strong and supple due to her love of dance and trampoline.

'She's a six-year-old Alsatian.'

'She?'

'Maxine.'

'Oh.'

'You assumed Max was a male, right?'

'I suppose—'

'You must learn not to take things at face value, Madeline.'

'I'll try.'

Ebb studied her for a while as if appraising a piece of art in a gallery. 'A child is a product of those who shape it and mould it with their misguided beliefs. No one blames you for getting a puppy at Christmas, Madeline. Least of all me. We're here to protect and nurture you, not to point fingers.'

Maddie wondered how chaining her to a bed was conducive to protecting and nurturing.

'Dogs have many qualities most humans can only dream of. When I say dogs, I mean proper dogs; not those stupid yappy things like my mother used to own. Bite you one minute, shag your leg the next. If I had my way, every one of those damned things would shame the shovel.'

Maddie was about to ask what "shame the shovel" meant, but then thought better of it.

'What do you think Maxine's best quality is?'

Ripping you to shreds, hopefully. 'I can't think straight with my arms like this.'

Ebb ignored her. 'Loyalty, Madeline. That dog would walk over broken glass and through a hail of bullets for me. She never complains. Unlike humans who dedicate their lives to whinging and whining.'

Maddie pushed herself up on the bed and tried to relieve the pressure on her wrists. Maybe she could kick out and kill him with a single blow to the temple.

'What about cats, Madeline? Do you like cats?'

'No.' The truth. They made her sneeze for starters.

Ebb smoothed out creases in the white duvet. 'Me neither. Nasty little killers. Have you noticed the way people excuse their behaviour by saying, *Oh, it's just what they do.* Really? Do they say the same about paedophiles and rapists? *It's just what they do?*'

'People are weak.'

'They are, Madeline. Weak and full of excuses. If your daddy was here, he'd be defending the education system. Denying the systematic brainwashing of whole generations of good young people. Correct?'

'Yes.'

Ebb pursed his lips. 'From the minute you can talk, they tell you to shut your mouth. Soon as you're old enough to wipe your own backside, they're force-feeding you with lies and teaching you to be a greedy capitalist pig.'

Maddie tried to measure the distance between her foot and Ebb's head.

'Remember assemblies?'

Maddie nodded.

'We had a deputy headmaster called Oxlade-Bullingdon. Everyone called him The Ox. A beast of a man. He used to parade up and down the stage during assembly, threatening this and threatening that. It's a damn good job they banned the cane. Oxlade-Bullingdon looked like a man who might have enjoyed thrashing children. Do they still have the cane at your father's school, Madeline?'

'I don't know.'

'Does he paddle his warped beliefs into the backsides of the innocent?'

Maddie grappled for an answer. It was impossible to think.

'Of course he does. Don't move. Don't talk. And above all else, don't think. Not unless you want Orwell's Thought Police to come knocking on your door and rattling your windows like Wee Willie Winkie. So much for free speech. Free speech, my eye. A headless chicken has more rights.'

'Can I have some water?'

Ebb blinked, as if coming out of a trance. 'Pardon?'

'Can I have a drink?'

'Yes. What would you like? I've got some Australian Chardonnay. It's rather good for the price.'

'I didn't think you allowed alcohol?'

'We do on special occasions, Madeline. Don't worry, I've squared it with Jesus.'

Maddie watched him leave the room. The muscles in her neck throbbed. The tips of her fingers throbbed. A thought: even if she kicked out and disabled Ebb, she would still be manacled to the bed. What then?

Ebb returned a few minutes later with a glass of wine and a pink and white striped straw. He held the straw to her lips. Maddie drained the glass without pausing for breath.

'Better?'

Maddie nodded. 'Yes.'

'Yes, Father,' Ebb corrected.

'Yes, Father.'

He put the glass down on a solid oak night table. 'That should help you to relax.'

'But why have you handcuffed me to the bed?'

'Because Satan lives in you, Madeline.'

'Satan?'

'Satan. Beelzebub. The Devil. Call him what you will.'

'He's not inside me,' Maddie protested.

'*You* don't *know* he's inside you, Madeline. But he is.'

'He's not.'

Ebb held a finger in the air as though testing wind direction. 'He has hijacked your soul, child. It is our job – our duty – to flush him out. The restraints are to prepare for Satan's resistance.'

Maddie searched her mind for a way to reason with a man that had lost all sense of reason. Her mind was all out of ideas. The wine had blunted her senses.

'And he will resist, Madeline.'

Maddie's lips suddenly went numb. 'He won't. I won't let him.'

'Satan already controls your tongue.'

'I—'

'Silence, Satan. Be still.'

Her eyelids felt so heavy. 'I wanna go home.'

'You'll be going back to the flames of Hell where you belong, Satan.'

Maddie closed her eyes. An image of her father flashed in her mind's eye. Pastor Tom, with his smiling blue eyes and arthritic hands drawn together in a gesture of prayer.

Chapter Eighteen

Ebb returned to the barn. An Alsatian walked on his right-hand side. The dog wasn't on a leash. It kept in perfect step with its master. Ebb stopped a few feet in front of the cross and snapped his fingers. The dog sat down and regarded Ben with alert brown eyes.

Ebb grinned at Ben. 'I'd like you to meet Max.'

Ben wondered if he should introduce himself to the dog. *Hi, I'm Ben, and I'm in a stack of shit right now, so please excuse me if I don't shake you by the paw.*

'Madeline thought Max was a boy.'

Whatever was she thinking?

'Just so you don't make the same mistake, Max is very much a girl, Benjamin. She's called Maxine.'

Ben didn't give a fig what sex the dog was. He was more concerned with why Ebb had brought the damned thing into the barn.

'Do you know that a dog can sniff out a single drop of blood in thousands of litres of water?'

Ben didn't.

'They can sniff out drugs. Cancer, even. Were you aware of that?'

'Not really.'

'Dogs are the most marvellous creatures. I was telling Madeline about the virtues of dogs not half an hour ago.'

'Where is Maddie?'

'Having a little nap at the moment. She likes dogs. Had an Andrex puppy when she was a little girl. Bought for her by her over-indulgent parents.'

If you've done anything to her...

'Do you know the most remarkable thing about Maxine?'

'No.'

'She can smell evil.' Ebb clicked his fingers. 'Can't you, girl?'

Max barked. The sound echoed around the barn like a gunshot. Saliva dribbled from her muzzle.

'What do you think, Benjamin? Can Maxine flush Satan out of you?'

'Satan's not in me.'

Ebb turned around and addressed the group. 'The Imposter speaks.'

Tweezer stepped forward. 'We must flush him out, Father. Destroy him.'

Ebb turned back to Ben. 'During the war, Russian guards would starve their dogs. Do you know why?'

Ben didn't. He didn't want to know, either.

'Take a guess.'

'Not enough food?'

'No. It was to ensure those dogs were hungry. Not just *grumbly tummy* hungry, Pixie-pea. Not just *get to bed with no supper* hungry. Not just *mummy's drank the dinner money again* hungry. No, sir. Not on your high heels. Those dogs were *rip off your arm and shit your fingers* hungry. That way, when they stood those insubordinate prisoners naked in the quadrangle and covered their frozen bodies with hot goulash, those dogs would be ready to eat them alive.'

Ben's mind refused to process any more information. A tear slipped down his cheek. He looked at the other members of The Sons and Daughters of Salvation standing a few yards away from the cross. How could they believe in such a crazy crock of shit? How could they stand there and do nothing?

Ebb continued: 'By the time two or three prisoners were turned into dog meat, the rest of them were ready to sing like birds.'

'Praise Jesus,' Tweezer said, as if by default.

'Praise Jesus,' Ebb agreed. 'I would say there's nowhere for Satan to hide when confronted with man's best friend.'

Ben's stomach lurched. What was Ebb going to do? Cover him with food and set his dog on him?

'Luckily for you, Benjamin, we do not condone such barbarity. Not even in pursuit of Satan.'

Tweezer studied Ben. 'Satan mocks you, Father.'

Ebb tightened his robe. 'He tries, Brother. He tries. But my patience is bolstered by the fortitude of Jesus Christ Himself. I'm in no rush. Satan will come out.'

Tweezer punched the air. 'Praise Jesus.'

'All mockers and the counterfeiters will be held to account in the court of the Lord Jesus Christ. The highest court in the universe. The Court of Correction.'

'Amen,' Tweezer rapped.

'Sinners shall be burned alive. No one shall be spared. It is written in the stars. We must build our spaceship and be ready. The old and the young alike shall be called unto Him.'

'The oldest is the youngest, and the youngest is the oldest,' Tweezer shouted.

'The pimp and the paedophile might seek refuge in the body of an old man, but does that mean we should take pity upon his frailty?'

'No, Father,' the group chanted.

Ben noticed Bubba staring at him. There was something in the big man's eyes. A fleeting flash of something that Ben couldn't quite put his finger on. Compassion? Fear? Understanding?

Ebb rattled on: 'Should we spare the child who will mature and cause misery to the world?'

Like you, Ben thought.

'No, Father,' the group chanted.

'What should we do?'

'Destroy him, Father.'

Ebb paced up and down like a victorious sportsman basking in the glory of victory. 'Satan comes in many guises. The poet, the politician, the thief, the vagrant. He hides like a thief in an alleyway at night. As he does to this poor wretch on the cross.'

Tweezer agreed. 'I smell Satan oozing from every pore.'

'He hopes we take pity on him. But do we take pity?'

'No, Father,' the group chimed.

'Do we turn a blind eye?'

'No, Father.'

Ebb stopped pacing and cocked his head to one side. 'Damn right, we don't. Because that would be as stupid as eating a raw chicken and wondering why you had a dicky belly. The deadliest spider on the planet isn't any bigger than a two-pence piece, but we don't invite it to stretch its legs and take a walk on our bodies, do we?'

'No, Father.'

Ben looked at the group. In the eerie yellow light cast by the lanterns, he couldn't distinguish their features. The lack of identity made them seem even more sinister.

'This wretch represents all that is wrong with the world.'

Ben's bladder threated to let go. 'I haven't done nothing.'

Ebb waved a hand dismissively. 'We hear your words, Satan. We hear them like wind on a hilltop. But we don't believe you.'

'I'm… just… me….'

Ebb ignored him. 'Max! Heel!'

Max fell in line beside her master. Ebb walked right up to the cross with the dog at his side. He ran his hands across Ben's legs like a faith-healer. 'I feel Satan's vibration.'

Tweezer crossed himself. 'May the Lord Jesus Christ protect us.'

Ebb finished his bizarre exercise. He then turned to the dog. 'Max! Seek.'

Max sniffed Ben's feet and shins. Her tail swished in the dusty air. The leather restraints suppressed Ben's natural urge to kick out. Max paid particular attention to Ben's right knee. She sniffed it for several seconds and then stepped back and barked.

Ebb hunkered down. 'What is it, girl?'

Max panted. Droplets of saliva fell on the dry earth floor.

Ebb put his hands either side of the dog's head and stared into her eyes. After several moments of what appeared to be deep contemplation, Ebb stood up. 'She smells Satan.'

Max barked, as if acknowledging Ebb's claim.

Ebb ruffled Max's head. 'Good girl, Max.' He then turned to Tweezer. 'Take Maxine to her kennel. There are treats in the kitchen under the sink. Give her two and make sure her water bowl is filled.'

'Yes, Father.'

'Just two treats, mind. There's a thin line between rewarding and spoiling.'

'Yes, Father.'

Ebb pursed his lips. 'Bring the blow torch back with you. I think it might be prudent to drive Satan from his hidey-hole.'

'Yes, Father.'

'Blow torch?' Ben shouted. 'Oh, God, no. This can't be happening.'

Ebb grinned. It was a grin that belonged on the back of a Wild West wagon selling snake oil. 'I'm sure you're familiar with the concept of fire, Satan.'

Ben moaned. His hands and shoulders already felt engulfed in flames.

'A nice hot fire should be right up your alley.'

'Please don't burn me,' Ben pleaded.

'Save your pitiful whimpering for the imps.'

'There's nothing inside me.'

'You can't have "nothing" in you. That's impossible, unless you're hollow.'

'I mean *Satan*. Satan's not inside me.'

'Denial is always the first port of call for the guilty. Your flagrant disregard for my authority tells me who's sailing your ship. Max has confirmed Satan's presence. Now we must act.'

Ben tried to push up and relieve the pressure on his shoulders. A flare went off in his knee. He screamed and gasped for air.

Ebb was unimpressed. 'Spare me the amateur dramatics. Your pathetic attempts to garner sympathy are wearing thin.'

'I'm… not—'

Ebb pointed a finger at Ben. 'You'd do well to speak only when spoken to.'

Ben closed his eyes. He recited the Lord's Prayer and asked Pastor Tom's God to spare him.

Ebb addressed the group. 'See how Satan controls Benjamin?'

'Yes, Father.'

'See how Satan distorts the truth?'

'Yes, Father.'

'Leave m-me alone, you f-f-f-fucking idiot,' Ben shouted.

'See how Satan decorates his tongue with profanity?'

The group did.

Ebb turned back to Ben. 'But I'm not listening, Pixie-pea. You words fall upon deaf ears.'

Ben twisted his head from side to side. He wanted to reach out and rip Ebb's tongue from his mouth. Poke out his eyes. Wrap his hands around his neck and squeeze the life out of him. But poor old Stutter-buck didn't even have the guts to say boo to a bat. He was born a coward, and he would die a coward. And Maddie would die right along with him because he didn't even have the balls to come here on his own.

'We shall wait for Brother Tweezer to return,' Ebb said. 'Then we'll see what you've got to say for yourself.'

Chapter Nineteen

Maddie was still half asleep when Tweezer came into the room. For a few seconds, as her brain scrambled to distinguish the difference between imagination and reality, she thought she was in a hospital, and Tweezer's robe was a surgical gown.

Tweezer smiled at her and stroked his goatee. 'How are you feeling?'

Maddie pushed herself up. The cuffs jarred her wrists. 'What?'

'Sorry, did I wake you?'

'What do you want?'

Tweezer sat on the bed. 'I was just wondering if there was anything I could get you?'

'The key to these handcuffs?'

'Sorry, sister. That's more than my life's worth.'

'And what is your life worth?'

'Pardon me?'

'What is your life worth? It's a simple question.'

'I'm only trying to be friendly.'

'Are you? I'd hate to see you when you're trying to be nasty.'

'I'm not nasty.'

'Really? So what do you call killing a man with a hammer? A friendly pat on the head?'

'That was a long time ago.'

'And that makes it all right, does it?'

'God has forgiven me.'

Maddie rolled her eyes. 'He told you that, did He?'

'He came to the Father in a vision and told him so.'

'And you believe that?'

'I don't *believe* it. I know it.'

Maddie looked away. 'Course you do.'

'This isn't about me, Madeline. It's about you, and what lives inside you.'

'There's nothing inside me.'

'You and Benjamin must be purged.'

'Where is Ben?'

'About to be exorcised.'

Maddie felt as if someone had dropped ice cubes in her blood. 'What do you mean, "exorcised"?'

'That's not for you to worry your pretty little head over. It's all going to be finished with by the morning. You two will have plenty of time to catch up later.'

'Why am I handcuffed to the bed?'

Tweezer moved closer. 'You know why, Madeline. For your inauguration.'

Maddie could smell tobacco on his breath. 'But what will happen?'

Tweezer seemed to consider this for a while. And then said, 'The Father will plant his seed in you.'

'I'm not letting him do that.'

'Pride is a sin, sister.'

'It's got nothing to do with pride. It's my body.'

'Not anymore it's not. You gave your body to The Sons and Daughters of Salvation the minute you arrived at Penghilly's Farm.'

'He's not touching me.'

'Resistance is pointless, Madeline. Brother Gerald would testify to that – if he could.'

Maddie closed her eyes. Maybe this would go away if she never opened them again. Just like when she was a little girl, and she used to shut her eyes to wish away the wicked witch with the tombstone eyes and the goo-green face hiding under her bed.

'You want my advice?' Tweezer asked.

The pungent smell of tobacco wafted up Maddie's nose, making her feel sick. 'What?'

'Just do as you're told.'

Maddie knew that the witch under the bed had a huge wart on the end of her nose. Oozing pus. One night, convinced that the witch's bony fingers had reached out and touched her, Maddie had screamed for her mother to rescue her. Screamed all the way to Rwanda. But her mother was dead. Dead and buried in the baked earth, with a simple wooden cross and a few pebbles to decorate her grave. Screaming for help now was as pointless as screaming for her mother had been all those years ago. Except this time the source of her terror was not just a figment of her imagination.

'Do you want a drink?'

Her father had taken her to Rwanda when she was twelve. Back to the village where her mother had died. She'd wanted to cry as she'd looked at that pregnant swell of earth marking her mother's grave, but no tears would come. Her only emotion had been anger. Anger at all the things she'd missed out on.

'Madeline?'

Her father had told her she had her mother's pretty green eyes. But that was plain daft. She had her own eyes!

'The world is evil,' Maddie whispered.

Tweezer agreed. 'Profoundly evil.'

'How could anyone do such a thing?'

'Do what, love?'

Maddie didn't feel his hand on her arm. She was back at the grave in Rwanda. Her father saying a prayer, giving thanks and praising Jesus. For what? Jesus was just a selfish liar.

Tweezer rubbed her arm in small circular motions. Saliva bubbled in the corner of his mouth as he snorkelled air through his bent and flattened nose. If Maddie had looked into that face, she might have seen a witch with a goo-green face and tombstone eyes.

Maddie looked up at the skylight. 'Why does God let so many bad things happen?'

Tweezer's hand moved down to Maddie's leg. 'God isn't responsible for what people do. He's our judge, not our instigator.'

Maddie didn't hear him. 'Maybe God's deaf, dumb and blind.'

Tweezer squeezed her thigh. 'God sees us, sister. God hears us. God knows us.'

'Maybe he's dead.'

'God isn't dead. He's immortal.'

Maddie suddenly realised Tweezer's hand was on her leg. She shook her arms and kicked out. The handcuffs clanged against the brass head rail. 'Get your hands off me.'

Tweezer jumped back and withdrew his hand. 'No need to be like that. I'm only trying to help.'

'Do you really want to help me?'

Tweezer nodded. 'Sure.'

'Then undo these handcuffs.'

Tweezer wiped his nose with his forefinger. 'I would if I could.'

'Yeah, right. Course you would.'

'Are you a virgin?'

Maddie resisted an urge to spit in his face. 'Piss off.'

'I'm only asking because I care about you.'

'What do you know about caring?'

'I could break you in if you're a virgin.'

Maddie's heart turned to lead. 'The day I let you near me is the day I die.'

Tweezer smiled. 'You might end up thanking me. I could save you a lot of pain. And I mean a *lot* of pain. Ebb uses *things*.'

'He's not coming anywhere near me.'

'Do you think you have a choice?'

'I'd rather die.'

'He'll take you whatever you might think.'

'I think you're sick.'

Tweezer inched closer. 'Between you and me, he prefers men. Ask Brother Gerald if you don't believe me. Oops! Silly me. You can't. Brother Gerald's dead. He died for the sin of homosexuality, which is a bit rich, considering the Father is that way inclined himself. Anyway, I'm telling you all this for your own good. The Father has to *do it* with *other things*.'

Maddie's stomach tightened. 'Leave me alone.'

'The Father calls it Purification. I prefer to call it bloody painful. Especially if you're a virgin.'

Maddie groaned and shook her head. Her mind tried to erect barriers to stop the words getting inside her head. 'No.'

'I'll be gentle with you.'

'Get out! Leave me alone.'

Tweezer stood up. He looked at Maddie with eyes forged in Hell. He untied the yellow sash around her middle. 'You're not in any position to issue ultimatums. This isn't a soap opera, Madeline.'

'Leave me alone.'

'You'll thank me for this in the long run. Trust me, you will.'

Maddie pushed herself as close as she could to the head rail. The cuffs bit into her wrists. She drew her legs up and squeezed them together as tight as she could.

Tweezer took off his robe and threw it on the floor. Tattoos marked most of his body. Scorpions, snakes, scales of justice. His erect penis appeared to sniff the air. His hair hung in greasy strips across his face.

'Get away from me,' Maddie screamed.

Tweezer grinned. 'I think you're begging for it.'

Maddie sobbed and drew her knees up to her chin. 'No... I'm... not....'

'All women are. Deep down inside, you're all begging for it.'

Maddie looked up at the darkening skylight. Where was God now? Where was He when you needed Him the most? In the same place He was when those savages raped and murdered her mother. Up in the sky making daisy chains with the angels.

Tweezer knelt on the bed and grabbed hold of Maddie's knees. He tried to force them apart.

Maddie squeezed her legs together with every last drop of energy in her body. 'Please don't do this.'

Tweezer forced his fingers between her knees, gouging her skin with his nails. 'I'm… trying… to… help… you….'

'By raping me?' Maddie shouted.

'I'm not going to rape you. I'm going to make things easier for you. You really don't get it, do you?'

Maddie spat in his face. 'Piss off.'

Tweezer withdrew his right hand from between her knees and wiped his face. 'Sister Emily couldn't walk for a week after Ebb had been at her. Do you want that?'

'I want to go home.'

Tweezer laughed. 'You ain't never going home, Madeline.'

'Rape is the most despicable thing a man can do.'

'*If* it's rape, yes. Maybe. But this is your inauguration, so don't confuse two issues. That's like saying a wet tee-shirt contest is a porn show.'

'In your twisted mind.'

'Sometimes the truth hurts. Now, do you want to make this easy for yourself, or hard? I'm running thin on patience, love.'

Maddie looked up at the skylight. 'All right. Do it, then.'

Tweezer's eyes narrowed. 'Are you sure?'

'Yeah. Go on. Do it.'

'Are you a virgin?'

Maddie didn't answer.

'You'll thank me for this. You'll enjoy it. I promise.'

Maddie opened her legs and lifted her feet off the bed.

Tweezer licked his lips. 'Come on, baby. Open the door. Let's do it.'

Maddie suddenly kicked out and caught Tweezer on the bridge of his nose with her left heel. The bone snapped. Blood gushed from his broken nose. He clutched his injured face with one hand. The other flailed by his side.

Maddie kicked him again. In the left eye. Tweezer grunted and fell sideways off the bed. His head struck the bare oak floor, rendering him unconscious.

Maddie sobbed and drew her knees up to her chest. Her whole body shivered. She closed her eyes and waited for Tweezer to get up off the floor and finish what he'd started.

Chapter Twenty

'Where is he?' Ebb demanded. 'I sent him to get a blowtorch, not build one.'

The Sons and Daughters of Salvation stood in line. No one offered an answer. Ebb turned to Bubba who was still standing beside the cross. 'Guard him.'

Bubba nodded and looked at the ground.

Ebb strode out of the barn like a sergeant major in pursuit of a missing recruit. By the time he reached the farmhouse, he was gasping for breath. He walked around the side of the building to the back door and stepped on a thistle. He yelped and hobbled into the kitchen. As soon as the inaugurations were done and dusted, Benjamin could help Bubba to tidy up the garden.

He stood in the middle of the room and called Tweezer's name. Tweezer didn't respond. Something moved in the corner of his eye. A shadow near the Welsh dresser. Ebb spun around to face it, heart thudding in his chest. He took a deep breath and tried to calm his nerves. Where in God's name was that idiot Tweezer? The house was quiet. Too damned quiet. Calm before the storm quiet.

'Tweezer?'

The silence in the house crept under Ebb's skin. He walked through the kitchen and into the hallway, keeping an eye out for unannounced guests. It wasn't unknown for Jesus to appear to him when he was least expecting it. Once, the great man Himself had appeared from the spout of a teapot and told Ebb to kill Brother Gerald. Told him in no uncertain terms to "castrate the traitor and subject him to death by a thousand cuts".

A mahogany grandfather clock at the end of the hallway read a quarter to ten. He watched the pendulum swing from side to side. Its steady tick sounded like a death-knell in the silence.

Ebb checked the lounge and then called up the stairs. 'Tweezer?'

A floorboard creaked, making Ebb jump. 'Tweezer? Are you up there?'

If Tweezer was, he wasn't saying.

'You'd better have a damn good reason for going AWOL.'

No response. Where the hell was he? He walked up the stairs and checked the Brothers' Room. Nothing. The Sisters' Room. Same. Both empty, save a few flies and the lingering smell of dope. How many times did he have to tell Marcus not to smoke that dreadful stuff inside the house? It was tantamount to mocking the Lord.

He walked along the landing and took a peek in the bathroom. Empty. He made a mental note to tell Sister Emily to pay close attention to the soap scum around the rim of the tub. It was no good showing the damned thing a bottle of Flash and hoping it would self-clean.

He looked up a second flight of stairs leading to his quarters. His haven. His space. His oasis. Tweezer wouldn't dare go up there without permission. Not if he valued his life. Ebb wiped perspiration from his eyes. The hairs on the back of his neck were standing proud.

Ebb cleared his throat. 'Tweezer? Are you up there?'

'Help me,' a muffled voice called back.

At first, Ebb thought his mother was playing tricks on him again. She could be a real joker sometimes. She was about as funny as a fart at the dinner table, but it didn't seem to deter her.

Ebb held onto the handrail for support. 'Who's there?'

'It's me. Maddie. Help me.'

Ebb walked up the stairs, mindful that his mother might still try to fool him. You needed to keep all the bulbs burning bright concerning that one. He reached the small landing outside his quarters and stood stock still. 'Madeline?'

'Help me.'

Ebb's blood froze. His heart fell into his feet. The front door was slightly ajar. And he'd closed it. He'd not bothered to lock it, because everyone had been in the barn with him except for Marcus who was on watch duty up the tower.

'Madeline? What's happened?'

'Tweezer tried to rape me.'

'Rape you?' Ebb said, his mind a kaleidoscope of scenarios. This had to be a trick. Satan playing games with him. 'Tweezer?'

'He's unconscious on the floor.'

Ebb laughed. 'And I'm Peter Pan.'

'It's the truth. I kicked him in the face and knocked him out.'

Ebb shoved the door back against the wall and stepped into the lounge. There was a fifty-inch flat-screen TV secured to one wall. He peered at the blank screen. His mother had once interrupted the evening news to announce that Ebb was on the FBI's top ten most wanted list. She'd even been wearing her trademark pink wig and sunglasses.

Ebb ripped the crucifix from his neck and held it out before him. He walked through the lounge on legs barely able to support his weight. He stopped in the bedroom doorway and peered inside. Madeline was still handcuffed to the bed. Her face looked strained, but that was to be expected with Satan controlling her.

'Help me,' Maddie pleaded.

Ebb ignored her pitiful appearance. Appearances could be deceptive. Vigilance was the key to survival. He took two steps towards the bed and addressed the waif. 'What have you done?'

'Nothing. He attacked me.'

'Who attacked you?'

Maddie nodded towards the blind side of the bed. 'That bastard.'

Ebb ignored the profanity. He walked around the foot of the bed and stared at Tweezer's naked body. Tattoos scarred every inch of his skin. Serpents. The scales of justice. Gangland graffiti. In Ebb's opinion, Tweezer's body looked like a billboard advertisement for Hell.

Ebb glanced at Maddie. 'You must have lured him here.'

'How the hell could I do that? He attacked me.'

Ebb grappled with the truth. 'He wouldn't betray me.'

'He tried to rape me.'

Ebb clutched the cross in both hands and thrust it out before him. 'I'm not listening to your filthy lies.'

'Who do you think untied my robe?'

'I have no doubt in my mind that Brother Tweezer untied your robe.'

'Thank you,' Maddie sobbed.

'I also have no doubt in my mind that you coerced him into doing so.'

'How in God's name am I supposed to have coerced him?'

'Because you're a seductress. A temptress. A vampire. You must have seduced him with telepathic messages.'

Tweezer groaned on the floor. Ebb thrust the cross at him. 'Get up and get dressed.'

Tweezer raised his head. 'Where am I?'

Tweezer's disorientation lent further proof to the fact that external forces controlled him. 'Get up. Right now.'

'You're sick,' Maddie said.

Ebb raised his eyebrows. 'Do you want to shame the shovel?'

'I don't have a clue what you're talking about.'

Ebb didn't like the look lurking in those beguiling green eyes. They were full of malice. Only time would tell whether she was beyond salvation.

Tweezer groaned. 'What happened?'

'You've been compromised, Pixie-pea. Get up and get dressed before your hideous body makes me puke.'

'Please undo my hands,' Maddie pleaded.

Ebb pointed the cross at her. 'Not while this court's in session, sister. What do you take me for: the fool on the hill?'

'I'm begging you. Please.'

Ebb ignored her and walked over to an oak dressing table. He took a hatpin from a drawer. He held it up in front of Maddie. 'My mother's. She liked hats. And wigs. And men.'

Maddie pushed back against the head rail.

'Don't fret. The pin's not for you. It's for Sleeping Beauty over there.'

Ebb walked to where Tweezer fumbled about on all fours. He bent over and jabbed the hatpin into the sole of the man's left foot. Deep. Almost right through to the other side.

Tweezer screamed and bucked like a wild horse introduced to a rodeo.

Ebb pulled the pin out. Blood oozed from the wound. 'Get up! It's time for the rabbit hole.'

Tweezer looked over his shoulder at Ebb. One eye was closed, the surrounding skin swollen and purple. His mouth and goatee beard were streaked red.

Ebb put the hatpin in the pocket of his robe. 'You're not looking too good, my friend.'

Tweezer gawked at him. His mouth opened and closed as if disconnected from his brain. Ebb resisted an urge to kick Tweezer's backside. 'How could you be tempted by Satan so easily?'

'I wasn't—'

'You've made a nasty mess all over my floor. It's a good job that the oak is sealed.'

'I'm sorry, Father.'

Ebb watched a bubble of snot and blood burst from the end of his nose and splatter on his top lip. 'You're supposed to be my number two. My main man.'

'I'm sorry, Father.'

Ebb snorted. 'Do you think sorry makes it all right?'

'No, Father.'

'Get up.'

Tweezer scrambled to his feet. Blood dripped from his nose and ran into his beard. He picked up his robe and put it on, fastening it around the middle with the yellow sash.

Ebb noticed Tweezer's hands were shaking. Perhaps he was still under the influence of the seductress. 'Go to the bathroom and clean yourself up.'

'I'm sorry, Fa—'

Ebb waved the cross at him. 'Satan has tempted you, brother. Compromised you. Save your apologies for the Lord Jesus Christ Himself. I've got better things to do than listen to the excuses of a sinner.'

Tweezer wiped his nose with the back of his hand. His good eye swivelled in its socket, coming to rest on Maddie. 'She—'

Ebb waved him away. 'Go.'

Tweezer hobbled out of Ebb's quarters, his injured foot leaving tiny spots of blood on the floor. Ebb studied Maddie. 'I suppose you think you're clever?'

'I just want to go home.'

Ebb laughed. A small throaty laugh that sounded as if it had been fashioned in a witch's cauldron. 'You're a slippery customer, all right. But I'm on to you. As Jesus Christ is my witness, I'm on to you.'

'I didn't do anything.'

Ebb pursed his lips. 'How did you do it? How did you seduce him?'

Maddie looked away.

'It's going to be a long night, Madeline. But I will purge your body of Satan if it's the last thing I do.'

Chapter Twenty-One

E bb escorted the prisoner down into the kitchen. Twice the prisoner had tried pleading his innocence, but Ebb had learned long ago that the truth was best extracted by time and torture. You could set your clock by that.

Tweezer looked at Ebb with his good eye and tried to smile. 'Would you like a brew, Father?'

Ebb took a deep breath and tried to summon patience. Tweezer was in denial. That was as plain as Sister Emily's face. 'A brew?'

'Yes, Father.'

'What kind of brew? A Hebrew?'

Tweezer snorted laughter. A mistake. His nose bled again.

'You disgust me, Brother Tweezer.'

Tweezer wiped his nose. 'Sorry, Father.'

'You have betrayed me.'

'She tempted me, Father.'

'I know she bloody well tempted you, you fool. I don't need you to tell me she's a nest of vipers.'

Tweezer bowed his head. Blood bubbled from his nose. 'I'm really sorry, Father.'

Tweezer's eyes put Ebb in mind of a wounded animal. 'The girl has just arrived. What do you expect her to be? Pure?'

'No, I—'

'She has all the sins of the free world raging inside her.'

Tweezer plucked a flake of dried blood from his beard. 'She might be a witch, Father.'

Ebb squinted at Tweezer as if he'd just challenged him to a dual at dawn. 'A witch?'

'Yes, Father. I think we might have to drown her.'

'You do, do you?'

'Yes, Father. It's the only way to rid her body of the evil inside her.'

'Perhaps we ought to put you both down the wishing well in the garden. What do you think about that?'

Tweezer clamped his mouth shut and focused his attention on his dripping nose.

'The girl's not a witch. She needs purging, nothing more than that.'

'She's dangerous, Father.'

Ebb ignored him. 'But you're a different kettle of mackerel, aren't you?'

'I didn't do—'

Ebb slapped the table. 'Save your tongue. If you tell me one more time that the girl lured you to the bedroom, I shall render your mouth incapable of speech. Is that clear to your ears?'

'Yes, Father.'

'You are supposed to be my right-hand man. What do you suppose that means?'

'I carry out your instructions, Father.'

'What else?'

'I serve the Lord?'

Ebb fought an impulse to bang Tweezer's head on the table. 'You're meant to set an example to the group. Do you think attempting to rape an uninitiated member is setting a good example?'

'No, Father.'

'I trusted you.'

'You can still trust me, Father.'

Ebb shook his head. 'Not anymore. You have proven yourself to be weak. Weak and open to attack. I fear Satan has attached himself to you.'

'No, Father. No, he's—'

Ebb held up a hand. 'Stop babbling. The weak always deny the truth, even when it's perched on their shoulders like a parrot.'

'Satan's inside the girl, Father.'

Ebb crossed his arms. 'I vividly remember your inauguration. I truly believed that we'd purged all traces of Satan from you when we tied you to a tractor and hauled your sinful body back and forth across the North Field.'

'You did, Father.'

'But I still see him standing before me, large as life, twice as brazen.'

'No, Father.'

Ebb held up a hand. 'You can no longer be trusted, Brother Tweezer.'

'I can. I swear on my life.'

Ebb walked over to the Welsh dresser and took a set of keys from a drawer. He selected a large silver key and walked to a door at the far end of the kitchen.

'What are you doing?'

'You're going down the rabbit hole, Brother Tweezer.'

Tweezer gawked at the door with his good eye. 'Please, Father. There's no need to put me down there.'

Ebb unlocked the door and opened it. 'You get settled in. I've got urgent business to attend to.'

'Please, Father.'

'Stop wittering and get down there.'

Tweezer limped past Ebb and peered into the basement. 'Please, Father. I don't like being locked in. I get claustrophobic.'

'Do you want to shame the shovel?'

'No, Father. It's just—'

Ebb walked up behind Tweezer and shoved him in the back. Tweezer rolled down the stone steps in a tangle of twisted limbs. His skull hit the concrete floor at the bottom. He hollered like a baby torn from its mother's breast. Ebb considered it quite an unseemly racket for a man who boasted gangland murder in his portfolio.

Tweezer crawled a few feet and then collapsed between the neat rows of cannabis plants.

Ebb slammed the door and locked it. Some people proved to be downright babies when the chips were down.

All the king's horses, and all the king's men, couldn't put Humpty together again.

Ebb jumped at the sound of his mother's voice. It seemed to come from the teapot. For one terrible moment, he thought the thing was sporting a pink tea-cosy. He rubbed his eyes. No cosies. Not even pink ones.

He shuffled out of the kitchen and went back to the barn. He was exhausted. It was all he could do to put one foot in front of the other. The Lord had seen fit to overload his schedule, which was fine by him, just as long as He didn't expect Ebb to perform miracles when dealing with Satan.

Bubba was still guarding the cross. Good old dependable Bubba. The big guy hadn't shown one stick of dissent since the night Ebb had cut out his tongue. In fact, Bubba had even shown a level of understanding concerning the need to remove his tongue after witnessing Cyril's execution. As far as Ebb was concerned, Bubba was too good a worker to dispense with, but too much of a liability to leave with an ability to tell tales.

'Everything all right, Bubba?'

Bubba nodded.

Ebb noticed a strange black aura around the big guy. Like a shadow with fuzzy edges. 'Are you sure you're okay?'

Bubba shuffled and grunted.

Ebb stared in disbelief as the aura broke ranks with Bubba's body and hovered in front of the cross.

'Are you okay, Father?' Sister Alice asked.

Ebb looked at her. There was a nasty buzzing noise in the back of his head, reminiscent of the time one of his *uncles* had hit him with a shovel when he was a child.

Sister Alice broke ranks and walked towards him. 'Father?'

Ebb closed his eyes. The ground swayed beneath his feet.

Sister Alice reached out and took his arm. 'You look… tired, Father.'

Ebb tried to smile. Tried to reassure her. He liked Sister Alice. She would be spared when the bunnies burned. 'I am tired, Sister.'

'Would you like to rest, Father?'

Ebb tried to open his eyes, but the lids were too heavy. It was as if someone had placed pennies on them after death. 'There's much work to do, Sister.'

'That's why you need to rest, Father. You need to be strong.'

Ebb ground his teeth as the buzzing in his head escalated. 'Satan is among us now. I can smell his foul breath on the wind.'

'We shall fight him, Father,' Sister Alice promised.

Ebb forced his eyes open. Satan was blocking his thoughts. 'Be careful.'

'We shall be vigilant, Father.'

Ebb's eyes rolled back in his head. 'It's time to put the bunnies to bed.'

'The bunnies?'

Ebb fell to the floor. He twitched and jerked like a man in the midst of an exorcism.

Chapter Twenty-Two

Ben watched the group fuss around their leader. He turned his head towards Bubba. 'Please help me.'

Bubba stared ahead, silent and still as a tombstone.

Sister Alice took charge of the situation. 'Get back and let the Father breathe.'

'What's up with him?' Sister Dixie asked.

'He's having an epileptic fit.'

'He looks like someone's plugged him into the mains.'

Alice knelt beside Ebb. 'Don't be so disrespectful.'

'I'm not.'

Alice grabbed Ebb's arms and pinned them down. 'It's okay, Father. It's okay.'

Ben pleaded with Bubba again to help him.

Bubba mouthed something unintelligible.

'He's going to kill me.'

Bubba shook his head. He reached out and touched Ben's shoulder.

'Will you help me?'

Bubba took his hand away.

'Why can't you talk?'

Bubba didn't answer.

'Sorry. Dumb question. Can you sign?'

Bubba stared ahead.

Ebb ceased thrashing about on the floor.

Alice turned to Emily. 'Fetch the Father some water.'

Emily scurried out of the barn, her bare feet kicking up puffs of dust.

Ebb peered up at Sister Alice. 'Where's the shovel?'

Sister Alice wiped his forehead with a white lace handkerchief. 'Shovel? What shovel, Father?'

Ebb pushed her hand away. 'Who are you? Declare yourself.'

'I'm Sister Alice, Father. You had a – turn.'

Ebb sat up and looked about him. 'I was attacked.'

'Attacked, Father?'

'By Satan.'

For the next five minutes, Ben watched the group fuss around Ebb, hanging onto his every word like medieval servants in the presence of a great messiah. Ben wouldn't have been too surprised if they'd all fallen to their knees and fought over the exclusive right to kiss his feet.

Ebb allowed Dixie and Alice to help him to his feet. He dusted himself down and tightened the black sash securing his robe. 'Get back into line. We need to drive Satan out. The sooner we get to grips with this, the better it will be for everyone.'

As the group reassembled behind him, Ebb pulled the hatpin from his pocket and walked over to the cross. 'Benjamin?'

Ben looked away.

Ebb turned back to the group. 'Satan scurries around inside Benjamin like a cornered rat. But let me tell you, he cannot escape the judgement of God.'

'Satan isn't inside me,' Ben shouted.

Ebb examined the pin. 'Satan is inside all sinners, Benjamin. And you are a sinner. The first step towards salvation is admitting your guilt.'

'How the fuck can I admit to something when I don't even know what it is?'

Ebb waved a hand. 'Blah, blah, blah. I expect nothing better than puerile denial and profanity from you. Let me help you. You have many things to choose from. Let's start with gluttony.'

Ben stared at the hatpin. 'Gluttony?'

'Are you guilty of the sin of gluttony?'

'I don't know.'

'Judging by the look of you, probably not. You look like a bag of bones after the butcher's dog has finished with them.'

Ben's mind refused point blank to think. He watched Ebb wave the hatpin in the air like someone attempting to cast spells.

Ebb held the pin up and placed his other hand on his chest. 'I admit to being guilty of the sin of gluttony once. I, too, have sinned. But let me tell you, as God is my witness, I opened my heart to Jesus. The Lord Jesus Christ brought me into the light.'

'Praise Jesus,' Sister Alice shouted.

Ebb turned to face the group. 'What was your sin, Sister Dixie?'

'Forgive me, Father, for I have sinned. I have committed the sin of lust.'

'Are you now cured of the sin of lust?'

Dixie bowed her head. 'Yes, Father.'

Ebb looked at Sister Emily. 'And you, child?'

'Forgive me, Father, for I am guilty of the sin of sloth.'

'How so, sister?'

Emily stared straight ahead with those expressionless eyes. 'I was lazy of mind, Father. I did not stand up for the things I believed in. I allowed myself to be led into temptation.'

'Are you now cured of the sin of sloth, Sister Emily?'

'Yes, Father.'

'Sister Alice?'

'Forgive me, Father, for I have sinned. I have committed the sin of avarice. I longed for the attainment of wealth and jewels and material possessions.'

'Are you now cured of the sin of avarice?'

'Yes, Father.'

Ebb turned to Bubba. 'Brother Bubba was guilty of the sin of pride, weren't you, my friend?'

Bubba nodded his head.

'Brother Bubba is now cured of his sin, aren't you, Brother?'

Bubba nodded, eyes staring straight ahead.

Ebb looked at Ben. 'Brother Tweezer was guilty of the sin of wrath. Brother Marcus, sloth. Lazy as a leech in a blood bank that one. Brother Gerald carried the sin of envy. Do you see where we're going with this, Benjamin?'

Up shit creek without a teaspoon, Ben thought.

Ebb pursed his lips. 'First thing you need to do is fess up, as our colourful American cousins might say.'

Ben looked from Ebb to the hatpin. He was willing to "fess up" to anything right now. Anything to make this lunatic go away.

Ebb took a deep breath. 'Gluttony, sloth, envy, avarice, pride, wrath or lust? Take your pick, Benjamin.'

'I am guilty of the sin of sloth, Father.'

'A lazy spirit?'

Ben agreed.

'Guilty of picking fruit from another man's tree?'

'Yes, Father.'

'Bathing in the sweat of his labour?'

'Yes, Father.'

'Climbing on the back of the weary traveller?'

Ben struggled for breath. 'Yes, Father.'

'Stealing a poor man's bread, that he should starve whilst you fill your bloated belly?'

Ben looked at his stomach and almost laughed. 'Yes, Father.'

Ebb bent over in front of Ben. 'Then we must purge you of your sin, Benjamin.'

'Please. I—'

Ebb jabbed the hatpin into the sole of Ben's right foot. Deep. Tweezer-deep, you might say.

Ben screamed. Molten lava flowed through his foot. His shoulders erupted in a fresh ball of flame.

Ebb stood up. 'You are guilty of the sin of sloth. May the Lord Jesus Christ forgive you.'

Ben writhed on the cross.

Ebb paced back and forth like an evangelist on a stage. 'Admission to sin is the first step on the road to redemption. Let it be known that Benjamin has now confessed to the sin of sloth. Now we can exorcise Satan from his body.'

'Satan's not in me,' Ben shouted.

Ebb held up a hand. 'Words are just wrappings for poisonous thoughts.'

'I'm telling the truth.'

Ebb waved the hatpin in the air. 'Your truth and my truth hail from different continents, Benjamin.'

Ben was about to protest, but arguing with Ebb was like arguing with fog.

'You are no better than the mealy-mouthed scum who litter the streets on a Friday night,' Ebb continued. 'They all talk a good fight, fuelled by the demon drink, but put them in a uniform and ask them to fight for Queen and Country, and they'd piss their pants at the first whine of a bullet.'

Ben tried to keep still. The slightest movement set off flares in his body. 'Can I please have some water?'

'You are in a period of fasting, Benjamin.'

'I feel sick.'

'You're bound to be queasy. Satan is like a rotten tooth. Your instinct is to resist the dentist, even though you know extraction will make you better in the long run.'

'I just want water.'

Ebb turned away and addressed the group. 'He will resist, but we shall be strong. Satan's instinct is to procure sympathy. But we must never be fooled by his foolery.'

'I'm not trying to fool any—'

Ebb turned around and clapped his hands at Ben like a teacher trying to form order in a classroom. 'Silence. I've suffered enough of your insubordination. Speak only when spoken to.'

Ben closed his mouth.

Ebb turned to Alice. 'Sister?'

'Yes, Father.'

'I want you to fetch a lighter, a flannel, and a bowl of antiseptic liquid.'

'Yes, Father.'

'What are you going to do?' Ben demanded.

Ebb turned around again. 'Do you think I want to give Satan prior knowledge of my intentions?'

Ben closed his eyes. He prayed to Pastor Tom's god. A god with compassion. A god who represented the power of good. A god that would surely condemn Edward Ebb to the flames of Hell one day.

Ebb closed his eyes. 'I ask you to guide me, Lord, as we seek to remove Satan from this wretched mortal being. I ask you to help me cleanse Benjamin's soul, that he may be pure and whole and ready to serve you.'

Ebb's bald head looked like a glass dome in the glow of the lanterns. He still had the hatpin clutched in one hand. His robe was open at the top, revealing a crop of black hair sprouting from his flabby chest.

Sister Alice returned five minutes later with a bowl of steaming water. She placed the bowl on the ground in front of the cross and then took a disposable lighter from the pocket of her robe. She handed it to Ebb. The smell of Dettol wafted up to Ben, reminding him of his mother's obsession with the stuff when he was a kid. Every cut and scrape would bring forth the Dettol, complete with cotton wool balls and a put-Humpty-together-again smile.

Ebb gave an exaggerated bow. 'Thank you, Sister Alice. Please join Sister Dixie and Sister Emily.'

Ben watched the three women link arms, Sister Alice in the middle. Ebb then instructed Bubba to stand in position beside the cross and remain vigilant.

Ben wondered what the hell for; he was hardly going to slip out of the restraints and spring from the cross like David Blaine, was he?

Ebb stood before Ben. 'Are you prepared?'

'How the fuck can I be prepared?'

'The Devil makes a fine fork of toasting your tongue, Benjamin. But taking hostage of your tongue will serve no purpose, other than to strengthen my resolve. Is that clear to both of you?'

Ben asked Pastor Tom's God to strike Ebb down. He wasn't listening.

Ebb looked up at the rafters. 'This sinner has confessed to the sin of sloth, Lord. A weak spirit who leeches upon the blood of others. He has shown a flagrant disregard for the welfare of others, and a propensity towards self-obsession. What shall be his punishment?'

Ben followed Ebb's gaze, half-expecting to see the Devil straddling a beam. Apart from dozens of cobwebs hanging from the rafters like ghostly hammocks, the beams were as bare as Ben's body.

Ebb clasped his hands in front of him. 'I ask you to guide us with your everlasting light, Lord. Guide us as we endeavour to drive Satan from Benjamin's body.'

'Let me go,' Ben shouted.

'By order of the Lord Jesus Christ, I command you to be silent, Satan.' Ebb fell to his knees and bowed his head right down to the ground.

For one crazy moment, Ben thought that God had answered his prayers and struck the bastard down with a heart attack.

Ebb stayed this way for almost ten minutes, occasionally bobbing his head up and down like a chicken pecking corn. He then climbed to his feet and addressed the three women. 'Jesus has spoken.'

'Praise Jesus,' Sister Alice shouted.

Tears shimmered in Ebb's bloodshot eyes. 'Jesus has accepted Benjamin's confession. Praise Jesus.'

'Praise Jesus,' the three women agreed.

'But Jesus has warned us to be wary. The lazy are inclined towards deception. We must leave no stone unturned in Benjamin's rehabilitation.'

'We shall watch him closely, Father,' Alice said.

Ebb turned to Ben. 'Are you ready to reject the ways of Satan?'

Hear no evil, see no evil, speak no evil, Ben's mind chanted like a mantra.

'Answer the Father,' Sister Alice said.

Ben was ready to crawl across hot coals to get off the cross. 'Yes.'

Ebb rambled on: 'Jesus has told me you are to complete fourteen days hard labour and fourteen days of fasting following the Night of Naked Reconciliation. Do you accept Jesus's ruling?'

'Yes.'

Ebb held the hatpin held out in front of him like a sparkler on Bonfire Night. He heated the tip of the pin with the lighter.

'What the fuck—'

'It's time for you to leave, Satan,' Ebb announced. 'Jesus has instructed me to mark you with the sign of the cross.'

'No... please... don't....'

Ebb ignored him. 'You will leave Benjamin's body, Satan. By the order of the Lord Jesus Christ. You are not welcome here.'

'N-n-n-no.'

Ebb scratched the red-hot tip of the pin across Ben's hairless chest. The skin sizzled and scorched as the hot metal burned into the flesh. Ebb then drew the pin down towards Ben's naval.

Ben screamed and twisted his head from side to side. Spit frothed in the corners of his mouth.

'Jesus suffered for you, Benjamin. He suffered so that a sinner like you might be saved.'

Ben opened his mouth to scream again, but unconsciousness afforded him temporary respite. His head rolled to one side, resting on his right shoulder.

Ebb turned to Bubba. 'You stay with him until I relieve you.'

Bubba nodded.

'Sister Alice, Sister Dixie? Go to my quarters and release Madeline. Take her to the Sisters' Room and see that she's comfortable.'

'Is that wise, Father?' Alice asked.

'Why do you ask?'

'Is she purged?'

Ebb regarded Alice as though she'd just questioned his sanity. 'Jesus Christ told me to release her.'

Alice bowed her head. 'Yes, Father. Sorry, Father.'

'I've got urgent business to attend to, so if you're done with the questions?'

'Yes, Father.'

Ebb turned to Emily. 'You can sanitise Benjamin's wounds. Then you are to return to the Sisters' Room. Do you understand?'

'Yes, Father.'

Ebb dipped the tip of the hatpin into the bowl of water and then walked out of the barn into the cool night air.

Chapter Twenty-Three

Ebb panted and wheezed as he reached the top of the fifty-foot tower. Either those steps were getting longer, or he was getting shorter. As soon as the weather cooled, he would embark on an exercise programme designed to offload weight. Not that he was fat. Not in relation to some of the gluttonous lard-arses waddling up and down the High Street, the contents of Pizza Hut jiggling in their jogging bottoms. The Lord had profound rules regarding gluttony.

Ebb blamed his propensity towards carrying a few extra pounds on a faulty gene inherited from his unknown father. It certainly hadn't come from his stick insect of a mother.

Marcus lurched around the corner. 'Father? What brings you up here?'

Ebb scowled and stared down the barrel of the rifle. 'Will you point that blessed thing in another direction?'

Marcus lowered the gun. 'Sorry, Father.'

'We've got problems.'

'Problems?'

Ebb was sorely tempted to poke him in the eye. Why did he always have to respond to a question with a question? Apart from being infuriating, it was damned well rude. 'Yes, problems. You know, puzzle, puzzle, riddle, riddle?'

'Sorry, Father. Is it the new recruits?'

'This isn't the army, Brother Marcus.'

'Sorry.'

'And stop saying "sorry". It's tiresome. It makes me believe you're hiding something.'

'I'm not hiding anything, Father.'

'The guilty flee where none pursues. Perhaps you've been having a toke on the wacky-baccy?'

'No, Father.'

'I hope not. Polluting your brain with that smog might prove a dangerous pastime, Pixie-pea. It's a long way to fall from the tower, don't you think?'

Marcus looked at the sheer fifty-foot drop. 'Yes, Father.'

'There used to be a lock keeper at Briers lock. Len Bunyan. Big Lenny, they called him. Big buffoon, more like. He was partial to a drink. So partial he ended up falling into the lock and drowning. Do you see the point I'm trying to make here?'

'Yes, Father.'

Ebb moved from water to flames. 'If you play with fire, you get burned.'

Marcus looked at him with those I'm-up-to-something eyes. 'Yes, Father.'

'And we all know what happens to bad bunnies. But I haven't climbed all the way up here to lecture you on the dangers of drug abuse. Suffice to say, a fool and his brain are soon parted.'

Brother Marcus cocked his head to one side like a dog trying to comprehend a mathematical equation. 'Yes, Father.'

Ebb cut to the chase. 'It's Brother Tweezer.'

'What about him?'

Ebb regretted his decision not to eat a Mars Bar before climbing the tower. Vanity had prevailed over good sense. His sugar levels were dangerously low. 'He tried to rape Madeline.'

'Tweezer? Are you sure?'

'Of course I'm bloody well sure. Do you think I'm in the habit of spreading malicious rumours?'

Marcus took a step back. 'No, Father. It's just a shock, that's all.'

'He defied me.'

'I can't believe he would go against you, Father.'

'Well he did. Fact. End of discussion.'

'When?'

'Whilst I was attending Benjamin's inauguration. He tried to force himself upon her.'

'I can't believe—'

'Do you doubt me?'

'No, Father.'

'You're not harbouring any ambition to be the Doubting Thomas of The Sons and Daughters of Salvation?'

'No, Father.'

Ebb felt faint. He gripped the guardrail. The sooner he got back down onto more secure ground, the better. He'd never liked heights. He couldn't wait to get back to his quarters where a nice big family-sized slab of Dairy Milk was waiting for him in the fridge.

'Did he actually rape the girl, Father?'

'No. Madeline kicked him in the face and rendered him unconscious.'

'So no real harm—'

'He shouldn't have been there. Period. I sent him to put Max in the kennel and fetch a blowtorch. I didn't tell him to go up to my private quarters and rape the girl. He knows he's not allowed up there under any circumstances. No one is.'

'Satan might have used the girl to lure Brother Tweezer to your quarters.'

Ebb took several deep breaths and tried to clear his head. 'I thought so at first. But Jesus came to me in the barn and told me the girl is blameless. I'm afraid the Devil is inside Brother Tweezer.'

Marcus looked away. 'Are you sure, Father?'

'Do you doubt me, Thomas?'

'No, Father.'

'Do you wish to undermine my authority?'

'No, Father.'

'Or perhaps you believe I've climbed all the way up here to tell you bedtime stories?'

'No, Father.'

'Perhaps you'd like to join Brother Tweezer down the rabbit hole?'

'No, Father.'

'It can be arranged. Benjamin and Bubba can replace both you and that useless article, Tweezer.'

'I'm sorry. I thought Satan might be playing games with you.'

Ebb smiled. 'Do you think the Devil is capable of playing games with me?'

'No, Father.'

'Perhaps all that wacky-baccy has addled your brain and denied you the ability to think?'

Marcus didn't answer that. He didn't need to. Ebb could see the guilt and shame resident in the man's bloodshot eyes.

'What are we going to do, Father?'

'What can we do? Sometimes the only thing to do when a building is overrun by the enemy is destroy the building.'

'Kill him?'

'It's the only course of action open to us. May the Lord have mercy upon his soul.'

'Tweezer's been a loyal servant. I shall pray for his spirit.'

With Satan running amok, Ebb thought it prudent to pay close attention to Brother Marcus as well. 'We must all pray for our dear lost soul.'

'He served you well, Father.'

Ebb gripped the guardrail. 'Not well enough, Pixie-pea. But I won't be fooled again.'

'No, Father.'

'Whichever way the wind blows, I shall not bend. However much the tide turns, I shall not drown. However much the earth moves, I shall stand resolute. Unfaltering. A monument to all that is sacred. Do you understand me, Brother Marcus?'

Marcus did. His head bobbed up and down like a lifebuoy in rough weather.

'I want you to come down from the tower. I want the farm put into lockdown until we've dealt with Brother Tweezer.'

'Yes, Father.'

'Carry out your duties with competence and diligence, and you might very well replace Brother Tweezer.'

'Me, Father?'

'No. I'm talking to that parrot perched on your shoulder!'

Marcus glanced at his right shoulder, and then looked back at Ebb with those shifty, glazed eyes. 'Thank you, Father.'

Ebb didn't think Marcus looked very grateful. He looked more like a kid who'd just swallowed a dose of bad medicine.

'Do we *have* to kill Tweezer? Can't we just try to drive Satan out of him first?'

Ebb fought a compelling urge to hurl Marcus from the tower. 'He is beyond salvation, Brother Marcus. I'm afraid he must shame the shovel.'

Chapter Twenty-Four

Ben's hands throbbed, sending shock-waves up into his arms. His shoulders and legs were white sheets of pain. He watched Ebb and Marcus walk into the barn. Marcus was carrying a rifle. Thankfully, it was pointing at the ground. The two men stopped in front of the cross.

Ebb looked up at Ben. 'How are you holding up, Benjamin?'

For one wild moment, he considered telling Ebb to fuck off and bury his head in a hole. Then he looked at the rifle. 'How do you think?'

'Has Brother Bubba been looking after you?'

Ben almost laughed at the absurdity of the question. He'd tried several times to engage Bubba in conversation, but Bubba had ignored him. Either the big man was as dedicated to the worthless cause as the rest of them, or too scared to act against them.

'I trust you are purged of all sin?'

Ben didn't answer. Arrows dipped in napalm pierced the back of his head.

Ebb turned to Bubba. 'What about you? Do you think the Devil has left our friend?'

Bubba nodded. He didn't make eye contact with Ebb.

Ebb asked Marcus for the rifle. He then told Bubba and Marcus to take down the cross.

Bubba unscrewed the crossbeam from the barn's wooden frame. The two men carried the cross to the middle of the barn and lowered it to the floor.

The blood drained from Ben's head. Three Bubbas and two Marcuses loomed above him. Two of the Bubbas pirouetted like ballerinas. 'I feel sick.'

Ebb grinned at him. 'You just need time to adjust.'

Ben looked away as Ebb's eyes left his face and orbited his head.

'Untie the restraints, Bubba.'

Ben felt pressure on his legs. It was as if Bubba was trying to bore a hole through his shin. But which Bubba? Bubba the mute or Bubba the ballerina?

'He'll need time to get his bearings,' Marcus said.

The pressure on Ben's legs intensified. He tried to call out and tell Bubba to be careful, but the words stuck in his throat like Post-it notes. He closed his eyes.

Ebb told Marcus to go back to the house and tell Sister Alice to put the girls in lockdown. Ben watched the words float around inside his head. White letters in an oily black soup. The letters spelled out something important. Ben tried to focus on them. Tried to string those letters together.

Ebb prodded Ben with his foot. 'Are you still with us?'

The letters formed a word in Ben's head: S – T – U – T – T – E –R – B – U – C –K.

'He's flaked out, Father.'

'I thought I told you to go to the house and tell Sister Alice to put the girls in lockdown?'

'Yes, Father.'

Ben watched the letters sink down into that oily soup. Deeper and deeper. The black soup was good once you got right down into it. A little scary at first, but once you took the plunge, it was as fine as an oil slick in a soup bowl could ever be.

Ebb kicked Ben's right hip. 'Benjamin?'

Ben swam deeper and deeper into the black ocean. It somehow seemed safer down there.

Ebb looked at him for a good while before turning to Bubba. 'Carry him back inside.'

Bubba nodded.

Ebb grinned. 'That's what I like about you, Bubba. You speak your mind.'

Bubba took a key from his overalls and unlocked the handcuffs.

'Take him to the Brothers' Room and keep an eye on him. He's allowed water, but no food. He'll be fasting for the next fourteen days. Do you understand?'

Bubba nodded.

Ebb slapped the stock of the rifle. 'Come on, then. Chop, chop. There's a million things to do before first light.'

***

The black ocean was choppy. Ben bobbed up and down in the water. Bile bubbled in his stomach and leaked into his throat. He could see shafts of light above him where the sun pierced the surface of the black water. He tried to swim, propel himself up through the water to reach the surface, but his limbs refused to move in the thick syrupy liquid.

Ben could see the hull of a ship just beneath the surface. No, not a ship. Way too small. A rowing boat. And Old Joe rowed that boat for all he was worth. Ben smiled. The smile peeled itself like a banana. Old Joe rowing a boat: that was just a joke to end all jokes. Old Joe, with one eye looking east, the other as blind as faith, paddling around in circles like a dog chasing its tail.

Three letters from the alphabet soup floated past him, rising to the surface. S – B – C. Ben tried to work out the significance of the three letters. An acronym? An invitation to play scrabble?

'Hey, whatcha doing down there?' Old Joe said from above him in the rowboat.

Ben tried to shout to Old Joe, tell him to throw down a lifeline, but the words formed into white bubbles in the black liquid and popped. Poof. Just like that. Like a dream he'd never had.

'I'll fetch you some water,' Old Joe said.

Ben wondered why Old Joe would want to fetch him water when he was surrounded by the stuff. Swimming in it, you might say.

High above him, the Stutter-buck of a motor stammered into life. Light shafted through the inky water. 'Benjamin?'

Ben tried to swim. Tried so hard to force those dead-end limbs to move. The light grew stronger, the sound of the motor louder. Something touched his lips. Something wet and cold. How was that possible? He looked up and followed the shaft of light to the surface.

'Benjamin?'

The rowboat vanished. The ocean vanished. Old Joe vanished. Ben looked up. Marcus held a green plastic beaker of water in one hand. The rifle was slung over his shoulder and held in place with a frayed leather strap. 'Sit up and you can have a drink.'

'Where's Old Joe?'

Marcus laughed. 'Old Joe? There's no one called Old Joe here, mate. You've been away with the fairies.'

'My name's not Benjamin. It's Ben.'

'Not anymore, brother. You're one of us now. Once the Father swears you in tomorrow morning, you'll be known as Brother Benjamin. You'd do well to remember that.'

'I need painkillers.'

'Sorry. No can do. We don't allow artificial substances. If you want to sit up, you can have a glass of water.'

'I'm in agony.'

'Pain is all in the mind.'

'You tell my fucking shoulders that.'

'Swearing's also against the rules. I'm telling you that as a friend, okay? Everyone curses once in a while. It's to be expected. But if you want my advice, make sure the Father is out of earshot.'

'I couldn't care less.'

'You'll learn. It's up to you whether you want to do it the easy way or the hard way.'

Ben forced himself to sit up. His shoulders and knee would never recover from his ordeal on the cross. He just wanted to dive back into the soothing black water again and never resurface.

Marcus handed him the water. 'Don't gulp it; you might throw up.'

Ben ignored him and drained the water in one long draught. Water had never tasted so good. So cold and invigorating. What the hell did it matter if he threw up? In the grand scheme of things, throwing up was the least of his worries.

Ben's stomach suddenly felt as if it was in the grip of giant pincers. He dropped the beaker on the floor and bent double.

Marcus put a hand on his shoulder. 'Whoa there, buddy. I told you to take it easy.'

Ben rocked back and forth on the bed. He dry-retched several times. Bile burned the back of his throat.

'I've got to go. I've got work to do. Brother Bubba will look after you if you need anything. Right, Bubba?'

Bubba grunted and rolled over on his bunk.

'You can have my bunk for the night,' Marcus said. 'There's a bucket in the corner of the room if you need to take a leak.'

Ben stared at the bare boards as Marcus walked out of the room and locked the door behind him. He'd never given much consideration to the concept of Hell. But now he knew for sure that Hell existed.

And he was in it.

Chapter Twenty-Five

E dward Ebb sat at the kitchen table, deep in contemplation. The Lord had laid plenty of food for thought at his table. Overladen it, you might say, but Ebb was old enough and wise enough to understand that Jesus would never ask him to do anything beyond his capabilities.

A fact clearly illustrated the night Jesus had told him to kill his own mother. Right out of the blue, like a midge on a hot summer's day, Jesus had interrupted Alan Titchmarsh during a gardening program on BBC Two to tell him that his mother must shame the shovel.

Uncle Reg, the latest in a long line on *uncles*, had been watching the TV whilst Ebb had been trying to do his homework at the dining table. Jesus had waited for Uncle Reg to nip to the loo before demonstrating the art of shaming the shovel. The great man had used a pumpkin as a substitute head. He'd smashed that thing to a pulp. Liquidised it. Beaten every drop of juice out of it. Jesus had also performed a miracle to rival His water into wine trick: He'd turned the flesh and juice of the pumpkin into blood and brain matter. His white robe had looked more like a butcher's apron than a holy gown. The program had concluded with Titchmarsh planting a row of runner beans in the blood-soaked ground and telling viewers about the importance of fertile soil.

Ebb had needed no second invitation to beat his mother to death. No, sir. But even at the tender age of sixteen, he knew a murder required proper planning. Especially the murder of a close family member. The police always looked in the victim's own backyard before they poked their noses further afield.

Knowing the right time to kill his mother was simple. She got drunk in the mornings, slept it off in the afternoons, and started again in the evenings. Easy-peasy, vodka and lemon-squeezy. He'd just have to find a good way to get himself out of school in the afternoon, nip home and smash her pumpkin to pieces with a shovel, and get back to school again without being missed. One problem though: teachers had a nasty habit of checking your attendance in class. Even Miss Parsons, and she was blind in one eye.

After weeks and weeks of trying to find a solution to his conundrum, the answer came by virtue of a cross-country race. With their usual lack of concern for kids that hated sports and loved chocolate, the school had set up a two-hour course, which at its furthest point ran close to the river. The plan was simple by design. All he had to do was leave the race, go home, bash his mother's head in with Uncle Reg's shovel, and rejoin the race.

But here was the main problem: it would take too much time to execute. And there would be teachers planted along the route to stop the kids from cheating. As the race drew near, Ebb had wrestled with the problem, night after sleepless night.

The answer had finally come to him in the early hours of the morning after a fretful night listening to his mother *at it* with Uncle Reg in the adjoining bedroom. All he had to do was cut across the dried-up brook at the back of the park to get home and back again without being seen. Then he just needed to injure his leg, so it looked as if he couldn't move. Nothing as radical as a break, because that would hurt like hell on a cheese toasty, but bad enough to swell it up so he could sit down and wait for someone to find him.

On the day of the race, Ebb consumed three Snickers bars to prepare for his *marathon*. The initial sugar rush soon dissipated and left him feeling sick as a dog. What if he threw up all over the murder scene? By the time he reached home, his heart was trying to beat its way out of his chest. There was a funny tingling sensation in his head.

He went to Uncle Reg's garden shed and put on a pair of surgical gloves stolen from the school science lab. Uncle Reg loved the garden. Said you couldn't beat home-grown vegetables. Jesus would have disagreed. Just ask the pumpkin He'd beaten to a pulp with the shovel.

Armed with Uncle Reg's shovel, he went inside the house and leaned the shovel up against the kitchen wall. He polished off four glasses of water. He then picked up the shovel and walked upstairs. Up the wooden hill to Bedfordshire, as his mother used to say when Ebb was still little and her brain wasn't so pickled. He made a mental note to raid her chocolate drawer before he left. She wouldn't be needing chocolate anymore.

It felt as if someone was whisking eggs in his stomach. He stood in his mother's bedroom doorway, the shovel dangling by his side. As predicted, Veronica Ebb was lying flat on her back on the bed that seemed to harvest uncles from the depths of its springs and lumps. The room stank of booze. He felt sure that if he lit a match, she'd erupt in a ball of flame. But he didn't want her to die in such an impersonal way. He wanted to *feel* her die. He wanted to *taste* her death. Savour it and digest it so he could relive it, over and over again.

This was for all the times she'd sent him to bed with a great big hungry bear growling in his tummy. For all the uncles who'd laid their hands on him when he was too little to fight back. All the times she'd woke him up with her howling fake laughter. The times her headboard had beat against his wall like a thumping reminder she was a whore. For all the times she'd called him Pixie-pea.

But mostly, it was for the time she'd thrown him down the stairs when he was seven years old and almost turned her Pixie-pea into a mushy pea. He'd been unconscious for close on a lifetime. He'd woken up to find her bathing his head with a cold flannel that stank of damp and TCP. A few days later, she'd had to take him to the doctor because he kept having fits. She'd made him tell the doctor he'd been sleepwalking and took a tumble down the wooden hill. Ebb had done what mummy had asked. The doctors had prescribed some gloopy medicine, and pills to control the fits.

As he looked at his snoring mess of a mother, a thought struck him. What about blood? If he smashed her pumpkin head to a pulp, he would get covered in blood. It was one thing feigning an injury, quite another trying to explain to the teachers why he was covered in blood.

The shovel saved him. The shovel told him to go to the spare room and put on a pair of Uncle Reg's overalls. That way, Ebb could stash the bloody overalls in the garden shed, along with the shovel, and get Uncle Reg locked up for life. Perfect. Ebb had almost fell to his knees and kissed the shovel. The shovel also told him to put his tracksuit on over his PE kit and wear his mother's pink wig, just in case he contaminated the overalls with any of his hair and skin.

The overalls hadn't fit. Uncle Reg was over six feet tall. The arms covered his hands, and the legs gobbled up his trainers and made walking a dangerous experience. He'd nearly tripped over twice on his way back to his mother's bedroom. But nearly was as good as never as his mother used to say when she'd had a mouth capable of talking sense. To make matters worse, it was hotter than Hell in three layers of clothing.

Ebb picked up the shovel. It made him feel warm and cosy inside. The shovel understood him. Loved him for who he was. He moved close to the bed and raised the shovel above his head. In his excitement, he forgot about the brass ceiling light that Uncle Tom had fitted when he'd occupied Uncle Reg's berth. The shovel clanged against it louder than a church bell at a wedding. One of the tiny glass shades smashed, raining a fine shower of glass down on the bed.

Veronica Ebb opened her eyes and gawked at her son. She looked like a chicken looking at the dreaded axe. She opened her mouth to say something. Perhaps to ask him why he was wearing her pink wig. Perhaps to beg forgiveness. Perhaps to say goodbye to her little Pixie-pea.

Ebb brought the shovel down on her face hard enough to splinter the bone in her nose. The corner of the shovel gouged her right eye.

Love of the shovel and hatred of his mother poured through Ebb in equal measures. He hit her again and again and again until exhaustion finally stopped him. Spent, he rested on the shovel, gasping for air and looking at the bloody pulp that used to be his mother's face.

Ebb grinned. 'You have shamed the shovel.'

Veronica Ebb's face resembled a giant hamburger with bits of eyeball and tooth ground into the mix. Ebb wanted to stay in that moment forever, locked in a cocoon of pleasure, but time was ticking. He removed the blood-soaked overalls and took them to the shed along with the shovel. He rolled up the overalls and stuffed them underneath Reg's workbench. He leaned the shovel against the wall.

By the time he'd got back to the cross-country course, nagging doubt had replaced elation. His head felt as if it housed a nest of baby birds, beaks open, waiting to be fed answers. To add to his problems, his plan to twist his own ankle wasn't so easy to implement as he'd imagined. Every time he tried to roll the ankle over, his pain threshold refused to let him. Perhaps he could smash his ankle with a rock? Again, same problem. Self-preservation blocked the move. Ebb looked up at the sky and howled. He needed Jesus to tell him what to do.

And so Jesus had. In the guise of a rook sitting high in the branches of a massive oak tree. Jesus had gone out on a limb for him, you might say. Told him to climb right up in that tree and throw himself to the ground.

Driven by desperation, and Jesus's encouragement, Ebb climbed halfway up the tree and leapt to the ground. His left foot landed on the rock he'd been considering using to smash his ankle with. His leg twisted and spilled him forwards onto the hard earth.

He'd spent the best part of an hour in agony under that tree, before Mr Gibbs, the sports master, found him. By then, he'd been convinced that there were vultures circling overhead waiting to feed upon his carcass. After first looking angry, then concerned, Mr Gibbs had called an ambulance on his mobile phone, and tried to pacify Ebb by telling him that only babies cried.

Ebb had spent the rest of the day in hospital having a plaster cast fitted on his broken left leg. By the time an ambulance took him home that evening, the house had been cordoned off with police tape.

He'd spent the following week recuperating at a neighbour's house. Two days after the killing, Uncle Reg was charged with Veronica Ebb's murder. The evidence was overwhelming. The only fingerprints on the shovel belonged to Reg. The blood-soaked overalls belonged to Reg. Reg the Veg was duly found guilty of murder and given a life sentence.

Ebb had left school that summer with no qualifications. He didn't even bother turning up for the exams. He'd stayed in the house as long as he could, but with no money to pay the rent, let alone the bills, he was soon forced to leave. All he took with him, in an old brown rucksack, was a change of clothes, his mother's pink wig, and the sunglasses she'd worn to cover her eyes when one of the many uncles had got handy with his fists.

He'd spent the next two years sleeping rough and begging on the streets. Fourteen years later, he'd exhumed his mother's skeletal remains and pinned them to the wall in the Revelation Room. It was a shame that the original shovel was unobtainable.

He'd gone back once and had a look at the old house. It now boasted new windows and a new front door. Reg the Veg's vegetable garden had been levelled off and grassed over. The shed was gone. In its place, a kids' swing and slide set. A strange mixture of sadness and nostalgia passed through him. A yearning. A longing to break in and go up to his mother's old bedroom and relive the beautiful experience of killing her.

But, of course, he knew better than that. Nothing could be allowed to get in the way of his destiny.

Chapter Twenty-Six

Maddie sat on the edge of her bed and stared at the floor. A filthy red rug covered the bare boards in the middle of the room. A single bulb hanging from the ceiling cast shadows across the room.

Dixie asked, 'What did Tweezer do to you?'

Maddie looked up. She thought Dixie might have been pretty, but life had marked her face with harsh edges. Her faded denim eyes *looked* kind enough, but Maddie didn't know if she could trust her. 'Nothing.'

'Sister Alice reckons he's in deep shit.'

'Language!' Emily said.

Dixie ignored her. 'Come on, Madeline. Spill. He must have done something bad.'

'He came into the room when I was handcuffed to Ebb's bed.'

Dixie raised her eyebrows. 'And?'

'I don't want to say anything out of turn.'

'Then shut up,' Emily said.

Dixie told her to go to sleep.

'I would if you two would shut up yacking.'

'Why don't you stop listening instead.'

'Whatever.'

'Moody cow.'

'So would you be if you were in my shoes.'

Dixie let out an exaggerated sigh. 'Oh no, not the dreaded phantom pregnancy again!'

'It's not a phantom pregnancy. It's real.'

'And who got you up the duff, then? The Tooth Fairy?'

'You can mock me all you like. I don't care.'

'Or maybe it was the Father?'

'Don't be revolting.'

'Nope. Couldn't have been him because he couldn't raise a smile when it comes to women.'

'I'm not interested in your filthy thoughts.'

Dixie laughed. 'Perhaps it was the Holy Ghost, then?'

'Piss off, Dixie. I'm not in the mood.'

Dixie turned back to Maddie. 'What did Tweezer do to you?'

Maddie tried to think. Her thoughts were lost in a maze. Finally, she relented and told Dixie about the attempted rape.

Dixie whistled. 'And you knocked that bastard spark out?'

'Yes.'

'What did Ebb say?'

'He told Tweezer to get dressed. Then he said something about *shaming the shovel*, whatever the hell that is.'

'Did Ebb do anything to you?'

Maddie shook her head. 'No. Sister Alice released me and brought me down here.'

Dixie chewed her index finger. 'You were lucky.'

'You call that lucky?'

Dixie did. 'It looks as if he spared you the initiation.'

Emily propped herself up on one elbow. 'He's all right if you don't antagonise him.'

'That's not what I remember you saying after your initiation. You couldn't walk for a week.'

'That's because I hurt my knee.'

Dixie rolled her eyes. 'Course you did.'

'He gave me wine earlier,' Maddie said. 'Kept going on about Satan being inside me.'

'If he met Jesus Christ himself, Ebb would be convinced that Satan was inside him.'

Emily crossed herself. 'You shouldn't mock Jesus.'

Dixie snorted. 'I don't need to mock Jesus with that crazy bastard on the loose. He does enough mocking for the rest of us put together.'

'How long have you been here?' Maddie asked.

'Christ knows. It must be at least three years, give or take a life sentence.'

Maddie's suddenly wanted her father. Wanted to feel his arms around her, holding her tight and reassuring her. 'I want to go home.'

Dixie walked over to Maddie and sat down next to her on the bed. 'I can't help you there, love. But I can help you learn to play the game and get through this if that's any help?'

Maddie's shoulders collapsed beneath the weight of the day. Her heart felt as if it was about to explode. Spill every emotion, every secret, every last piece of her.

Dixie held on to her as Maddie rocked back and forth on the bed. She cried for her mother, lost to a worthless civil war in Rwanda. She cried for her father, who would never see her again. And she cried for a life already over before it had begun.

After a few minutes, Dixie pulled away and rubbed Maddie's arm. 'At least that bastard never got a piece of you. That's one up to you.'

Maddie nodded.

'Brother Tweezer has always been all right with me,' Emily said.

Dixie rounded on her. 'Really? Maybe you can be Tweezer's bitch one day.'

'You don't know me at all, do you? Just because I believe in what we're doing.'

'Believe in what we're doing? Do you really think we're going to build a spaceship and go to Heaven?'

'Yes.'

'Then you're more stupid than I thought.'

Maddie remembered Emily's letter home. 'What spaceship?'

Dixie rolled her eyes. 'Ebb tells everyone he's building a spaceship ready for the Rapture. What he really means is he's getting members to milk their families to pay for his lavish lifestyle. You've been up in his room, Maddie. Does it look the same as the rest of the farmhouse?'

'It looks like a penthouse suite.'

'Exactly. He'll ask you to get your parents to cough up, just like he asked Dozy over there to ask hers. How much did he ask for, Emily?'

'None of your business.'

'A hundred grand?'

'None of your business.'

Dixie laughed. 'You sound like one of those villains going "no comment" to the cops.'

'Go to Hell. I know who I am and where I'm going.'

'First she reckons she's pregnant, now she thinks she's going to Heaven to give birth to the new baby Jesus.'

'Mock me all you like, Dixie. But it's you who will pay the price on Judgement Day. Not me. Not Sister Alice. You. You and all those non-believers who think it's clever to mock Jesus.'

'I'm not mocking Jesus. Just you.'

'You've so got it coming to you, Dixie. You and your filthy mouth.'

'And you've got a cuckoo in your nest.'

Emily ignored her. 'If you've got any sense, Maddie, you won't listen to a word she says.'

'Please don't fight,' Maddie said.

Dixie glared at Emily. 'She's as batty as Ebb.'

'I'll report you to the Father if you don't shut up, Dixie.'

'Would that be the same upstanding Father who grows cannabis in the basement?'

'He doesn't.'

'Yes, he does. Marcus sells it on the streets, along with a shitload of other drugs. Do you know what he calls it? The Crop of Christ. The Crop of fucking Christ? How sick is that?'

'You're lying,' Emily said.

'It's good shit. I've had some. Me and Marcus sometimes sneak out to the barn and have a toke.'

Emily sat up. 'You're a liar. Marcus doesn't take drugs.'

Dixie took a deep breath and continued. 'The basement is massive. Marcus says Ebb's got cannabis plants growing under artificial lights. There's even a ventilation thingy to keep the plants healthy.'

'That's all just a great big fat lie. Marcus doesn't take drugs, and he certainly doesn't sell them. He goes to Oxford to spread the word of Jesus.'

'He's a dealer, you stupid girl.'

Emily stood up. 'That's a lie, Dixie. Take it back.'

'It's not a lie. He sells heroin, crack cocaine, weed, amphetamines. You name it, he sells it.'

'You'll rot in Hell for all your lies,' Emily shrieked.

'And you'll get a slap in a minute.'

'He wouldn't sell drugs. It's wrong.'

'What do you care?'

Emily opened her mouth to speak.

'Well?' Dixie persisted.

Emily sat back down on her bed. 'God is watching you.'

'Fuck God.'

'You are so going to Hell, Dixie.'

'I don't care what you say, you silly little cow. I know it's true. Marcus helps Ebb cultivate it. As for all the other gear, Ebb gets it from the contacts I gave him.'

'Contacts?' Maddie said.

'Dealers I used to know when I was on the game. I used to carry drugs for my pimp. Ebb picked me up one day. I could tell straight away he wasn't your run-of-the-mill punter. There was something odd about him. You get this kind of instinct for weirdos. You have to. Anyway, he came cruising along in this battered old Vauxhall Nova looking for a pickup.'

'More lies,' Emily muttered.

Dixie ignored her and carried on. 'We used to operate out of my pimp's flat. I took Ebb back there, but he told me he didn't want sex. Well, like I said, I had a feeling about him. I mean, telling a whore you don't want sex is like telling a barber you don't want a haircut, right? So I'm thinking he's going to ask me to do something sick. You wouldn't believe what turns some of those perverts on. But no, not Ebb. He paid me fifty quid so he could show me Jesus.'

'What's wrong with that?' Emily said.

'I thought he was trying to trick me. Maybe *Jesus* was a code name for something. I was intrigued. I hated what I'd become. I wanted out. I'd been selling myself since I was fourteen. Selling myself and taking drugs to numb the pain.'

'That's terrible.,' Maddie said.

'You don't know the half of it. Anyway, the more time I spent with Ebb, the more I realised he wasn't just using me. The more he spoke, the more convinced I became he was genuine.'

Emily rubbed her stomach. 'He is genuine.'

'He told me he had somewhere safe I could go. Somewhere I would be protected. All I had to do was steal my pimp's money and drugs. And trust me, the flat was swimming in the stuff. Plus all the gold chains, watches and medallions.'

'You stole it all?' Maddie asked.

Dixie nodded. 'We planned it for weeks, right there in the heart of Jazz's shitty little empire. The day we made off with everything was the best day of my life.'

'Stealing is also a sin,' Emily reminded her.

Dixie turned on her. 'Considering Ebb instigated the whole fucking thing, I won't lie awake at night worrying about it. Anyway, we took off with the best part of a hundred grand, bags of cocaine, weed, gold, the lot.'

'Liar.'

Dixie ignored Emily. 'On the day we did him over, he was waiting to do a huge drugs deal. Ebb hid under the bed and waited for him to come home. Ebb had a gun and a hunting knife. As soon as Jazz opened the safe, Ebb came out from under the bed. Jazz's face was a picture. He couldn't have looked more surprised if an alien had landed a spaceship in the middle of the flat and invited Jazz to tea.'

Maddie tried to digest what Dixie was telling her. It was like trying to digest a fifty-course meal.

Dixie took a deep breath and continued. 'If it wasn't so scary, it would've been funny. This little bald fat dude pointing a gun at the man who'd made my life a misery for longer than I could remember. Jazz opened his gob to say something and Ebb blew half his face away. Just like that. Poof. Jazz's head exploded. There was blood and bits of brain all over the wall. He fell to the floor, twitched a few times, and that was the end of Jazz.'

'She's making it up,' Emily said.

'We stole all the money in the safe. Jewellery. Drugs. Everything. Stuffed it into two massive holdalls and walked out of that flat as calm as you like.'

Maddie looked at the floor. What did you say to something like that? Congratulations? It pays to plan?

'Just before we left, Ebb shot Jazz another five times. Then he knelt down and prayed for his soul. I puked on the way back to the farm. I was both excited and scared witless. For the first time since I was a kid, I was free. Free of Jazz. Free of punters. Free of beatings. I didn't know that within a month I'd be wishing to Christ I was back at that flat and working the streets.'

The lights went out. Darkness wrapped itself around Maddie like a thick black fog.

'Try to get some rest,' Dixie said. 'It'll be a long day tomorrow.'

'Especially for sinners,' Emily mumbled.

Dixie sighed. 'Especially for the deluded.'

Chapter Twenty-Seven

Ebb unlocked the basement door and turned to Marcus. 'Be on your guard.'

Marcus wrapped a finger around the trigger. 'Yes, Father.'

'He may be dangerous. Particularly if he's wounded.'

'Yes, Father.'

'That's not to say I want you turning him into a colander if he dares to move. Just be attentive.'

Marcus nodded.

Ebb opened the basement door, making a mental note to keep a careful eye on his new deputy. Brother Marcus looked as if he might be open to invasion. He took a few tentative steps down into the basement.

Tweezer was lit up beneath overhead lights suspended above the cannabis plants. He sat with his back against the wall, one leg splayed out at a crazy angle. Ebb thought Tweezer looked like an image drawn from a child's imagination.

He stopped halfway down the steps and turned to Marcus. 'Keep the gun trained on him at all times.'

'Yes, Father.'

'And please remember he is no longer a member of The Sons and Daughters of Salvation.'

'Okay.'

'He is an enemy of The Sons and Daughters of Salvation, and therefore a prisoner. First thing tomorrow, I shall instruct Brother Bubba to build a cross for him.'

'Yes, Father.'

'We must cancel all street operations for the time being. Once Tweezer is dealt with, I want you back up that tower. The Imposter might well use telepathy to call his cronies. The farm can stay in lockdown until we've got ourselves on an even keel.'

'But I—'

Ebb flapped a hand and moved down a few more steps. 'Tweezer?'

Tweezer regarded Ebb with his good eye. The other one looked like an overripe plum. He mumbled something unintelligible and waved an arm in the air.

'Remember that Satan is within him, Brother Marcus. Don't be fooled by his pitiful pleas.'

'My leg's ba-roke,' Tweezer said, the word snapped in two by a sob.

Ebb faced the man who had betrayed his trust. The Judas Iscariot of The Sons and Daughters of Salvation. 'Broken, my eye. You've probably just sprained your ankle.'

Tweezer didn't agree. 'It's ba-roke.'

'I'll tell you what you've broken, Pixie-pea. Your pledge to The Sons and Daughters of Salvation. How's about that for getting yourself bowled out for a duck?'

'I didn't—'

Ebb held up a hand. 'Save your lies.'

'I'm not lying, Fa-ther.'

'You went to my room. Guilty or not guilty?'

'I only—'

'Guilty or not guilty?'

Tweezer looked away. 'Guilty, Father.'

'You then tried to force yourself on Madeline. Guilty or not guilty?'

'Not guilty, Father. She enticed me.'

Ebb produced the bottle of acid from the pocket of his robe. 'Perhaps the holy water shall tell us the truth?'

Tweezer attempted to burrow through the stone wall with his back. 'No, Father. Please. I haven't done nothing.'

Ebb reached the bottom of the steps and uncapped the bottle. He drew the last of the acid into the dropper and squeezed the contents onto Tweezer's bare foot. The foot which was joined to the ba-roken leg. He then threw the bottle at Tweezer's head. Fortunately for Tweezer, Ebb's aim was diminished by exhaustion. It smashed on the wall behind him.

'Be gone, Satan.' Ebb commanded.

Tweezer screamed. He writhed and bucked on the floor like an enthusiastic student of breakdance. His head banged against the stone wall. Snot bubbled from his nose. His lips stretched wide in a rictus grin. He looked as if he might be on the verge of turning into a rabid animal. Ebb had once researched the phenomena of shape-shifting, and although he didn't subscribe to the notion, he conceded that anything was possible whilst under the spell of a demon. Particularly the type proclaiming squatters' rights in Tweezer right now.

Ebb turned to Marcus. 'See how Satan resists?'

Marcus nodded and trained the gun on Tweezer.

Ebb stepped back as Tweezer attempted to shape-shift into a snake and slither across the floor. 'I command you to keep still, or Brother Marcus will shoot you. Do you understand?'

Tweezer stopped writhing. His good eye narrowed. Ebb didn't trust that eye. He checked Tweezer's mouth for signs of a forked tongue. 'What are you?'

'I don't understand, Father.' The words came out flat and compressed. Pitiful, even.

Ebb wasn't fooled. 'Are you a snake?'

Tweezer shook his head. His good eye swivelled from Ebb to Marcus. 'I'm just me, Father.'

'That's what I fear most. Perhaps I should fetch Max to flush you out.'

'No, Father. Please….'

Ebb turned his back on him. He wasn't about to let Satan engage him in a war of words. 'Come down here, Brother Marcus.'

Marcus walked down the steps. When he reached the bottom, Ebb took the gun off him. He aimed it at Tweezer's uninjured leg and pulled the trigger.

The shot echoed around the basement walls. Tweezer screamed and arched his back. Blood blossomed like a liquid rose from a ragged hole just above his kneecap. He huffed and puffed on the floor as if making ready to visit the Three Little Piggies.

Ebb lowered the rifle and addressed Marcus. 'Fetch Max.'

'Yes, Father.'

Ebb turned back to Tweezer. 'What do you think about Brother Marcus taking over your role as second-in-command?'

Tweezer clutched his wounded leg and panted like Max in the midday sun. 'That… fucking… drug… addict?'

Ebb smiled. 'Said the rapist.'

'I never raped no one.'

'Really?'

'Really.'

'And why was that? Did you suddenly see the light?'

Ebb watched Tweezer's lips try to wring an answer from his addled brain. 'Or perhaps Madeline spurned your unwanted advances by kicking you in the face.'

Tweezer wiped his mouth. His hair was pasted to his head in greasy strips. 'She seduced me.'

'Why would she want to seduce you?'

Tweezer wiped blood from his leg and pawed the wound. 'I've no idea, Father.'

'You're hardly a catch, are you?'

Blood oozed between Tweezer's fingers. 'She deceived me, Father. Just like she's deceiving you now.'

Ebb smiled. 'Perhaps you ought to put your finger in the wound. Like the little Dutch boy who stuck his finger in the dyke.'

Tweezer regarded Ebb with an eye stoked with malice. 'Huh?'

'That's dyke as in dam, not a lesbian.'

Tweezer looked away and focused on his bleeding leg.

Ebb pointed the rifle at him. 'I suggest you speak the truth from now on if you want to enter the Kingdom of Heaven, Pixie-pea.'

Tweezer snarled and raised his muzzle. 'Fuck you.'

Ebb took a step back. 'I wondered when Satan would announce himself.'

'You're fucking nuts.'

Ebb aimed the rifle at Tweezer's head. 'Don't cast stones at me, Pixie-pea. I'm just the messenger.'

Tweezer clawed his leg. 'I'm sorry, Father. It's just I'm in such pain.'

Ebb studied Tweezer's good eye for signs of Satan. The man was certainly displaying schizophrenic behaviour. 'Jesus suffered upon the cross for you, Brother Tweezer.'

'I know, Father.'

'But do you?'

'I know Jesus suffered for me, Father.'

'Actions speak louder than words through a bullhorn, Pixie-pea. And your actions tell me you regard Jesus's suffering to be banal.'

'That's not true, Father. I've done everything you've ever asked of me. Everything. I even killed Brother Gerald for you.'

'For me?'

'Yes, Father. You said—'

'I hope you're aware that God is watching you?'

'Yes, Father. But—'

'Brother Gerald was a sinner. Just like you are. And sinners must be punished. The Bible says so. The Scriptures say so. And Jesus Christ Himself says so. I did not order Brother Gerald's execution, the Lord Jesus Christ ordered it. Fact!'

'I'm not saying—'

'Brother Gerald committed the sin of homosexuality. He deserved his punishment. But never confuse God's will with mine. Brother Gerald suffered death by a thousand cuts because that's what God decided.'

Tweezer gawped at Ebb. 'I've never let you down, Father.'

Ebb raised his eyebrows. 'Madeline might beg to differ.'

'I never—'

Ebb held up his free hand. 'Save your lies, rapist. I want you to focus all your attention on crawling to the other end of the room. Do you think you can manage that without tripping over your tongue on the way?'

'Why?'

Ebb pointed the rifle at Tweezer's head. 'Yours is not to reason why, Pixie-pea.'

Tweezer groaned and rolled onto his front. 'My legs. Oh, God, my legs.'

Ebb was unimpressed. 'My legs, my eye. Use your arms to pull yourself forward.'

Tweezer inched forwards, mewling like a cat with its tail caught in a mousetrap. He stopped after a few feet and looked over his shoulder at Ebb. 'Why are you doing this, Father?'

'Move.'

'I don't want to go in the Revelation Room.'

'That's too bad, Brother Tweezer, because that's where you're going.'

'I don't want to die, Father,' Tweezer whined.

'Then you should have thought about that when you attacked Madeline.'

'I didn't attack her.'

'God will be the judge of that. Get moving. A slug on a sleeping pill could move faster than you.'

'My legs are broken.'

'One of your legs is broken. The other one is wounded. There's a difference.'

'There's no difference in the fucking pain.'

'Perhaps you need a bullet up the backside to hurry you along?'

Tweezer didn't. He put his head down and inched forward.

178

'The Imposter will be pleased to see you. That's if he's still alive. He looked in bad shape the last time I saw him. He's a tough nut to crack, I'll give him that.'

Tweezer reached the other end of the room. He lay on the ground panting and wheezing and sobbing. They didn't make men like they used to. Ebb blamed it on the overuse of comforters in infancy. And antibacterial wipes. And indulgent mothers who perched themselves on the edge of baby-boo's crib waiting for the first murmur of discontent.

'Move away from the door,' Ebb instructed.

Tweezer rolled over and whimpered.

Ebb felt scorn tempt his trigger finger into action again. Was this really the same man who'd used his bare hands to kill? Subjected Brother Gerald to death by a thousand cuts? He leaned the gun against the wall and took a bunch of keys from his pocket. 'Move one whisker, and I'll kill you. Is that clear, Pixie-pea?'

Tweezer minced his words through clenched teeth. 'Yes, Father.'

Ebb inserted a brass key into the lock and turned it anti-clockwise. He opened the door and picked up his rifle. The Imposter was still tied to the chair where Sister Alice had left him. He looked ragged, to say the least. 'I've brought you some company.'

The Infiltrator didn't seem very appreciative. He thrashed from side to side in the chair, thus proving you needed little fuel in the tank to start an engine.

Ebb turned his attention back to Tweezer. 'Get in!'

'Please, Father, I don't want to go in the Revelation Room.'

'Once you're settled, I'll fetch you some water.'

'I don't want water.'

'There's no point in throwing temper tantrums, Pixie-pea.'

Tweezer didn't move. 'Please, Father. I'll do anything. Please.'

'If you want me to shoot you, then I will. It's up to you.'

'And what happens if I go into the Revelation Room?'

Ebb smiled. 'I'll make sure you get a fair hearing.'

'No, you won't. You'll just murder me like you did all those other poor sods in there.'

'Have you been given the powers of prediction?'

Tweezer looked up at Ebb, his good eye burning as bright as a church candle. His hair was splayed out in wild clumps above his ears. His ridiculous goatee beard was almost white with froth and dribble. It was a good job that Max wasn't too fussy about what she ate. He would make sure he chopped Tweezer up into indistinguishable lumps for her. Ebb had learned the skill of butchery from the internet. It was simple when you got down to the bare bones of it. There wasn't that much difference between a pig and a man when it came to butchery, except a man kicked up a lot more fuss about going to meet his maker.

A shadow moved in the corner of Ebb's eye. He snapped his head round, fearing that the Imposter might have somehow slipped his bonds. No. Still tied to the chair. Ebb rubbed his eyes and focused all his attention on Tweezer. He ached for his bed. For the feel of the cool cotton sheets. Perhaps a good bottle of red and a box of Milk Tray to calm his shattered nerves.

Perhaps when things settled down, he could take a trip to London and indulge himself in the services of a rent boy. Sex was so much more enjoyable without the restrictions of relationships. He'd allowed himself to fall in love once with Brother Gerald. Never again. Once smitten, twice shy.

'Get in. Now!' Ebb shouted.

Tweezer crawled into the Revelation Room.

Ebb waited for him to get a good way inside and then followed him in. Peace and serenity washed over him. This was his place of renewal and rejuvenation. Of solace.

The Imposter tried to speak, but his efforts were in vain. Sister Alice had secured his lips with duct tape as instructed. The chair rocked precariously.

'See how the Imposter fights his fate, Brother Tweezer?'

Tweezer didn't respond. He lay face down on the floor, motionless. Ebb jabbed his backside with the rifle. 'Come on, sleepyhead. You'll have plenty of time for rest later.'

Tweezer didn't respond.

Ebb studied him with caution. Experience had taught him that Satan could strike without warning. There was a slim possibility that Tweezer might have passed out, but Ebb hadn't built his empire by taking risks. He aimed the rifle at Tweezer's backside and pulled the trigger.

As expected, Tweezer was feigning unconsciousness. He roared back to life, screaming and bucking. The shot echoed around the Revelation Room. Tweezer made frantic efforts to clutch his backside and eat the floor at the same time.

Ebb waited for him to settle down before trying to reason with him. 'Why do you fight me so?'

Tweezer whined and sobbed like a child with a scraped knee.

There was little point in engaging with a burnt bunny. Not when he was destined to shame the shovel. 'Have some dignity, Brother Tweezer.'

Brother Marcus called out from the Cannabis Room. 'Father?'

Ebb steadied himself. He'd never allowed Brother Marcus access to the Revelation Room before. That special privilege had only been afforded to Tweezer, Bubba and Alice. But now it was time for Marcus to step up to the plate. 'Come on in.'

Brother Marcus walked into the Revelation Room with Max panting and slobbering on the leash beside him. He stopped just inside the door, eyes wide, mouth hanging open.

'Welcome to the Revelation Room.'

Marcus stared at the Imposter. 'He's... still alive, then?'

Ebb ignored him. He didn't have time to discuss the Imposter right now. He walked over to the wall where three skeletons were secured to their crosses with twine. Each had a small leather-bound book lodged in its ribcage, documenting its life and association with Ebb.

Marcus gawked at the skeleton with the pink wig and sunglasses.

Ebb snapped his fingers and pointed at the skeleton to the right of his mother's. 'This is Brother Gerald. He died about a year before you arrived.'

'Died? How?'

Ebb prodded Brother Gerald's pelvic area with the rifle. 'Guilty of the sin of homosexuality. Tweezer subjected him to death by a thousand cuts.'

Marcus's mouth hung open. Ebb's mother would have said he looked as if he was trying to catch flies. The man would need to sharpen up considerably if he wanted to take Tweezer's place. 'Do you know the principle of death by a thousand cuts, Brother Marcus?'

Marcus shook his head. His eyes seemed drawn to Ebb's mother. Particularly the wig perched on her head.

Ebb ploughed on. 'It's an old remedy. You hoist the accused up in a net, so as tiny portions of flesh are poking through the holes. Then you chop away until the job is done. Can't say for certain how many times Brother Gerald was cut. A thousand might be a bit of a stretch.'

Marcus looked from Ebb's mother to the Imposter and then back again at Ebb's mother.

'I'll tell you this much: that man could scream. Two barn owls left their roosts that night, didn't they, Brother Tweezer?'

Tweezer didn't answer him. He seemed too concerned with trying to breathe and plug up holes in his leaking body.

Ebb excused him on the grounds of compassion. 'Brother Gerald tried to seduce me.'

Marcus looked at Ebb with peek-a-boo eyes. 'Seduce you?'

Ebb crossed himself and gazed at Brother Gerald's grinning, cavernous mouth. The mouth that had performed oral sex on him. Whispered promises of love. Threatened to betray him when Ebb had refused to acknowledge that they were an equal partnership. The mouth that had threatened to take all his money and leave The Sons and Daughters of Salvation.

'I tried to save him,' Ebb said, 'but he was beyond salvation.'

Marcus pulled on the end of his nose as if trying to flush thoughts from his brain.

Ebb smiled. The Revelation Room was a lot to digest in one sitting. Tweezer hadn't reacted when Ebb had first showed him the skeletons, but then Tweezer was a psychopath and a rapist.

Ebb didn't think it prudent to tell Marcus that Brother Gerald had rescued him from the streets. Given him a home in his flat. Educated him and taught him the importance of widening his vocabulary. Introduced him to religion and the art of lovemaking. These facts were like discussing the foetus in relation to the man. Important, but unnecessary.

Brother Gerald had even sold his flat and persuaded Cyril Penghilly that his rundown farm would be better served as a commune and a place of worship. Brother Gerald had befriended Cyril in church after the farmer's wife had died, but Ebb hadn't been interested in such trivialities. All he'd been concerned with was building The Sons and Daughters of Salvation into a thriving community.

Ebb had been truly shocked the day Jesus had come to him in the form of a watermelon to tell him of Brother Gerald's traitorous nature. Even more surprised when Jesus had insisted he elicit a confession from Brother Gerald by tying him to the bed and torturing him with a razor blade and vinegar. By the time they'd hoisted Brother Gerald up in an old fishing net in the barn, the man had admitted to the crimes of perversion, jealousy, greed and envy. Praise Jesus.

'Things were good with Brother Gerald for a while. But when Satan is buried deep within, I'm afraid there can only be one outcome. The transformation was terrible to see. Terrible.'

Marcus held Max's leash a little too tight for Ebb's liking. 'Let go of Max, Brother Marcus. You're in danger of throttling her.'

Marcus dropped the leash. He looked as if he might be about to throw up. Or run. Or challenge the wisdom of Jesus Christ.

'Are you okay?'

'Yes, Father. Just a bit—'

'Shocked?'

'A little, Father.'

'Don't be. Even I doubted Jesus's wisdom at first. But He does not lie. Take that poor wretch on the floor. What do you see?'

'Tweezer?'

'What else?'

'A man who's wounded, Father.'

'Do you take pity on him?'

'A bit. I still don't believe—'

Ebb held up a hand. 'He tried to rape Madeline.'

'I know, Father.'

'Rape her and subject her to the most terrifying ordeal imaginable. Now he garners pity, because that is always Satan's trump card, is it not?'

Marcus nodded.

'So let's not be fooled. The man is alive with demons, just as Brother Gerald was before him. We must root out evil as we find it before it takes hold and destroy us all. Do you understand?'

'Yes, Father.'

Marcus's eyes seemed to contradict his words. He'd have to watch him carefully. He moved on to Cyril. 'This is Brother Cyril. He wasn't a *member* of The Sons and Daughters of Salvation. It might be prudent to describe him as more of a founder.'

'What happened to him?'

Ebb was in no mood to go into detail. He didn't bear Cyril Penghilly any malice. It had simply been a clash of ideals. Cyril believed the farm belonged to him. Ebb didn't. What Cyril failed to remember was that Ebb had given him the sum of eighty thousand pounds to secure the services of the farm. Well, technically Brother Gerald had given him the money from the sale of his flat, but you didn't want to split hairs on a bald head.

'He wanted to go east, I wanted to go west. He died without fuss or fanfare.'

Marcus looked at the skeleton as if trying to seek the truth from its bones.

Ebb moved on and pointed the rifle at the skeleton in the pink wig. 'And this is the mother of all creation.'

'Who is it?'

'I shall discuss her in more detail when we have more time.'

'It's his fucking mother,' Tweezer shouted. 'His own fucking mother.'

Ebb pointed the rifle back at Tweezer. 'Lies fall from your tongue like confetti at a wedding, my friend.'

Tweezer propped himself up on one elbow. 'I'm not lying. It's his own mother. He battered her to death with a shovel.'

Ebb considered emptying the rifle into Tweezer. But bullets were too good to waste on his sorry soul. 'Perhaps I should set Maxine upon you? Help you with the truth?'

'It is the truth.'

Ebb ignored him and turned his attention back to Marcus. 'God will be the judge of him.'

'Yes, Father.'

Ebb wondered if he should reconsider his decision to trust Marcus. There was something unsavoury lurking in the man's eyes. He might be good at dealing drugs. A competent musician if your ears were inclined towards trashy pop music. But was he really up to the mark for dealing with the finer points of faith?

He walked to the far corner of the room and rested the gun against the wall. He then picked up his shovel. It was a pity he hadn't been able to retain the services of the shovel that had shamed his mother. That would have been the icing on the wig. But this one still felt good in his hands. Weighty. Balanced. Bubba had sharpened the edges with an angle grinder in the workshop. Sharpened them to guillotine status.

He walked to where Tweezer lay mewling on the floor like a tomcat that had just had its balls bitten by a shit-house rat. Ebb hummed. A tuneless hum, born of contentment rather than melody. He liked the analogy of Tweezer and a tomcat. Unfortunately for Tweezer, his strutting days were over. He'd pounced on the wrong bird when he'd assaulted Madeline.

Chapter Twenty-Eight

Ben lay on his bunk. Every bone in his body felt broken, every joint on fire, every nerve on high alert. The dark accentuated his suffering. He had no idea of the time, or how long he'd been lying there. He wanted to get up, get his joints moving, but pain pinned him to the bed. Crucified him, you might say.

His father was dead; he'd been close to death when he'd interrupted youth club with that awful phone call. What Ben couldn't understand was what had possessed him to think he could somehow rescue him. Now they were all going to die, right here on this stinking farm. Cause of death: stupidity.

There was a sliver of moon framed in the sash window. It looked like a small 'C' carved upon the black canvas of sky. *C* for *condemned*. Ben arched his back to relieve the stress at the base of his spine. The movement ignited pain in his tortured limbs. He sank back onto the lumpy mattress and tried to relax. Tried to breathe into the pain the way Pastor Tom had taught him to all those years ago when he'd jumped from the conker tree. The pain didn't seem to have much regard for relaxation techniques.

He gasped for air in the stifling heat of the room. He always slept with his bedroom window open at home. No such luxury here. He turned his head to one side. He could just see Bubba silhouetted in the dim light of the moon. 'Are you awake?'

Bubba nodded.

Ben eased himself over onto his right side. 'Why can't you talk?'

Bubba didn't respond.

Ben's mother would have asked Bubba if the cat had got his tongue. They had a cat at home. CJ. No one quite knew why he was called CJ, but CJ didn't care. He killed things for fun at night and came home for his breakfast in the morning just the same.

Ben suddenly realised how dumb the question was to a man who couldn't speak. 'Sorry. I wasn't thinking.'

Bubba grunted.

'Do you want to communicate with me?'

Bubba nodded.

'I'll ask you some questions. Just nod your head for yes and shake your head for no. Okay?'

Bubba sat up on his bunk and nodded.

'Ebb said you worked for Cyril when he took over the farm. Is that right?'

Bubba nodded.

'Ebb said Cyril had an accident with a tractor. Is that right?'

Bubba shook his head.

'What happened to him?'

No answer.

'Did Ebb do something to Cyril?'

Yes.

'Did Ebb kill him?'

Yes.

The insides of Ben's things went clammy, like when he was a kid and about to throw up. 'Did you see him kill Cyril?'

Bubba nodded and thumped the wooden bed frame.

Ben forced himself to get up. He hobbled across the room to Bubba's bunk. 'Why did Ebb kill him?'

Bubba shrugged.

'Did Ebb do something to you?'

Bubba nodded.

'What did he do?'

Bubba pointed to his mouth and then rested his forefinger on his lips.

'He cut out your tongue?'

Bubba nodded.

'I'm so sorry.'

The moon cast an eerie glow across Bubba's face. Tears shimmered in his eyes. He drew his index finger across his throat.

Ben didn't need words to understand Bubba's simple message. They were all going to die.

Bubba stood up and walked over to the window.

Ben wanted to tell Bubba that it would be all right if they stuck together. If they made a plan. Together they could be strong. Ebb had control because individually they were weak. If solidarity could bring down the Iron Curtain, toppling Ebb ought to be a doddle.

Come on, Stutter-buck, what are you going to do?

Images swirled in his head. Thirteen again. Stuck in the conker tree. Kids standing around the tree like a lynch mob in an old Western movie. Kids throwing sticks at him. Throwing conkers at him. Calling him *Stutter-buck. Chicken shit. Yellow-belly.*

Come on, Stutter-buck, whatcha gonna do? Stay up in that tree all night?

Such a long way down. Fifteen feet, give or take a tall tale. Might as well have been a hundred. 'L-leave me alone.'

It had been all right climbing the tree. Charlie Cory had helped him up onto the first branch by lifting him onto his shoulders. They'd all promised to help him down. Made him feel important. Like Superman for the day. He'd thought climbing the conker tree would help him to be accepted by them. He'd been dumb enough to believe that the stuttering kid with the mop of frizzy hair could be one of the normal guys. Wrong. He would never be one of the normal guys. Not then. Not now. Not ever.

Come on, Stutter-buck. Jump. Use your hair as a parachute.

'S-s-s-stop it.'

He sounds like a helicopter. Time for lift-off, Stutter-buck.

'I c-c-can't.' He needed to pee. His bladder felt like a swollen river about to burst its banks.

Do you want mummy to come and hold your hand, Stutter-buck?

'L-l-l-leave me alone.'

Stutter-buck, Stutter-buck, useless fuck….

His father would be waiting at home for him. Grumpy old daddy bear waiting to pounce on him if he arrived so much as a minute late. And, boy, was he going to be late. To add to his woes, his new trousers would be all messed up if he jumped.

He was nothing more than a useless Stutter-buck. Too chicken to jump out of a conker tree. Too chicken to fight back. Too chicken to reclaim his identity from the thieves who'd stolen it.

The other kids had all gone home for tea around five, leaving Stutter-buck glued to the branch of that conker tree. High above him, birds twittered and poked fun at him long before social media cottoned onto the idea.

Stutter-buck didn't jump from that tree. *Not on your nelly* as his father was apt to say. He slipped off the branch after his legs had gone as numb as his brain. Slammed into the ground and fractured his right knee on impact. Pastor Tom had found him lying at the base of that tree an hour later, sobbing his heart out like a little baby.

Ben looked at Bubba. 'I never jumped. I s-slipped. I'm a c-c-coward. A useless c-coward.'

Chapter Twenty-Nine

Ebb raised the shovel above Tweezer's head. 'You have shamed the shovel.'

Tweezer writhed on the floor and looked over his shoulder. 'No, Fa—'

Ebb brought the shovel down in a sideways arc designed to decapitate. Tweezer rolled out of the way with the dexterity of a man possessed by Satan. The shovel slammed into the concrete floor inches from Tweezer's head.

Ebb's heart stomped around in his chest like a petulant child. Before he had time to raise the shovel again, Tweezer pounced. He grabbed Ebb's left ankle and yanked hard enough to spill his assailant on top of him. The shovel slipped out of Ebb's hands and clattered to the floor beside them.

'Help me,' Ebb squawked, as Tweezer poked him in the eye. One of Tweezer's rings ploughed a furrow in Ebb's cheek, deep enough to draw blood. Ebb clutched his injured eye.

Taking advantage of his opponent's distraction, Tweezer bucked and threw Ebb sideways. He then rolled over and pinned Ebb to the floor with his forearm across his throat. Ebb responded by kicking and thrashing and making noises that belonged to the mortally wounded. Tweezer pushed down harder, resting all his weight on Ebb's throat.

Ebb stared into those murderous eyes. Deceitful eyes. The eyes of Brutus. Puke decorated Tweezer's goatee beard. Ebb wanted to cry out for mercy, but the pressure from Tweezer's arm closed off his throat.

Spit foamed on Tweezer's lips. For some reason, it reminded Ebb of Briers Lock. Snot and blood dribbled out of his nose in equal measure. Ebb could see every blackhead and blemish on his attacker's contorted face. To Ebb's horror, Tweezer leaned closer. Ebb could smell his foul breath. For one terrible moment, Ebb thought Tweezer was going to kiss him.

Tweezer opened his mouth wide. Like a vampire about to strike terror into a neck. But he didn't bite his neck. No, sir. That callous swine had far worse intentions. He closed his mouth over Ebb's nose and bit down, right through to the bone. He then chewed his way through sinew and gristle before wrenching a chunk of Ebb's mangled nose from his face.

The centre of Ebb's face exploded in a ball of flame. The flames leapt into his brain and set his thoughts on fire. Ebb tried to scream, but his throat was still pinned beneath Tweezer's weight. His legs kicked out like a dying fly stranded on its back.

Ebb didn't see Max attack. He didn't even feel the dog's teeth rip into the bottom of his right leg. His injured nose commanded control of all his senses. But as Max bit deeper and shook Ebb's leg from side to side, the pain ripped up into his groin and seized him by the balls.

Ebb tried to scream, but only managed to squeak and hiss. His hips gyrated as he tried to dislodge his attacker. His bare feet scraped against the concrete floor, tearing the skin and drawing blood.

A gunshot. Way off in a distant galaxy. Perhaps a shooting star come to save mummy's little Pixie-pea.

Tweezer screamed. He released his grip on Ebb's nose as the bullet hit him in the back of his neck. Tweezer stared at him with eyes that seemed to hatch from their sockets. He panted and dribbled like a rabid dog. His lips were stained crimson. A grimace stretched those bloodied lips into a wide clown's grin.

Ebb's throat whistled and wheezed and did its best to scream. Stars danced and popped before his eyes. A loud thudding noise boomed in his ears. All the things he'd done for Tweezer. Saved his miserable life when the outcast had turned up at The Sons and Daughters of Salvation with no crib for a bed.

Tweezer opened his mouth and yawned blood.

Another shot echoed around the walls of the Revelation Room. Max released Ebb's leg as Marcus shot her in the back. Max howled and whined as the bullet smashed through her ribs and punctured one of her lungs.

Marcus fired again. This time, the bullet hit Tweezer in the base of his spine. It severed the spinal cord and killed him. Tweezer fell forwards and treated Ebb to fifteen stones of dead weight. By the time Marcus managed to haul Tweezer off him, Edward Ebb was unconscious and drowning in the rabid waters of Briers lock.

Ebb regained consciousness five minutes later to find Brother Marcus hovering over him like an expectant father trying to figure out how to deliver a child. Most of his hair had escaped his ponytail in wild, sweaty strands.

'Are you all right, Father?'

Ebb gasped for air and prayed that the Lord would give him the strength to survive this awful unprovoked attack. He could see Tweezer lying face down on the floor a few yards to his left.

Ebb's throat was one step short of strangled. 'Tweezer?'

'He's dead, Father.'

Ebb tried to speak; it was like trying to summon words from a bog. The middle of his face felt as if it had been used to launch a rocket into space.

'I shot him,' Marcus elaborated.

Ebb wheezed and coughed. 'Maxine?'

Marcus looked away. 'She's still breathing.'

Ebb found his voice. 'What do you mean? What have you done to her, you idiot?'

'I shot her, Father.'

Ebb willed his body to rise up and beat Marcus to a pulp. 'You did what?'

'I had to, Father. She attacked you.'

This was all the fault of the Imposter. Ever since that swine had shown up, everything had gone wrong. The Imposter had somehow orchestrated the whole thing. As soon as he had sufficient bounce in his bones, he would get answers out of him by blood or by stone.

'You'd better pray that Maxine doesn't die, Brother Marcus.'

'I'm sorry, Father. I didn't know what else to do. She attacked you. She must have got confused with everything that was going on.'

Ebb glared at Marcus. 'That dog means more to me than anything else on this planet. So you'd better pray she doesn't die.'

'I could take him to a vet, Father.'

'Max is not a "him",' Ebb wheezed. 'He's a she. And you're not taking her to any vets. The same rule applies to animals as it does to people. We must never interfere with God's will. If she is to die because of your gross incompetence, then that is God's intention. Do you oppose God?'

Marcus shook his head vigorously. 'No. No, of course—'

'Pray, Brother Marcus. Pray with all your heart.'

'Now, Father?'

Ebb ignored him. Either Marcus was trying to bait him, or he was as dumb as a muddy puddle. He pointed at Tweezer's body. 'Shoot him.'

'But he's already dead, Father.'

'Are you a doctor?'

'No, Father.'

'Then what qualifies you to award a death certificate?'

Marcus picked up the rifle and emptied three more bullets into Tweezer's corpse. He lowered the rifle. 'That's all the bullets gone, Father.'

Ebb didn't care. A thousand bullets might not be enough to kill a heinous creature like Tweezer. You could never be certain. Of that he was certain. 'I need treatment. That swine's bitten my nose.'

Marcus peered at Ebb's wounded face. 'Can you walk, Father?'

The mention of walking made Ebb's injured leg throb. 'I don't know. Help me up.'

Marcus helped him to his feet and then buzzed about him like a fly wondering whether to offload its eggs. 'Shall I fetch Sister Alice?'

Ebb shook his head. A mistake. His brain bounced off the sides of his skull.

My poor little Pixie-pea, his mother said, from beneath the shroud of her pink wig.

Ebb told her to shut up.

Marcus raised an eyebrow. 'Pardon, Father?'

Ebb regarded Marcus warily. He was more than aware that evil spirits could hop from one body to another like a virus in a Russian winter. It might well transpire that all the bunnies would need to be burned after this sorry episode. It might be prudent to start again with Benjamin and Madeline. Perhaps those two could breed a new generation of Sons and Daughters of Salvation. At least a new generation could be raised up pure and proper without fear of interference and risk of contamination.

Has Pixie-pea bitten off his nose to spite his face?

Ebb gawked at his mother's skeleton. He was sorely tempted to go over there and dismantle her, bone by bone.

Marcus turned his attention to the Imposter. 'I still don't get what he was doing up that tree.'

Ebb was in no mood to discuss the him. 'Perhaps he was trying to rescue a cat.'

'We don't have a cat.'

Ebb snorted. A huge mistake. He ignited the afterburners idling on the spot where his nose used to be. He beat his fists against his sides and panted like a woman in the throes of labour. When the agony had subsided enough to allow the passage of words, Ebb chose them carefully. 'I don't know why he was up a tree with a long-range camera, any more than I know why you seem to persist in babbling nonsense every time you open your mouth. But I'll tell you this much: if he's a cop, and any cops show up here, that's the end. Over and out. Roger that?'

Brother Marcus looked at him with those blank-canvas eyes.

Ebb tried to summon saliva into his mouth. 'Everyone is to come to the Revelation Room. We shall pray. And then we shall set the fire.'

'Fire?' Marcus squawked.

Ebb was now convinced Marcus had the leadership qualities of a chimpanzee. He clearly didn't have a brain capable of independent thought. One thing was for certain in these dangerous times: he was in no mood to let his nose burn whilst Brother Marcus fiddled. 'I want you to help me up to my room. Then get Sister Alice.'

'Yes, Father.'

'Then get dressed in your overalls and get back up that tower. If any cops show up, I don't want you to engage them in a shoot-out. This is not the OK Corral. You come and tell me so as we can get all the bunnies down the rabbit hole.'

'The rabbit hole?'

Ebb thumped the floor. 'Down here, Pixie-pea.'

'Yes, Father.'

What a mess, Ebb thought. *What a great big, tub-thumping mess.*

Chapter Thirty

'Oh, Father,' Sister Alice cooed, looking at Ebb and stroking his head with her long slender fingers. 'What on Earth happened?'

Ebb tried to force a smile. *A try to be a brave little soldier whilst you fib to the doctor about how you fell down the stairs* kind of smile. 'Brother Tweezer attacked me.'

Sister Alice looked as if an invisible hand had slapped her across the face. 'Attacked you? Whatever for?'

'Did Brother Marcus not tell you?'

'He told me you were hurt, Father. He said nothing else.'

Ebb gargled blood and swallowed a thick clot. 'Brother Tweezer had the Devil inside him. Brother Marcus shot him.'

Alice's eyes doubled in size. 'Shot him?'

'I'm afraid he had little choice. Brother Tweezer was out of control.'

'I thought Brother Tweezer was pure.'

Ebb laughed. It sounded like a frog trying to learn to croak. 'This is the very reason I tell everyone to be on their guard.'

'Where's Brother Tweezer now?'

Ebb swallowed another clot and almost gagged. 'In the Revelation Room. He's dead.'

'Oh my God.'

'Maxine, too, I fear.'

'That's terrible, Father.'

Blood dribbled onto his top lip. 'We've got a crisis on our hands. A crisis of gigantic proportions.'

'But if Brother Tweezer's dead, I don't see—'

Ebb held up a hand. 'I fear Brother Marcus was contaminated when he killed Brother Tweezer.'

'Contaminated?'

'Satan is more than capable of jumping from one host to another. Especially in circumstances such as these.'

'Do you think Satan is inside Brother Marcus?'

'It's a certainty.'

'Is it wise to let him have possession of a rifle, Father?'

Ebb tried to sniff with a nose that was largely missing from its post. 'It's best not to alert Satan. Let him believe that he's fooled us. That way we can buy time.'

Sister Alice peered at the congealing wound festering in the middle of Ebb's face. 'You need to go to a hospital.'

'I'm not going to hospital. Not with the group in such disarray.'

'Then let me call a doctor.'

'No. I'm not having any agent of the state setting foot on my premises.'

'I know you always want to put yourself first, Father, but the wound needs treating. It might need suturing.'

Ebb shifted on the bed and tried to make himself comfortable. His beautiful king-sized bed had turned itself into a bed of nails. 'Suturing, my eye. It needs bathing and dressing. There's TCP and bandages in the medicine cabinet. You'll find a small plastic bowl in the cupboard beneath the basin. It might be prudent to give it a swill out. I usually use it for soaking my feet.'

Alice straightened up and headed off to the en-suite bathroom. 'As you wish, Father.'

Ebb watched her go. He wished all the members of The Sons and Daughters of Salvation behaved with the same level of decorum and dignity as Sister Alice. Unfortunately, the rest of them seemed to be mutinous trouble makers who needed constant observation and appraisal.

As for Madeline, his mind was torn in two. One part of him believed that Brother Tweezer was guilty as charged. But there was still a tiny sliver of doubt. What if she had enticed him? It was well within the capabilities of Satan to use such tactics. Money wasn't the root of all evil; seduction was.

Act in haste, repent at leisure.

Ebb twisted his head to one side as his mother's hot breath blew against his left ear. He could even smell stale booze, which was particularly scary considering Tweezer had robbed him of the best part of his nose. 'Go away. Leave me alone.'

'Pardon, Father?' Sister Alice called from the bathroom.

Ebb didn't hear her. All his senses were tuned in to that hot breath.

All the bunnies must burn, Pixie-pea.

Ebb opened his mouth to disagree and then clamped it shut. His mother had a point. Apart from Sister Alice, how could he trust any of the others? Sister Dixie was nothing more than a pay-as-you-go whore. Sister Emily was a decent housemaid, but utterly dispensable. Bubba was a dangerous mute, and Brother Marcus a glorified drug dealer with the brain capacity of a pebble.

By the time Sister Alice returned with a bowl of warm water laced with TCP, a length of bandage and a bag of cotton wool balls, Ebb was convinced that he would have to start afresh with The Sons and Daughters of Salvation. Make a clean sweep. Even Madeline and Benjamin would have to be sacrificed. He couldn't afford to take any more risks. You only needed to take a peek in the Revelation Room to understand how dangerous it was to trust people.

Alice cleared the bedside table and placed the bowl on top. She put the bag of cotton wool balls on the bed, took one out and dipped it in the water. 'Are you ready, Father?'

Ebb nodded, his mind cast adrift with thoughts of burning bunnies.

Alice dabbed his wounded nose with the cotton wool.

Ebb screamed as the rocket took off again from its launch pad.

Sister Alice withdrew the cotton wool ball from Ebb's nose and stepped away from the bed. 'I told you that you needed medical attention.'

Ebb was in no mood to listen to reason. He was too busy piloting his own internal rocket. He beat his fists against the white cotton sheet as though trying to transfer the pain. After close on two minutes, the rocket switched off the burners. Ebb lay panting on the bed, his neck contorted at an awkward angle.

Sister Alice studied him the way someone might study a dangerous animal. 'You must let me call a doctor.'

'No,' Ebb wheezed. 'No doctors. Just get me sleeping pills. There's some in the medicine cabinet.'

'Okay.'

'And there's a half bottle of whiskey under the kitchen sink.'

'Is it wise to drink alcohol and take sleeping tablets?'

Ebb hoped that Sister Alice wasn't going to get all motherly with him. He was in no mood to be anyone's Pixie-pea. 'I've had half my face bitten off by that madman. I don't need any lectures about pain relief.'

'Yes, Father. Sorry, Father.'

Ebb watched her walk out of the room. Tears leaked down his cheeks. He resisted an urge to wipe them away in case he touched the pothole in the middle of his face. As he tried to shift his neck into a more comfortable position, a terrible thought struck him: What if Tweezer had AIDS? Or hepatitis? Or syphilis? He had a sudden urge to phone the hospital and demand a blood transfusion.

The more he considered it, the more convinced he became that Tweezer was a carrier of some horrendous disease. It was well known that syphilis turned its victims as mad as a Mormon. It made perfect sense when you considered the man's lifestyle prior to joining The Sons and Daughters of Salvation. Those bikers were always at it like spring bunnies in a meadow.

By the time Sister Alice returned with the sleeping tablets and the bottle of whiskey, Ebb was already preparing for death. He relayed his fears to Sister Alice.

Sister Alice did little to allay those fears. 'Let's just deal with one thing at a time.'

He washed down three sleeping tablets with all the whiskey. *Straight down the hatch* as Reg the Veg might have said in his more liberated days. He then handed the bottle back to Alice and eased himself down on the bed. 'As soon as I'm asleep, tend to the wound and bandage it.'

'Yes, Father.'

Sister Alice's spiky grey hair put him in mind of stalactites. 'I am the moon,' he said, as he drifted off into beautiful black oblivion.

Chapter Thirty-One

Alice walked into the Sisters' Room and stood just inside the door. It was almost eight o'clock in the morning. She smiled and clapped her hands together as if bringing a class to attention.

Dixie unzipped her sleeping bag. 'What do you want?'

The smile slipped from Alice's lips. 'I would advise you to keep a check on your manners.'

'Would you now? And who put a rod up your backside?'

'I know being crude is the weapon of choice for women like you, but as of today I'm in charge, so you be careful how you speak to me, Sister Dixie. Very careful.'

Dixie sat up and rubbed her eyes. 'In charge? You? Why?'

Alice puffed out her flat chest. 'The Father is currently indisposed.'

'Indisposed? What's that supposed to mean? Why can't you talk in plain English?'

'Sorry, I forgot about your council estate background. Brother Tweezer attacked the Father. There. Is that plain enough for you?'

'Tweezer attacked Ebb?'

'He's called *Father*. Show respect.'

Emily lifted her head up from the bucket between her knees. She looked at Alice with bloodshot eyes. 'Why did he attack the Father?'

'Because Satan was inside him.'

'Who? Ebb or Tweezer?' Dixie asked.

Alice ignored her. 'Brother Tweezer has been dealt with, and the Father is recuperating. I'm not here to discuss the ins and outs of it with you.'

Maddie feigned concern. 'Is the Father hurt?'

'Nothing a few days' rest and some TLC can't cure.'

'I shall pray for him,' Maddie said. 'If there's anything I can do to help....'

'Thank you, Madeline. I shall bear that in mind. In the meantime, I'm afraid the farm has got to remain in lockdown. All I ask is that you girls try to stay patient whilst we get things back to normal.'

Emily wiped her mouth with the back of her hand. 'For how long?'

'As long as it takes. We're a man light with Brother Tweezer's departure. Marcus is manning the tower, and the Father is confined to bed. I know it's not ideal, but—'

'So what are you saying?' Dixie said. 'You don't trust us?'

'I'm not saying anything of the sort. I trust Sister Emily and Madeline implicitly.'

'But not me?'

'No.'

Dixie snorted. 'Fuck you.'

'That's one for the Father when he has recovered.'

Maddie tried to diffuse the situation. 'Wouldn't it be better if we all pitched in and helped?'

'Yes, it would,' Alice said. 'But the Father has instructed me to keep the farm in lockdown, so that's what I will do.'

'I suppose you'd jump off the tower if *he* told you to?'

'Save your sarcasm, Dixie. I don't care what you say. God is watching you, and I will report your behaviour to the Father.'

Emily peered into the slop bucket. 'How long's this going to last? I keep throwing up.'

'A day or two, tops. No longer than that.'

'A day or two?' Dixie said. 'And what are we supposed to do if we need the toilet? Crap on the floor?'

'Use the bucket.'

'How are we meant to use the bloody bucket with Emily hogging it day and night?'

'I'm not hogging it.'

Dixie looked at Emily as if she wanted to ram the bucket over her head. 'And where are we supposed to empty it? Out of the window? Oh, no, oops, forgot, the window's locked.'

Alice held up a hand. 'For God's sake. I'll come in twice a day and empty it.'

'I can't stay locked up in here,' Emily said.

'You'll be fine,' Alice assured her.

'No I won't. You don't understand. I *need* access to a toilet.'

'I've just told you: I'll come in and empty the blasted bucket.'

Dixie grinned. 'Language, Sister Alice, language.'

Emily gripped the rim of the bucket. 'But I'm throwing up all morning. And my bladder's weak. I need access to a toilet.'

'You've probably got a tummy bug. I'll bring you some bottled water with breakfast. It'll help to flush it out of your system.'

'I'm pregnant,' Emily blurted.

Dixie shook her head. 'Not the famous phantom pregnancy again.'

'It's not a phantom pregnancy. It's real.'

'Shall I tell you how she got pregnant?'

'Shut up, Dixie. You know nothing about me.'

'She fantasised that Brad Pitt came in through the bedroom window and made love to her in his latest movie.'

Alice crossed herself. 'Pregnant? How?'

Dixie laughed. 'Don't you know about the birds and bees?'

'I'm not a whore like you.'

'Fuck you.'

Alice glared at Emily. 'Who got you pregnant?'

'I don't want to say.'

'Let's see,' Dixie said. 'If it wasn't Brad Pitt, that leaves four possibilities. Was it the resident rapist, Tweezer?'

Emily peered into the bucket as though the answer might lay among the bile and the urine. 'Leave me alone.'

Dixie forged ahead. 'Then there's the Father, but he only runs rent boys up his flagpole. So that just leaves Bubba and Marcus. I'm still putting my money on Brad Pitt.'

Emily lifted her head up from the bucket. 'It's Marcus.'

Alice's jaw slackened. 'Brother Marcus?'

'We're in love.'

'In love?' Dixie said. 'That magic mushroom wouldn't know what love was if it bit him on the arse.'

'Shut up,' Emily shouted.

Maddie watched the three women facing each other like wronged victims on a reality TV show. All it needed now was Jeremy Kyle to come waltzing out from behind the wardrobe and offer counselling.

'Copulation is strictly forbidden.' Alice said.

'We're in love.'

'You're far too young to know the first thing about love, you silly girl.'

Emily bent back over the bucket. 'Leave me alone.'

'She's lying,' Dixie said.

'I'm not lying.'

Alice shook her head. 'The Father will go spare when he finds out.'

Dixie rounded on her. 'Then don't tell him.'

'Don't tell him? What happens when she starts showing?'

'We could get rid of it.'

'I'm not getting rid of it. Marcus said the Father will understand.'

Alice's eyes flashed in the morning sunlight. 'And you believe him, do you?'

'Yes.'

Dixie rolled her eyes. 'Marcus just told you what you wanted to hear to get inside your knickers. Trust me. All men do.'

'Even if Marcus does carry a torch for you,' Alice said, 'you'll end up getting burned by it. Oh, God, child, what in heaven's name were you thinking?'

'I love him.'

'How far gone are you?'

Emily didn't answer.

Dixie walked over to Emily. 'Look, if you really are pregnant, there's no way on earth Ebb will give this his blessing. If you want my advice, you'll get rid of it. There are pills you can use. I've used them myself, dozens of times.'

'What you've done in your sordid past bears no relation to this mess,' Alice said. 'You know full well the use of medication is prohibited.'

'And the alternative is?' Dixie said.

'The answer lies with God,' Alice said. 'God and Father Ebb.'

'You can't tell him.'

Alice stepped out onto the landing. 'I have no choice.'

'Yes, you do,' Dixie shouted, as Alice slammed the door and locked it behind her.

Maddie looked at Dixie. 'Now what are we going to do?'

'I haven't got a clue. Stupid bitch. She doesn't have to tell him. She wants to tell him.'

'What will Ebb do?'

Dixie chewed her nails and glared at Emily. 'What did you go and tell her for?'

'I had to. Marcus said the Father will understand.'

'Marcus is so full of shit.'

Maddie was inclined to agree. 'We have to get out of here.'

'The only way out of here is in a coffin,' Dixie said. 'I've seen first-hand what that bastard's capable of.'

'I don't care what anyone else says,' Emily said. 'I'm going to have this baby.'

'Yeah, right,' Dixie said. 'And we're all going to come to the Christening and shove a silver spoon in its gob.'

Chapter Thirty-Two

S ister Alice crossed the landing to the Brothers' Room. She unlocked the door and stepped partway into the room. 'We've got a slight problem.'

Ben's heart capsized. 'Is Maddie all right?'

'Madeline? Yes, she's fine. I'm afraid it's the Father. He's had an accident.'

Ben hoped the accident turned out to be fatal.

'Brother Tweezer attacked him. The Father wants everyone to stay in lockdown for the time being.'

'Why did Tweezer attack him?'

'Not now. I've got a million things to do.'

'How long are we supposed to stay locked up for? I can barely bend over, let alone crap in that stupid bucket.'

'Please refrain from being crude, Benjamin. The Father doesn't tolerate profanity.'

Ben groaned. Reasoning with Ebb and his cronies was like trying to reason with mud. He wondered if he could force his way out of the room before Alice reacted. 'I'm in absolute agony.'

'Your pain is nothing compared to the Father's. Believe me.'

'I need painkillers.'

'We don't allow medication.'

Ben snorted. An action Ebb might have envied with his missing nostrils. 'And does that rule apply to Ebb?'

Alice stepped back as if the words had physically assaulted her. 'Don't you ever call him that. Show respect.'

Ben ignored her. 'Why don't you answer the question instead of hiding behind all this b-bullshit?'

'I'll pretend I never heard that.'

'So what am I supposed to do? Lick my wounds like a dog?'

'Don't be so dramatic.'

'What if I was bleeding to death? Would you just stand there and watch me die?'

'It's not up to me who lives and who dies. It's up to God and God alone. Your life is in His hands. What makes you think you have the right to challenge God's will?'

'I'm in agony thanks to your so-called leader.'

Alice looked Ben up and down. 'You don't look as if you're in that much pain to me.'

'No? How do you think it feels to have pins stuck in the soles of your feet? Or acid poured on your hands?'

Alice crossed herself. 'That was holy water.'

'Holy water, my arse.'

'That it burned you only reinforces Satan's existence within you.'

'And you believe that?'

'I know that.'

Ben looked for traces of the woman who'd existed before Ebb had filled her head with dangerous nonsense. 'I wonder what your husband would make of all this crap.'

'Don't you dare speak about my husband.'

'What was his name again? Robert? Rodney?'

'Stop it.'

'Do you think he'd be proud of you?'

'Roger would be immensely proud of me.'

'For denying medical attention to someone in desperate need?'

'He would understand.'

'What about Ebb? Would your husband approve of him?'

'Show some respect.'

'I mean, come on, who's the evil one here?'

Alice stepped back towards the door. 'Forgive him, Lord. He knows not what he says.'

'Religion is nothing more than a made-up load of bullshit used to control people.'

'You'll go straight to Hell for that.'

'Has Ebb ever told you about Cyril?'

Alice looked behind her. 'You don't fool me with your filthy lies.'

'Do you want to know what Ebb did to Cyril?'

Alice didn't. Her hands fumbled for the door.

'He killed him. And then he cut out Bubba's tongue to stop him speaking about it. How's that for compassion?'

'You're lying.'

'Why else do you think Bubba can't talk?'

'Bubba can't talk because he's mute.'

Ben shook his head. 'Bubba can't talk because Ebb mutilated him.'

'Liar,' Alice shouted.

Ben turned to Bubba. 'Isn't that right?'

Bubba nodded.

'He doesn't talk because God has declared him mute. It has nothing to do with the Father.'

'Can you hear yourself?'

'The Lord can hear you,' Alice retorted.

'What has the so-called Father done to qualify for such a grand title? Murdered innocent people? Cut out people's tongues? Poured acid on people?'

'You can concoct all the fairy stories you like. My ears are deaf to your vile lies.'

Bubba moved towards Alice.

'Hear no evil, see no evil, speak no evil,' Ben said. 'Is that it, Alice? Turn a blind eye?'

Alice stepped out on to the landing. 'Get away from me.'

'Stop her,' Ben shouted.

Bubba made a grab for the edge of the door. Alice slammed it, crushing two of his fingers in the jamb. He yanked his hand free and held it to his chest as if trying to revive it with his heart.

Alice closed the door and locked it. 'You'll pay for this. By God, you will.'

Ben tried to respond. Tried to summon a smart-arse answer. 'Bitch,' was the best he could do.

'You two will both go to Hell for this.'

'See you there,' Ben shouted.

Ben heard her walk across the landing and up the second flight of stairs to Ebb's quarters. He turned to Bubba. 'I'm sorry.'

Bubba looked at Ben the way an injured animal caught in a trap might look at a hunter. If Bubba could speak, he might have told old Stutter-buck he'd been perfectly happy working on the farm and minding his own business before Ben and Maddie had turned up.

'Are your fingers broken?'

Bubba looked at Ben as if to say what the hell do you think? He then walked over to his bunk and sat down. He bent so far forward his head was almost touching the floor. Conversation over.

'We have to do something.'

Bubba stared at the floor and nursed his injured hand.

Ben walked to the window and peered out through a net curtain of grime. Above the tower, dark clouds gathered in the sky like a funeral procession mourning the loss of liberty.

Come on, Stutter-buck, jump. Make like a parachute and j-j-j-jump.

Alice was right. They were dead. And no stupid plan could do anything to alter that.

Chapter Thirty-Three

Ebb looked up at Sister Alice and tried to process the words spewing from her mouth like the staccato rasp of machine gun fire. 'Stop. Stop. Stop. Slow down.'

'The Devil's in them, Father. Right inside them. They're rotten to the core.'

Ebb dry swallowed. 'Fetch me water and painkillers.'

Sister Alice looked at Ebb as if he'd just requested a fresh turd for lunch. 'Pardon, Father?'

Ebb called upon all the saints within him for restraint. 'Water. I need water and painkillers.'

Sister Alice opened her mouth to say something else, but then seemed to think better of it.

Ebb sincerely hoped that she would rid herself of hysteria by the time she returned. The remains of his nose felt as if it was still clamped between Tweezer's manky teeth. As for his leg, that had been reduced to a butcher's bone. He would need a tetanus jab sometime soon. And antibiotics. Not that he blamed poor Maxine for his mangled leg. No, sir. Tweezer's unprovoked attack had just confused the poor animal.

He looked up at the skylight. Dark clouds rolled across the sky. How he longed to feel fresh air in his lungs. The cool invigorating summer breeze on his face. A rent boy clamped to the end of his pecker. But now was not the time to indulge in fantasies. Not while Brother Tweezer lay rotting in the Revelation Room along with dear Maxine. There was a slim chance that the dog was still alive, but he didn't dare raise his hopes. One thing *was* for certain, though: if that dog was dead, Brother Marcus would be burned at the stake. Ebb had raised that dog from a pup. To lose her now would be tantamount to losing half of his heart.

Sister Alice returned with a glass of water and the painkillers. 'Shall I help you up, Father?'

Ebb nodded and allowed Sister Alice to help him into a sitting position. A grenade exploded in his mangled nose. Ebb hollered and beat his fist against the bed.

'Are you all right, Father?'

Why did everyone seem to ask him questions designed to elicit murder? 'Do I look all right?'

Alice didn't answer. She fed two paracetamol caplets into his eager beak. He washed them down with the glass of water. His throat felt like a sandpit. Water dribbled down his chin. He tried to relax, but it was a big ask. A corpse in the throes of rigor mortis was suppler than he was right now.

Ebb studied Sister Alice's plain poker face for signs of the Devil. It was becoming difficult to distinguish who was and who wasn't contaminated. 'Right, now tell me what's happened.'

Sister Alice relieved him of the glass. 'I don't know where to begin, Father.'

'The beginning should serve you well.'

'Sister Emily is pregnant,' Alice blurted.

Ebb studied the woman's face for signs of mischief. There was nothing detectable. But that didn't mean he should drop his guard. 'Pregnant?'

'She is carrying Brother Marcus's child.'

A surge of energy passed through Ebb. For a few seconds, the afterburner in his nose was put on the back-burner. 'This is a joke, right?'

'I wish it was, Father. I'm as horrified as you.'

Ebb tried to link his thoughts to coherent speech. It was like trying to hitch a trailer to the wind. 'Horrified? Horrified? Please tell me that this is a joke.'

'Perhaps we could abort the child, Father?'

'Abortion is the contraception of the Devil. How could you even dare to make such a suggestion?'

A nasty tic tugged at the corner of Alice's mouth. 'I'm sorry, Father. It was Sister Dixie's suggestion, not mine.'

'I shall pray for her. You claim Brother Marcus is the father of this bastard child?'

'That's what Emily says, Father.'

'Fetch that heinous weasel from the tower.'

'There's something else, Father.'

Ebb's brain couldn't could cope with any more bad news. 'What?'

'Benjamin and Brother Bubba tried to attack me. They tried to get out of their room.'

'The sooner I'm up and running, the better it will be for everyone.'

'Benjamin was saying things about you, Father.'

'Benjamin? He doesn't know the first thing about me.'

'He claims you killed Brother Cyril.'

Ebb's heart stopped. There was no way on God's earth Benjamin could know about Cyril. Bubba couldn't talk. And even if he could talk, he was Polish for Christ's sake. The bugger didn't know a stitch of English. 'Benjamin's not been here five minutes. How could he make such a preposterous claim?'

Alice looked away. 'I'm sorry, Father. It's just what he said. And then they tried to escape. I only just got out in time.'

Ebb ignored Sister Alice's heroics. Benjamin had to be in possession of special powers. The kind only afforded to demons. Terror tweaked his balls and then squeezed them in a vice-like grip. So Satan had at last declared himself ready for the final showdown. Ebb had known all along that this day was coming. Right from the time Jesus had appeared in that gardening programme all those years ago, telling him that his mother must shame the shovel.

'Are you all right, Father?'

'What *exactly* did Benjamin say?'

'He said that you killed Cyril, Father. Why would you want to kill Cyril? I thought he had an accident with a tractor.'

Ebb felt like reaching up and wrapping his hands around that turkey neck and squeezing the chicken bones out of her. 'Never mind accidents with tractors. What else did Benjamin say?'

'He said that you cut out Bubba's tongue because he saw you kill Cyril.'

Ebb sat up in bed and swung his legs over the edge. The room swam in and out of focus. His head throbbed, and his nose bleated like a lost lamb on a hilltop.

'You need to rest, Father.'

'Rest?' Ebb squawked. 'You think I should rest when Satan is among us?'

'But you're not well, Father.'

Ebb rubbed his eyes. 'Satan is in our midst.'

'I don't think—'

'He is spreading his filth and lies like a deadly virus.'

Alice looked away. 'He cannot defeat us, Father.'

Ebb hacked phlegm. 'Can't defeat us? We have Sister Emily pregnant with Brother Marcus's spawn. Brother Bubba attacks you, and Benjamin makes wild accusations. And you say Satan can't defeat us?'

'Is it true, Father?'

Ebb looked at Sister Alice. She was all fuzzy around the edges. There were tiny silver balls clinging to the spikes of her hair. 'Is what true?'

'What Benjamin says about you killing Cyril and cutting out Bubba's tongue?'

Ebb nodded. 'All true, your honour. I killed Cyril because he was contaminated, and I spared Bubba because he was a good worker. I simply removed his ability to tell tales.'

After seeming to consider this for a few moments, Alice nodded. 'You did the right thing, Father.'

Ebb slapped his thigh. 'Damn right I did the right thing. The Lord Jesus Christ Himself told me to do it.'

'Praise Jesus.'

'If the Lord Jesus Christ told me to jump off Mount Sinai, I would jump. If the Lord Jesus Christ told me to leap into the flames of Hell and rescue a fallen angel, I would jump.'

A noble man indeed, Pixie-pea.

Ebb ignored his mother. 'I did what was right. That's all any of us can do.'

Alice bowed her head. 'Yes, Father.'

'I am not bound by man-made laws. I follow Jesus Christ. I am answerable only to the Redeemer and the shovel.'

'You did what you thought best, Father.'

Tears formed cataracts over Ebb's eyes. 'There is no law in the land that can interfere with God's will.'

'Praise Jesus.'

'I would walk over hot coals in blistered feet for the Lord. I would sleep upon a bed of rusting nails for the Lord.'

Sister Alice wept. She plucked a tissue from a box of Kleenex on Ebb's nightstand and dabbed at her eyes. 'I love you, Father.'

'We are nothing more than mortal servants. We are not here to question the workings of the Lord. We are here to carry out his instructions without fear or favour.'

'Amen.'

'The trouble that Satan has brought to our door may seem insurmountable, Sister Alice, but I shall pray for resolution. I shall ask Jesus what must be done to defeat this enemy.'

'I shall pray, too, Father.'

Ebb tried to stand on his injured leg. A hot poker prodded him in the groin. 'Fetch Brother Marcus.'

'Yes, Father.'

'And don't give him any hint that we know of his evil deed.'

'What if he asks why he has to leave the tower unmanned?'

'Tell him we need to sort out Brother Tweezer.'

'Yes, Father.'

Ebb waited for Sister Alice to leave the room. He limped over to his mirrored wardrobe and peered at his mummified face in

215

the glass. His eyes squinted back at him over the parapet of a thick white bandage cordoning off his nose. His lips were cracked and peeling. A large scuff mark disfigured the top of his head. He wouldn't have been at all surprised to see a crown of thorns perched on top of his head and a cross pinned to his back.

'This is all the work of the Imposter,' Ebb told his reflection.

The reflection agreed. And rightly so. Everything had gone from bad to worse since that agent of the Devil had turned up in the tree overlooking the farm.

You're a sight for sore eyes, Pixie-pea.

Ebb watched his mother's gruesome image appeared in the mirrored door. Her pink wig sat precariously on top of her head. One of her eyes was bruised and swollen. A Woodbine cigarette dangled from her pink lips. She looked like the Barbie doll from Hell.

'Go away,' Ebb whispered.

She didn't. The puffed and bruised eye winked at him.

All the burnt bunnies are hopping mad.

'Shut up,' Ebb screeched.

Come home, Pixie-pea. The house is on fire and the bunnies are all gone.

Ebb gawked at that winking eye. What he'd give right now for the corner of a shovel. Unfortunately, that piece of equipment was otherwise engaged in the Revelation Room.

Ma puffed on that Woodbine like a steam train. Her hideous features vanished behind a cloud of smoke. Ebb hobbled over to a fire extinguisher secured to the wall. He lifted it out of its bracket, released the pin, and aimed the nozzle at his mother's image.

His mother laughed. A witch's cauldron kind of laugh. He was about to pull the trigger when the smoke cleared in front her face. But it was no longer Veronica Ebb's face. It was Cyril's leathery chops; not so much lived in as ransacked.

Cyril grinned. *You should have gone west, young man.*

'Cyril?'

Cyril saluted. *That's me. But you can call me bunny.*

216

'You're not there,' Ebb shouted. He squeezed the trigger and emptied a stream of pressurised foam at Cyril's face. The foam obliterated all traces of the farmer from the mirrored door.

Exhausted, Ebb dropped the canister on the bare oak floor. It landed with a hollow thud and rolled several feet before coming to rest. Job done. That would teach Cyril to fiddle with his bunnies. He staggered back to the bed and sat down. His brain felt as if it was filled with treacle.

You can lead a bunny to fire, but you can't make it burn, Pixie-pea, his mother said from beyond the wardrobe doors.

Ebb summoned all the strength within him to retrieve the discarded extinguisher. He raised it above his head and hurled it at the wardrobe door. The glass exploded and fell to the floor in a waterfall of fragmented shards.

I won't always be able to pick up the pieces, Pixie-pea.

Ebb stumbled over to the bed and collapsed on top of the cool cotton sheet. His wounds begged Jesus for forgiveness. His heart banged in his chest like a blacksmith's anvil. He rolled onto his back and looked up at the skylight. His mother's face appeared in a cloud. The cloud resembled his mother's pink wig.

Ebb closed his eyes and begged Jesus for guidance. Jesus didn't seem to be in any mood to offer direction, other than to reiterate Ebb's belief that all the bunnies should go down the rabbit hole.

His mother, God rot her soul, offered to tuck Pixie-pea in and read him a bedtime story. Ebb ignored her. She could mock him all she liked. Her caustic tongue was the least of his worries.

Where the hell was Sister Alice? He'd asked her to fetch Brother Marcus, not give birth to him and raise him up on cornbread and potato wedges. He was beginning to have a nasty feeling about Sister Alice. What if she deserted him and formed a union with Brother Marcus? What if the pair of them were plotting against him right now? He was in no position to fight back. Tweezer's barbaric attack had weakened him considerably.

Ebb forced himself off the bed. He had a shotgun stashed in the back of the wardrobe, and he was willing to risk the wrath of

Cyril's ghost to get it. Anyway, the farmer was as dead as yesterday. He'd ploughed his last furrow and planted his last seed in God's earth almost ten years ago. Ghosts were just illusions conjured up by the mind in times of stress.

He skirted around the broken glass and gripped the edge of the right-hand wardrobe door. It took him all the strength he could muster to slide the door along a runner littered with broken glass. He forced it about halfway along before it ground to a halt and refused to budge. He had just enough room to squeeze inside.

Watch out for the monsters, Pixie-pea.

Ebb didn't like it inside the wardrobe. A shiver unfurled a white flag at the top of his spine. The shotgun was propped against the wall at the back of the wardrobe. He started to whistle. *Onward Christian Soldiers.* Designed to ward off evil spirits. And jokers. And mothers in pink wigs.

Run piggy, run piggy, run, run, run, before farmer gets you with his gun, gun, gun.

Ebb panicked at the sound of Cyril's voice. He yanked clothes off the hanging rail and hurled them onto the bedroom floor, just in case the farmer might surprise him and launch an unprovoked attack. His best Armani suit landed in a heap a few feet shy of the bed. He would have to deal with the aftermath of his actions later. Suits could be dry cleaned. Shirts could be ironed. Wardrobe doors could be replaced.

He gasped for air. With most of the contents of the rail now relocated on the floor, Ebb grabbed the shotgun along with a box of cartridges. He retreated before his mother got any bright ideas about locking him inside. And she would. She enjoyed locking him in confined spaces. Just ask his childhood if you wanted proof.

He closed the door and moved away from the wardrobe as quickly as his injured leg would allow. He put the shotgun and the box of cartridges down on the bed and then turned to face the mirrored glass.

'Not so brave now, are you?'

Cyril and his mother exercised their right to remain silent.

He hoped with all his heart he didn't have to use the gun on Sister Alice. He didn't want to kill her. She'd been a loyal servant. Almost like a mother. Unlike that uncle-dunking witch pinned to a cross down in the Revelation Room, sunglasses hiding the hallmarks of tainted love.

It was becoming increasingly obvious that Tweezer's poison had infected Brother Marcus. But Sister Alice? Surely not.

'Why has thou forsaken me, Lord?'

The Lord didn't answer. Probably engaged in denying Tweezer entrance into the Kingdom of Heaven. And rightly so. The Lord had no place for rapists at his top table. The best Tweezer could hope for was purgatory.

Ebb picked up the shotgun. It felt weighty. Both barrels were still intact, no bank-robbing villain had mutilated it with a hacksaw. He checked the safety catch. On. Good. He knew it was loaded because Cyril Penghilly had always kept it loaded. Cyril had been rather fond of his Smith and Wesson twelve-gauge pump-action shotgun. Cyril pronounced it *Smiff and Wasson*. He claimed it could take a cow down from a hundred yards. Ebb thought Cyril inclined to exaggeration, but he didn't doubt the gun's potency. It certainly looked dangerous.

Dangerous enough to shoot the moon, Pixie-pea.

Ebb jumped and almost squeezed the trigger. He gawked at the wardrobe doors for signs of his mother. His reflection peeked back at him from behind the bandages. He looked like a bank robber who'd put on his mask all wrong. There were dark smudges beneath his eyes. He needed a holiday. Not just a weekend in London. A proper holiday.

'When my work is done here, I'm emigrating,' he promised his reflection. 'Thailand. The Philippines. Cambodia. Africa.'

Somewhere with a vibrant sex trade, Pixie-pea?

Ebb released the safety catch and squeezed the trigger. The force of the blast threw him off balance. His mother's reflection shattered into a thousand glass fragments. He dropped the gun and fell back onto the bed. His right shoulder felt as if it had been butted by one of Cyril's bulls. Dozens of tiny pink wigs danced before his eyes.

Chapter Thirty-Four

Brother Marcus stood at the top of the tower and surveyed all. The courtyard and outbuildings looked tiny from his perch fifty feet above the ground. Almost far enough away to look like a child's toy farm. But Penghilly's Farm was no toy.

Marcus tried to shake the image of Tweezer's dead body from his head. He couldn't. He was now a cold-blooded killer with a guilty conscience to prove it. It was written in Tweezer's blood down in that chamber of horrors, the Revelation Room. He couldn't even claim self-defence, because he'd not been defending himself; he'd been defending the Father.

To make matters worse, if they could actually get any worse, he'd killed Max. Once the Father knew that his beloved pampered mutt was dead, the shit would really hit the fan. Marcus was sorely tempted to leap from the tower and leave his life in a heap of broken bones on the courtyard floor below.

He rested the rifle against the railings and peered over the edge. How long would it take to hit the ground? Ten seconds? Twenty? How long before his spine was shoved up through the top of his head? Would there be anyone waiting to escort him to Heaven?

After what you've done?

'I had no choice.'

Tweezer was like a brother to you. Tweezer looked after you when you joined the group. He took you under his wing.

'I had to save Ebb.'

Bullshit. You shot the wrong man. You know it, I know it, and Uncle Tom Cobley knows it.

'I had no choice.'

If you jump, what happens to Emily?

Marcus gripped the rail like a man on the world's most dangerous rollercoaster ride. Marcus had loved Emily from the very first day he'd seen her in Oxford. Loved her vulnerability and her stubbornness, both of which she had in equal measures. Loved the way she looked at him with her head cocked to one side. The way she smiled. The way they made love.

She's pregnant, for Christ's sake.

Marcus shook his head. Women were always missing periods and getting sick in the mornings.

So you're just going to abandon her like you've abandoned everything else in your life?

He looked at the rifle and laughed. 'So shoot me.' He put one foot on the bottom rail and stepped up so as his waist was level with the top. He noticed how dark the sky looked. As dark as his heart. The wind whispered conspiracy theories among the trees.

He wondered whether to go head first or feet first? Or maybe hang over the side.

A woman's voice suddenly interrupted his thoughts. 'What in God's name are you doing?'

For one bizarre moment, Marcus thought that his guardian angel had spoken to him.

'Brother Marcus?'

He looked over his shoulder and saw Sister Alice walking towards him. He jumped off the rail.

'What are you doing?'

He picked up the rifle and aimed it over the guardrail. 'Nothing. I was just trying to exercise my legs. I'm as stiff as a board.'

Alice pursed her lips. 'You want to be careful on that rail. One slip and you'll make a nasty mess all over the courtyard.'

Marcus laughed. The laugh sounded as hollow and lost as he felt inside.

'The Father wants to see you.'

Marcus's heart stopped. 'Why?'

'Because you've been a naughty boy.'

'I haven't done nothing.'

'I wouldn't call getting Sister Emily pregnant "nothing." I'd call it a big fat *something*.'

Marcus tried to swallow. 'Pregnant?'

'That's what I said. Pregnant. Up the duff. Bun in the oven.'

Marcus looked at Sister Alice as if she'd just issued a death warrant. 'She's not pregnant.'

'The girl's pregnant, all right. And according to her, you're the father. Anyway, I'm not here to get into a lengthy discussion about it. The Father wants to see you, and if you want my advice, you'll accept what's coming to you.'

'Emily's lying.'

'Young girls don't lie about such matters.'

Marcus snorted. 'Don't they?'

'No, they don't. Do you want to know how I know this?'

Marcus didn't.

'Because for reasons beyond my comprehension, young girls are invariably in love with those who take their virginity. And Sister Emily is clearly in love with you.'

Marcus stalled for time. 'It could be Tweezer's.'

Alice wasn't having any of it. 'No. It's yours. And now you must answer for your actions.'

Marcus looked over the railing. Maybe he could throw himself over the edge before Sister Alice had time to react. But there was something about that smug look on her face that seemed to invite confrontation. He levelled the gun at his accuser. 'You're not in any position to tell me what to do.'

'Put the gun down.'

'You can't tell me what to do.'

'That's where you're wrong. I'm in charge now.'

'Since when?'

Alice stared at the rifle. 'Since you and Tweezer betrayed the Father.'

Marcus's shoulders shook. The rifle suddenly felt so much heavier. The first drops of rain fell as if the clouds were shedding tears of grief. 'I haven't betrayed anyone.'

'First you get Sister Emily pregnant, and now you aim a rifle at me? What do you call that?'

'I didn't get Emily pregnant.'

'Tell it to the Father.'

Marcus tried to relax his shoulders. 'I'm not going anywhere.'

Alice spread her hands out in front of her. 'Come on, Marcus, don't be stupid. Put the gun down.'

'No.'

'I won't tell the Father.'

'Yeah. Right.'

Alice crossed herself. 'Forgive him, Lord. He knows not what he does.'

'I know what I'm doing,' Marcus lied.

'You can still be saved.'

Marcus didn't want to be saved. He wanted to get as far away from Penghilly's Farm as possible. 'Save your crap. I'm not listening.'

Alice stepped closer. Just a half step. 'You have Satan within you. That isn't your fault, Brother Marcus.'

'You move another inch, and I swear to God I'll kill you.'

'Is that what you want to do? Kill an innocent woman?'

Marcus hacked a small laugh. 'You're not an innocent woman.'

'I love you, Brother Marcus. Please don't make this hard on yourself. I only want to help you.'

'Do you?'

Alice nodded.

'And what do you think Ebb will do? Give me a pat on the back and put an arm around my shoulder?'

'He'll help you. Just like he helps everyone.'

'Have you ever been in the Revelation Room?'

Alice hesitated. 'No.'

Marcus saw a look in Alice's eyes that seemed to contradict her words. Just a fleeting moment of recognition. 'You ought to go down there. It's a riot. He's got three skeletons pinned to the wall.'

'Don't be silly.'

'One of them is wearing a pink wig and sunglasses. It would be funny if it wasn't so fucking sick.'

'You're deluded.'

'And then Ebb tried to kill Tweezer with a shovel.'

'The Lord is watching you, Brother Marcus. He's watching you and keeping a count of all your lies.'

'Do you know what that mad fucker called it?'

'Called what?'

'Attacking Tweezer with a shovel, you stupid cow.'

'How should I know?'

'*Shaming the shovel.*'

'You're hysterical, Marcus. You're not thinking straight.'

'Shaming the fucking shovel. What the hell's that supposed to mean?'

'I think you're suffering delusions, Brother Marcus.'

Marcus didn't hear her. 'Tweezer grabbed hold of Ebb and tipped him over. Bit a chunk out of his face. Would've killed him, too, if I hadn't shot him in the back.'

'You did the right thing.'

'I shot him in the fucking back, for Christ's sake.'

'I shall pray for you.'

Marcus gawped at her. What was he going to do now? He couldn't stay up here arguing the rights and wrongs of Ebb's empire with this deluded woman. Perhaps he ought to just shoot her in the leg and get the hell out of there.

And leave Emily to rot? It's your fault she's here!

Marcus tried to reason with himself. He would never have brought Emily to Penghilly's Farm if he'd known what was in the Revelation Room. Street-dealing was one thing, wholesale murder and shaming shovels? Jesus Christ, what a mess.

'Please, Marcus. Just think about this, for everyone's sake.'

Maybe he would have time to get Emily. Take Ebb's Land Rover and be miles away before anyone realised. Ebb was in no fit state to come after him. Or Tweezer. That only left Benjamin, Bubba and the girls.

What if Alice bleeds to death?

Marcus dismissed the thought. He couldn't afford to get held up by compassion. He'd already made one monumental mistake by shooting Tweezer instead of Ebb; he wasn't about to make another by showing concern for Sister Alice; she seemed as mad as Ebb.

Alice moved with the speed and dexterity of a cheetah. She grabbed the end of the rifle before Marcus could even register what she was doing. Instinct caused him to squeeze the trigger. Alice twisted the rifle to one side. The bullet narrowly missed a red kite circling the farm.

'Let go, you fucking bitch.'

Alice held onto the rifle like a starving dog with a bone. She twisted the barrel left and right in sharp, jerking movements. Marcus tried to match her, tugging the rifle with every ounce of strength left in his body. They danced around the top of the tower like a couple performing some strange African ritual.

Alice screamed and bared her teeth. She pulled Marcus towards her and then thrust him away. He let go of the gun and fell back against the guard rail. Alice tried to turn the gun around, but Marcus pushed himself away from the rail and leapt forward. He grabbed her by the throat and dug his nails deep into the soft flesh.

The rifle clattered to the ground. Alice screeched and tried to prize his fingers away from her neck. Marcus dug deeper. He could feel her windpipe. He heard an awful hissing noise as she tried to draw in air. Marcus squeezed harder. He had to kill her. It was a simple matter of survival. Kill or be killed.

Alice stopped resisting. Her body went limp. Her knees buckled.

Marcus relaxed his grip. How long did it take to strangle someone? Seconds? Minutes? He didn't have a clue, but enough was enough. He'd settle for unconscious. All that mattered was getting away from Penghilly's Farm.

As Marcus let go of her neck, Alice struck for a second time in as many minutes. This time, she poked him in his right eye with her forefinger. Her fingernail sliced into the eyeball.

Marcus screamed and lurched backwards.

'You're going to die for what you did.'

Marcus clutched his injured eye. A white-hot needle lanced his brain. His other eye tried to keep a watch on Alice, but tears drew a misty veil across it.

Marcus saw a ghostly vision of Sister Alice bending over to retrieve the rifle. He stepped forward and kicked her in the side of her head with his heel. Although the blow wasn't hard enough to put her out of action, it halted her progress.

She stumbled sideways. 'You can't defeat me. God is on my side.'

Marcus rubbed his injured eye. He should have shot the bitch when he'd had the chance. He glanced at the rifle lying on the deck. Through his blurred vision, the rifle now had two handles and three barrels.

Alice rushed at Marcus, hands outstretched like a monster in a horror movie. She tried to grab him around the throat, but he seized her wrists and twisted them around. The left one snapped like a dry twig.

Alice screamed and tried to bite his face.

Marcus let go of her hands and shoved her backwards over the top of the three feet high guardrail. He could no longer afford to think about right and wrong. He picked up the rifle and hurried towards the steps.

By the time he reached the bottom of the tower, his hands were shaking like an alcoholic in dire need of a drink. He forced his mind to focus on rescuing Emily and getting as far away from Penghilly's Farm as possible. They could start again. Get jobs.

Have kids. Buy a nice little house by the seaside. Do all the things normal people did.

His father had always warned Marcus that he would end up in trouble, and his father had been right. He was in the deepest shit imaginable. Locked-away-for-life trouble, and the sooner he disappeared, the better.

Marcus approached Sister Alice's motionless body with caution. A pool of blood had spread out beside her head. One of her eyes stared up at the sun. The other was closed. A few flies buzzed around her like hesitant kamikaze pilots. If she wasn't dead, then she was the world's greatest actress. She was also the keeper of the keys now that Ebb and Tweezer were both out of action. That meant he would have to search her body for them if he wanted to let Emily out of the Sisters' Room.

He moved a few steps closer. Goosebumps hatched on his arms. Sweat dribbled into his eyes. His wounded eye reacted to the salty intrusion of the sweat. How on earth was he going to search the pockets of a corpse? To make matters worse, he needed to put down the rifle to go through her pockets. That meant he would be defenceless.

Come on! You can do this. Thirty seconds, tops.

More flies joined the others circling the corpse. Black dots peppered Alice's yellow overalls. What did the bloody things have? A fly grapevine?

Marcus knelt beside Alice and laid the rifle on the ground. 'Alice?'

Alice's open eye winked at him.

Marcus shook his head. That didn't happen. No way. That was just his mind playing tricks. He swatted the flies with the back of his hands. He then fished in her left-hand pocket for the keys. Nothing, save a hot slab of dead thigh. Just touching it caused bile to rise into his throat.

Don't puke. Not now. Get a grip.

Maybe he should just go. Forget Emily. Look after number one. What was the point in risking his neck for a girl who'd thought nothing of dobbing him in to Sister Alice and the Father? He could live without Emily. He'd been doing all right before he'd met her. No, scrub that, better than all right. Plenty of drugs. Free rein to deal. The girls on the streets liked him. Ebb trusted him. All things considered, life was cool before Emily Hunt had turned his world upside down.

You love Emily.

So what if he did? What was love, anyway? It was just a word. There were plenty more fish in the sea. Particularly down on the coast. He could find another Emily and start again.

And spend the rest of your life wondering what happened to her? For once in your life, do the right thing.

Marcus crawled to the other side of Alice's body. Through her blood. He could feel it soaking through the thin fabric of his overalls. Alice's arm was in the way of her pocket. As he pulled it out of the way, her closed eye flew open and treated him to an icy stare.

Marcus gagged. A fly landed on his hand, showing no distinction between the dead and the living. Thinking Alice had reached out and touched him, Marcus screamed and jerked his arm away.

Alice seemed to watch him with those sightless eyes. Her lips were peeled back. Blood trickled from one corner of her mouth.

Marcus dry-retched several times.

Get a grip. Don't look at her face.

He fished in Alice's pocket and was rewarded with a small bunch of keys. Overcome with a curious mixture of relief and hysteria, he brayed laughter and stuffed the keys in his pocket. He then scrambled to his feet, retrieved the rifle and headed back towards the farmhouse.

Chapter Thirty-Five

Ebb pumped the empty cartridge out of the shotgun, just as Cyril had shown him many years ago when Cyril still had arms to pump with. He also remembered Cyril telling him that another cartridge would automatically load into the chamber. So that was him armed and ready to go looking for deserters.

It was as clear as the crucifixion itself that something bad had happened. Sister Alice wasn't coming back. Call it intuition. Call it premonition. Call it one big disaster after another. The truth was as plain as pasta: she'd either deserted him, or she'd been attacked by that retarded deviant, Marcus.

The traitor had already shown he was more than capable of murder; just ask that gaping hole in Brother Tweezer's back if you wanted proof of what that pudding was capable of. It took a special kind of coward to shoot a man in the back. A man without heart. A man without compassion. A man who deserved to be pinned to a cross in the Revelation Room.

Most of Ebb's clothes lay in a crumpled heap on the floor, decorated with fragments of glass. No big shakes. He would treat himself to a brand new wardrobe once he got to Thailand. He walked out of the bedroom and into the lounge, his robe hanging open. His stomach wobbled and obscured his feet. A strict diet of rice and Thai chicken should do wonders for his figure. To hell with being a vegetarian. A man needed protein to put a spring in his step. But this was no time to fret about his appearance. Not when there was a goose on the loose with a pickled egg.

***

Marcus entered the farmhouse by the back door. He stood in the kitchen and tried to listen for movement. The only thing he could hear was the sound of his heart thumping in his ears. Still, with Alice and Tweezer dead, and the Father incapacitated, it was unlikely that anyone would oppose him now.

He tiptoed past the huge pine table where The Sons and Daughters of Salvation had shared so many happy meals together. The floorboards creaked beneath his bare feet. The rifle felt slippery in his sweating palms. He wanted to put it down and wipe the sweat away, but he didn't dare let go of it; it was as if doing so would conjure Ebb from his sickbed.

He walked into the hallway. Why couldn't he breathe properly? His lungs felt as if they had surgical stockings wrapped around them. He stopped and rested against the wall, the rifle dangling by his side. It would be so much easier just to leave Emily behind. It would only take two minutes to get to the barn where the Land Rover was parked and make his getaway. Then he would be free. Free forever.

You'll never be free. Not if you leave Emily behind. Your conscience will haunt you until your dying day.

'I can't do this,' Marcus whispered to the empty hallway.

And what do you think Ebb will do to Emily? Let her keep the baby and raise it up as his own? Or do you think he'll kill them both and put them down in the Revelation Room?

He pushed himself away from the wall and moved towards the stairs. He removed the safety catch on the rifle and prayed to God that he wouldn't have to kill anyone else. By the time he reached the Sisters' Room, he was convinced he was going to throw up. He fished in his pocket for the keys, unlocked the door and pushed it open.

Dixie gawped at the rifle. 'What the fuck….'

Marcus put a finger to his lips. 'Shut up and listen. We haven't got time for questions. We're getting out of here.'

Emily stood up and put a hand to her mouth. 'What's happened?'

'Ebb knows about us. Tweezer's dead. Alice is dead. And if we don't get out of here, so are we.'

'Alice?' Dixie said. 'Who killed Alice?'

'I said no questions. We're going to nick the Land Rover and get the fuck out of here.'

'Where are we going?' Emily asked.

'As far away from here as possible.'

Maddie asked, 'But what about Ben?'

'I'm only taking you three. Ben and Bubba will have to make their own arrangements. If you've got a problem with that, then you can stay put. I don't give a shit.'

'I can't leave without him. We came here looking for Ben's dad.'

Marcus's jaw dropped. 'His dad?'

Maddie nodded. 'He's a private investigator. He was looking for Emily.'

'Looking for Emily? Why? This isn't making any sense.'

'It's a long story.'

Marcus suddenly looked as if he'd seen a ghost. 'Jesus Christ! He must be the dude in the Revelation Room. The Imposter.'

'You know where he is?' Maddie said.

Marcus nodded.

'Then we've got to go and get him. Ben, too.'

Emily asked Maddie why Ben's dad was looking for her.

'We haven't got time for this now,' Dixie said. 'But Maddie's right; we can't just leave them behind.'

Marcus looked at each woman in turn. 'All right. But we have to keep quiet. Ebb's only one floor above us.'

***

Edward Ebb hobbled down the stairs using the handrail as a crutch. The shotgun dangled by his side, primed and ready to fell the very Devil himself. His injured leg throbbed and competed with his nose for attention. He tried to focus on nice things, like chocolate and rent boys, but his mind only seemed interested in pain.

A noise on the landing. A door closing. All thoughts fled from his head. He stood stock still about halfway down the stairs. His heart banged against his ribcage, pumping blood into his ears. He let go of the handrail and held the shotgun out in front of him.

Sister Emily's whining voice drifted up the stairs. 'But where are we going to go?'

'As far away from this shit-hole as possible.'

Brother Marcus this time. Ebb crept down another two steps and watched the leaving party as it gathered outside the Brothers' Room. They were so busy whispering and conspiring that they failed to notice the shotgun aimed at their miserable heads. Brother Marcus fiddled with a bunch of keys.

How could they betray him like this? How could they be such a dirty, filthy miserable bunch of Judas Iscariots? He walked down the last few steps and stood a few yards away from the traitors. 'Going somewhere?'

Marcus dropped the keys. He made a grab for the rifle propped against the wall.

Ebb fired. The blast boomed around the landing. Marcus clutched his chest and fell against the wall. He slid to the floor, leaving a trail of blood behind him.

'That's right, Pixie-pea. You get it off your chest,' Ebb shouted, as Marcus came to rest in a heap on the floor. He pumped a fresh cartridge into the chamber and made an instant decision to shoot Dixie with his last cartridge. She was the one most likely to cause a fuss when he was out of ammunition.

Dixie walked towards him, teeth bared, Satan riding shotgun on her tongue. 'You crazy bastard.'

Ebb squeezed the trigger and blew half of Dixie's chest away. He watched a why-hast-thou-forsaken-me-Father look creep into those gypsy-blue eyes. And then he watched death draw the curtains on her miserable prostitute life.

The landing certainly needed a lick of paint now, not to mention a damned good scrub. Sister Emily and Sister Madeline would have had some busy days ahead of them if they weren't both bound for the rabbit hole.

Screams circled Ebb's head like vultures. Sister Emily knelt beside Brother Marcus, her head pressed against the remains of his chest. Young girls didn't know which side of their toast was buttered, and which side was burnt these days.

Ebb pumped the gun and released the spent cartridge. 'Would you two girls like to join Brother Marcus and Sister Dixie at God's table?'

Madeline looked at him with eyes like obituaries. He would excuse her for now because she was in shock. 'I suggest you both do as you're told from now on, if you want to remain in charge of your lives.'

Chapter Thirty-Six

After locking Emily and Madeline in the Revelation Room, Ebb went back to his living quarters and reloaded the gun with three fresh cartridges. It was one thing bluffing the women, quite another, Bubba and Benjamin. Or the Brothers Grimm as he now referred to them.

He'd managed to struggle into his black Nike tracksuit and matching Nike trainers. It had been a right royal bitch getting the tracksuit bottoms over his bandaged leg, but at least he now felt a lot more comfortable and better dressed for the journey ahead.

He studied himself in the one remaining wardrobe door. Black was a good colour. It made him look streamlined. Athletic, even. Black was also a suitable colour for mourning. The colour of grief.

He'd asked Emily and Madeline a dozen times where Sister Alice was, but either they weren't telling or they didn't know. He'd put his chips on ignorance, considering they'd both been in lockdown prior to Brother Marcus's failed rescue attempt.

Both girls had reacted badly to the Revelation Room, but they would just have to get used to it. They wouldn't be in there for long. Jesus had already instructed him to burn the bunnies as soon as possible. A new life beckoned. He would miss Penghilly's Farm, but when Jesus told you to burn bridges, you bought matches and tested wind direction.

He was sure that Sister Emily and Madeline didn't have too much to fear. Jesus would forgive them their sins and allow them safe passage to Heaven. It was unfortunate that Sister Emily had been foolish enough to let Brother Marcus impregnate her with his filthy seed, but he didn't think Jesus would hold that against her. She was still young. Her heart was open to abuse. The Lord would understand her immaturity and forgive her. Ebb would say a special prayer for Sister Emily. And Madeline. May God forgive them both.

Poor Maxine was dead. Slain by that hideous fool Marcus. He hoped that God would see fit to punish Marcus appropriately. Perhaps St Peter would mount his head on a spike outside the Pearly Gates.

Maxine would have to be buried somewhere on the farm. He didn't want her to burn with the bunnies. She was way too precious to perish in the flames. Considering Maxine had consumed most of Brother Gerald, it would be like burying Brother Gerald as well. It would certainly ensure a fertile soil for whoever took on the farm after him.

How are you going to get Max out of the Revelation Room, Pixie-pea? He weighs a ton.

Ebb jumped. He turned to face his mother's reflection in the wardrobe door. 'If you're referring to Max, the dog is a *she*. For your information, she's called Maxine.'

His mother puffed on a Woodbine. *He'll be all dead weight. And poor little Pixie-pea's a wounded soldier.*

'Shut up, whore.'

Sticks and shovels, Pixie-pea, sticks and shovels.

An idea. A good one. 'Bubba can carry her up the steps.'

Risky, Pixie. What if that streak of lightning ups and bolts?

Ebb turned away from the wardrobe. He'd had enough of shooting the breeze. 'He won't be going nowhere with a shotgun aimed at his head.'

You can't go nowhere, Pixie-pea. You can only go somewhere.

Ebb ignored her. He hobbled through his living quarters and stepped onto the tiny landing. There was so much to do before the bunnies burned. All traces of his existence had to be removed from Penghilly's Farm. Clothes, personal possessions, documents, weapons and just about everything that could be traced back to him.

He wished with all his heart that Sister Alice was still alive to help, but intuition told him she'd already been killed by that fraudster, Marcus. Why else would she be missing? It was beyond comprehension to even consider that she'd deserted him. Well, he'd just have to manage on his own. And he would. He'd single-handedly built The Sons and Daughters of Salvation from a humble concept into what it was today. You didn't accomplish such a feat by being a woolly-minded mammoth.

With the taste of Thai chicken on his tongue, and visions of burnt bunnies hopping about in his head, Ebb limped down the stairs to put the last two bunnies in the pot.

***

Ben stared out the filthy window at the motionless body lying on the ground. He couldn't tell for certain who it was, but he thought it might be Alice. The hair looked grey, but it was impossible to tell for sure with the sunlight casting shadows across the courtyard. It was also raining. Sunshine and rain. The magic ingredients for making a rainbow cake as his mother used to say when he was still young enough to think it was funny.

He'd watched Marcus search the body and then walk off towards the farmhouse. Not long after that, he'd heard two shots ring out on the landing. Maddie was dead. He knew it. There was a huge black hole in his heart telling him so. Pastor Tom would never know what had happened to his daughter. Not even a mound of earth in Rwanda to mark the spot. And it was all Ben's fault. If Stutter-buck had possessed one ounce of courage, one shred of decency, he would never have let Maddie get anywhere near The Sons and Daughters of Salvation.

Hindsight's a wonderful thing.

Ben shook his head. 'I'm just a useless c-coward.'

Bubba put a hand on Ben's shoulder, making him jump. Ben turned to him. 'Maddie's dead.'

Bubba shook his head.

Tears pricked the backs of Ben's eyes. He thumped his chest. 'She is. I c-can f-feel it inside.'

Bubba formed his thumb and forefinger into an *O*.

'She's not okay. She's dead. We're all d-d-dead.'

Bubba put both his hands on Ben's shoulders. He looked at Ben with those clear blue eyes that so reminded him of Pastor Tom. *Don't give up*, Bubba's eyes said. *Never give up.*

***

Ebb stood on the first floor landing and looked at the corpses of Brother Marcus and Sister Dixie. 'Planning to leave, were you?'

Dixie and Marcus kept shtum. Traitors the pair of them. After all he'd done for them, and this was how they repaid him. By God, you certainly found out who your friends were in a crisis.

How you gonna get them down the rabbit hole, Pixie?

Ebb spun around, expecting to see his mother standing on the stairs. Nothing, just strands of cobwebs decorating the dirty walls with silver streaks. His heart felt like a kid on a bouncy castle. He swallowed hard. His throat still felt crushed from where Tweezer had attacked him. He wouldn't be at all surprised to learn that Tweezer had inflicted permanent damage to his windpipe.

'Bubba can carry them down to the Revelation Room once Benjamin is locked away,' Ebb said. He reached down and plucked the bunch of keys from a puddle of blood.

Dixie leered at him with her best *are you looking for a good time?* grin.

Ebb studied her for a while. It was a shame how things had turned out with Sister Dixie. She'd shown so much promise to start with. Perhaps one day, when the dust had settled, he'd find it in his heart to look upon Sister Dixie fondly again. He was rather proud of the way they'd disposed of the pimp who'd controlled her miserable life with drugs, threats and sexual depravity.

He wiped the keys on his tracksuit and opened the door to the Brothers' Room. Bubba and Benjamin were standing together by the window, locked in an embrace. For one incredulous moment, he thought the two of them had embarked on a love affair. He pointed the shotgun at them.

'Lockdown is over. We have work to do.'

Benjamin looked at him with bankrupt eyes. 'What work?'

'The Lord's work.'

Ben laughed. 'The Lord's w-work? Is that what you c-call it?'

Ebb didn't care for the whiny tone of Benjamin's voice. Or for that stammer rearing its ugly head. It spoke volumes for possession. As did Benjamin's warning to Sister Alice about Cyril's death and the removal of Bubba's tongue. 'Don't question me. Put your hands on your head and walk out of the room.'

Ben did as instructed. Bubba followed him.

Ebb backed away a few steps. 'Not you, Bubba. You stay put. We've got work to do. I'll be back in ten minutes.'

Ebb waited for Ben to get onto the landing before throwing the bunch of keys on the floor. 'Lock the Brothers' Room and then get down the stairs.'

'Where are we g-going?'

Ebb smiled. 'The Revelation Room, Pixie-pea. Now move.'

Chapter Thirty-Seven

Ben walked down the basement steps and through the Cannabis Room with his mind in meltdown. He didn't care what happened to him anymore. As long as it was quick. Maybe a bullet to the back of the head.

The cannabis plants tickled his bare arms. Ebb told him to stop as they neared a door at the far end of the room. There was a large silver key protruding from the lock.

'Before you go into the Revelation Room, I want you to remember it is a sacred place. It must be treated with the utmost respect at all times.'

Ben almost laughed out loud. The image of the two corpses on the landing burned like lanterns in his mind. Unlike the body at the bottom of the tower, he'd had no trouble identifying Marcus and Dixie.

'I can't watch you all the time, Benjamin, but the Lord Jesus Christ is always watching you. Please remember that. The Lord Jesus Christ tells me everything.'

'Really? I'd n-never have g-guessed.'

'Unlock the door and go inside. We haven't got enough time to wait for you to finish a sentence.'

Ben was just about to tell him to piss off when Ebb spoke. 'I'm sure Madeline will be pleased to see you.'

Ben's breath froze. 'M-Maddie?'

'Yes, M-Maddie. Now get inside and shut the door behind you.'

Ben opened the door and stepped inside. Maddie and Emily were bent over a man lying in the corner of the room. The man looked dead.

'Close the door, Pixie-pea,' Ebb shouted.

Ben shut the door. He didn't hear Ebb lock it. Tears spilled down his cheeks. 'M-Maddie?'

Maddie hobbled towards him, her bare feet scraping against the concrete floor. The sunshine had vanished from her eyes. Her overalls were unzipped almost to the waist.

'I'm so s-sorry.'

Maddie's blonde hair looked almost brown in the dim light. It hung in loose strands over her shoulders. She stood in front of Ben. 'At least we've found your dad.'

'My d-dad?'

Maddie pointed at the man with Emily. 'He's over there, Ben.'

Ben tried to take everything in. Tried to register what he was seeing. Tweezer and Ebb's dog lying dead in the middle of the room. The skeletons pinned to the far wall. The pink wig and sunglasses perched on one of the skulls. Emily kneeling beside his father. Poor bedraggled Maddie with the sunshine missing from her eyes. There was a terrible stench. Like mould and excrement mixed with a splash of piss. Or death, perhaps.

'Your dad's alive,' Maddie said. 'But I don't think he'll last much longer if we don't get him out of here.'

'Alive?'

Maddie took Ben's hand. 'Come on. He's talking a bit.'

They limped over to Ben's father, hand in hand, Maddie's right foot dragging against the concrete floor. Ben wanted to pick her up and carry her, tell her everything would be all right, but he barely had enough strength to support himself.

Geoff Whittle had one eye open. The other was swollen shut. 'Dad?'

Geoff opened his mouth to speak. Ben noticed one of his front teeth was missing. 'You… took… your… time….'

'I'm s-sorry.'

Geoff coughed and wheezed. 'Not… your… fault….'

'It's best not to speak too much,' Emily said.

Ben felt a sudden urge to shake Emily. He asked Maddie, 'Does she know why we're here?'

'She knows, Ben.'

Emily held her hands up. 'And I'm sorry. Okay? But how was I to know this would happen?'

Maddie toucher Emily's arm. 'You didn't.'

'I loved Marcus. And now he's dead. And we're all going to die. How sorry do you want me to be?'

Ben looked at his father. It had gone past the time for blame. Emily was right; they were all going to die. 'Can't we s-sit him up?'

'I think both his legs are broken,' Maddie said. 'He can't feel anything below the waist. And he's been shot in the left shoulder and the right knee.'

'J-Jesus.'

'They shot him when he was up a tree trying to get photos of Emily.'

Ben hunkered down. He reached out and stroked his father's forehead. He didn't know what to say.

Geoff revved breath into his lungs. 'You… did… okay….'

Ben shook his head. He'd done shit, as usual. 'I sh-should have called the p-police.'

Geoff shook his head slowly. The effort seemed to drain the last dregs of energy from him.

'I know one thing,' Maddie said. 'We're not giving up.'

'What do you propose we do?' Emily said. 'Rugby tackle the Father when he comes through the door?'

'I don't know. But we can't just give up. We've got to fight.'

'I'm pregnant, in case you've forgotten.'

Maddie ignored her. 'How are you, Ben?'

'Okay,' Ben lied.

Maddie looked at Ben and chewed her lip. 'What did he do to you?'

Ben looked away before he started blubbing like a baby. 'N-nothing.'

'Maybe we can talk about it later, huh?'

Ben didn't believe there would be a *later*. 'Maybe.'

'We could ask Ebb for some water,' Maddie suggested. 'Try to negotiate with him.'

'Why would he give us water when he's going to kill us?' Emily said.

Maddie turned away. 'You don't know that.'

Emily looked at Tweezer's corpse. 'Really? So Tweezer's just resting, is he? And what about Marcus and Dixie? Just having a nice long soak in a bloodbath, are they?'

Maddie groaned. 'We have to stay positive.'

Emily rolled her eyes. End of conversation.

Ben's brain pounded against his skull. He looked at his father. Geoff Whittle was barely breathing. Blood leaked from his nose. Stutter-buck couldn't even muster words of comfort for a dying man.

Chapter Thirty-Eight

Thunder rolled across the blackened sky as Ebb stared at the lifeless body of Sister Alice. Rain lashed down on her corpse as if God himself was mourning her tragic loss. Lightning flashed across the sky.

Ebb felt an overwhelming urge to take an axe from the woodshed and chop Brother Marcus into a thousand pieces. It was obvious what had happened now. You didn't need a degree in whodunit to figure this one out. Poor Sister Alice, his fallen angel, had gone to the tower as instructed, and Brother Marcus had thrown her from the top. And then Brother Marcus had attempted to flee the scene with Dixie, Emily and Madeline.

But he didn't have time to wallow in grief like a hippopotamus in mud. Not while the Devil was on the loose. There would be plenty of time for reflection when he got to Thailand.

He pointed the shotgun at Bubba, his faithful Polish workhorse. 'Take her to the basement.'

Bubba had already carted the bodies of Marcus and Dixie to the Cannabis Room. To be fair, Bubba hadn't been in any position to refuse, but credit where credit was due, Bubba had performed well.

Bubba hoisted Sister Alice onto his shoulders. Lines creased his face. Ebb marvelled at the man's strength. He was built like a beanpole and as strong as an ox. Loyal, too. Not like the rest of them. Bubba would be rewarded for his efforts; he could die first before the fire was set.

By the time they reached the Cannabis Room, Bubba was panting like Maxine on a hot day. Marcus and Dixie both lay twisted in a tangled heap to one side of the Revelation Room door.

Ebb spat on Marcus's back with all the contempt he could muster. 'Unlock the door and take Sister Alice into the Revelation Room. Put her on the floor with Tweezer and Maxine. Okay?'

Bubba grunted.

Ebb wished he hadn't cut out Bubba's tongue; it was like trying to communicate with an ape. 'Then come back outside and put Sister Dixie and Brother Marcus inside with them.'

Bubba unlocked the door and walked into the Revelation Room. Ebb followed him inside. He looked over at the three bunnies conspiring with the Infiltrator in the corner of the room. 'You stay right where you are. Anyone so much as twitches, and I'll blow Bubba's head off.'

Bubba heaved Alice onto the floor. Her right arm landed on Maxine's muzzle. Ebb tried to make allowances for Bubba's clumsiness. He must be dog-tired.

Not as dog-tired as Maxine, Pixie-pea.

Ebb ignored his mother and pointed the shotgun at Bubba. 'Right, get the other two. Any funny business, and I'll shoot the three wise monkeys in the corner.'

Bubba dragged the bodies of Marcus and Dixie into the Revelation Room one at a time. He then stood with his hands on his hips, panting and gasping for air.

Ebb took aim and fired. The shot hit Bubba in the chest. The force knocked him backwards. He gawped at Ebb with a *what did you do that for?* look in his eyes. Ebb didn't like the look of that look. It suggested Satan might be lodging in that beanpole Pole after all.

Bubba clutched his wounded chest and staggered backwards. He fell against the skeleton of Ebb's mother. Bizarrely, Veronica Ebb seemed to pat Bubba on the head with her long, skeletal fingers. *There, there! Don't fret. Mummy's here.*

Bubba slid down the wall, dismantling the skeleton as he went. He sat motionless against the wall with his chin resting on his chest, eyes closed. No pennies required. With all the bones scattered about him, he put Ebb in mind of the world's greediest cannibal. Dark red blood bloomed on his bright yellow overalls. His right hand seemed to search the ruins of his chest for a heartbeat. His other hand rested in his lap beside Veronica Ebb's leather-bound book.

Ebb made a mental note to make sure he took all the Books of Revelation with him before the bunnies burned. And his mother's pink wig and sunglasses. Her bones would have to stay put; he didn't fancy trying to get through customs with her rattling around inside a suitcase. He was travelling light to Thailand.

'Is the Imposter still alive?' Ebb asked the three wise monkeys.

They didn't answer. For all Ebb knew, they might be using telepathy to communicate. 'Sister Emily?'

Sister Emily blanked him. No matter. Ebb was old enough and wise enough to know that you could lead a chicken to corn, but you couldn't make it peck. 'You have betrayed me, Sister Emily.'

Emily looked away.

'I took you in. Gave you food and shelter. Introduced you to the Lord Jesus Christ. And how did you repay me?'

Sister Emily rubbed her belly, comforting the bastard child.

Ebb pointed the gun at her stomach. 'By committing the vile act of copulation.'

'We loved each other,' Emily shouted, stroking her belly as if it was a crystal ball about to reveal the future.

Ebb smiled. 'Love?'

'Something you wouldn't know anything about.'

'Don't you dare mock me. I love Jesus Christ with all my heart.'

'You love no one but yourself.'

'Save your breath. I'm not listening to any more of your guff. Just remember that God is watching you and keeping a count of all your lies.'

'Watching me? What about you? A coward who's about to kill a mother and her unborn child?'

'A whore and her bastard child,' Ebb corrected. 'Anyway, God doesn't recognise the illegitimate offspring of a union between a whore and a hyena.'

'Mary Magdalen was a whore,' Maddie said.

Ebb addressed the pile of bodies on the floor. 'See how Satan leaps from tongue to tongue like an epidemic in a Third World country.'

Ben moved a few steps towards Ebb. 'L-l-let them g-go.'

Ebb turned the gun on Ben. 'What's the matter, Nostradamus, you got a frog hopping about in your throat?'

'P-please.'

Ebb shook his head. 'If you shut up and do as you're told, you won't have to suffer. You keep babbling like a brook, and you'll wish your mummy had been sporting a migraine the night you were conceived. Do I make myself clear, Pixie-pea?'

Ben looked at the floor.

'I've got chores to do, and then I need to speak to Jesus. I suggest you all take this opportunity to get down on your knees and pray to God for forgiveness.'

'Us?' Emily shouted.

Ebb ignored her. He had no time to argue the toss with a tart. He backed out of the Revelation Room and closed the door behind him. He propped the shotgun against the wall and locked all the bunnies in the boiler.

Sister Alice's death had left a huge hole in his heart. He couldn't believe that God had allowed Marcus to throw her from the tower. Why hadn't God stepped in and thrown that low-life gypsy from the tower instead?

God moves in mysterious ways, Pixie-pea.

Ebb looked among the cannabis plants for signs of his mother. For once, he felt inclined to agree with her. God could certainly be a puzzle with a piece missing at times. But it was not his place to question the motives of the Lord. He was a humble servant, and he would do well to remember that, even when stricken with grief.

He was about to pick up the shotgun when he realised there were no longer any threats necessitating the use of weapons at Penghilly's Farm. Not physical ones, anyway. All the bunnies were either dead or about to burn. His mother might well try to unsettle him, but her days of locking him in cupboards and throwing him down stairs were long gone.

Now the time had come, he was glad to be making a clean break from Penghilly's Farm. It had run its course. Served its purpose. Scrambled its eggs. He'd gone way beyond the call of duty during his time here. In future, he'd make sure he was a lot more ruthless and vigilant. He'd trusted too many people. Been too forgiving. He wouldn't make the mistake of letting emotions blur his vision again. No, sir. It didn't bear thinking about what might have happened if he hadn't come down the stairs when Brother Marcus was about to let the bunnies go.

One thing was for certain: he needed urgent medical attention. His injured leg felt as if a white-hot needle was suturing the wound. As for his nose, that mangled lump of meat was in danger of rotting away altogether. Tweezer's rancid teeth had surely given him tetanus. His first port of call would have to be a hospital. He'd have to blame Maxine for the assault on his nose, but under the circumstances he didn't think the Lord would mind a little white lie.

Better to be safe than sorry, Pixie-pea.

Ebb resisted an overwhelming urge to rifle among the cannabis plants and weed his mother out. But he had to stay focused. She was just trying to unnerve him. Pull him off course. He hobbled up the stone steps, staring straight ahead, singing Onward Christian Soldiers as heartily as his injured throat would allow.

He walked into the kitchen. He didn't bother closing the door behind him. No one could escape from the Revelation Room. Not unless Harry Houdini's ghost was acting as an advisor to the bunnies.

He made his way up the two flights of stairs to his living quarters in the converted attic. His injured leg hampered his progress, but he refused to give in to it. He was no quitter.

It was a real shame he needed to torch his living quarters. He always felt a great sense of peace when he was up there. He would often lay awake at night, looking up at the stars. They reminded him of tiny specks of hope.

Careful not to cut himself on the fragments of glass, he took the rest of his clothes out of the wardrobe and threw them onto the bed. It would be a shame to burn them, but clothes could always be replaced.

With the wardrobe cleared out, he moved on to his oak dresser and added socks, vests and Calvin Klein boxers to the pile on the bed. He then retrieved a glass jar from behind a stash of gay pornographic magazines in the bottom drawer. He held the jar up to the light. Bubba's tongue no longer looked capable of telling tales. The formaldehyde had preserved it well, even though it no longer looked tickled pink to see him.

Poor Bubba was now sitting up at God's top table, and Ebb certainly didn't deny the wiry Pole his eternal peace. If anyone deserved a rest, then it was that tongue-tied Pixie.

Ebb put the jar down on the bed. His head was pounding like a steam press.

What are you gonna do if they stop you at customs with a pickled tongue, Pixie?

His mother's voice seemed to come from beneath his underwear. The thought of her being anywhere near his boxers turned his stomach sour. But, for the second time that day, he felt inclined to listen to mama. It *would* look suspicious hobbling through customs with nothing to declare other than Bubba's tongue, a pink wig and the three Books of Revelation. Perhaps it might be prudent to bury the tongue and the books somewhere in England before heading off to pastures new. The wig and sunglasses wouldn't cause any suspicion, other than indicating a tendency towards transvestitism.

He went to the wardrobe and grabbed a small black holdall. He put the glass jar in the bottom and then covered the jar with a smattering of socks and boxers. He added a Bible and a small silver cross from his bedside table. He emptied the contents of his bathroom cabinet into the holdall, along with the pills and potions from the kitchen cupboards. He would have taken his stash of chocolate from the fridge, but the heat would only turn it into treacle. Instead, he scoffed two Mars Bars and washed them down with a bottle of Lucozade Sport.

After an hour of rummaging through his quarters, he hobbled down the stairs, through the kitchen and out to the barn. How he wished Sister Alice was with him. She had a good eye for detail. And a calm and ordered mind. At least she did before Brother Marcus defied the will of Jesus Christ and threw her from the top of the tower.

Putting the holdall on the passenger seat of the Land Rover, Ebb retrieved two ten-litre cans of petrol from the back of the barn and returned to the farmhouse. He put one can on the kitchen table and then climbed the stairs to his quarters for the last time.

Even though he was glad to be leaving, some of his fondest memories were wrapped up in Penghilly's Farm. But this was no time for sentimentality. No, sir. His memories would always be locked inside his head. The value of his work would never be forgotten.

He took the cap off the can and emptied petrol over the clothes on his bed. Leaving a trail of petrol between the bedroom and the living room, he moved out of his quarters and down to the first floor landing. He doused the beds with fuel in the Brothers' and Sisters' rooms and then continued down the stairs leaving a trail of petrol behind him.

He threw the empty can onto the floor in the hallway and walked into the kitchen. He took the second can off the table and unscrewed the cap. If he'd had more time, he might have tried to rig up explosives. Gone out with a bang, you might say. But Satan had forced his hand somewhat.

The ventilation system in the Cannabis Room would fan the flames. The bunnies would all get as high as kites before they burned. Obviously, that depended on whether God was in a merciful mood. Ebb didn't think it wise for the bunnies to pin their hopes on God's mercy. God wouldn't forget all their lies and treachery in a hurry. No, sir.

He poured a good splash of petrol on the gas cooker and then limped down the basement steps. He would turn on all the rings before he left. The sugar rush from the Mars Bars and the Lucozade was already wearing off. His throat felt like a bog about to conjure toads. He placed the can on the floor. The smell was overpowering. The ventilation system seemed to stir up the stench.

Maybe you should have tied the bunnies up, Pixie.

Ebb shook his head. There was no time for that. He had a shotgun to keep those rabbits in their burrow. One move, and he would pebble-dash the walls with what remained of their corrupted minds.

He picked the gun up. Two cartridges left. More than enough for a few loose bunnies.

Chapter Thirty-Nine

B en sat on the floor beside his father. The old man was as good as dead. There was a nasty gurgling noise in the back of his throat that reminded Ben of blocked drains. Ben held his hand. He didn't care about dying anymore. Death just meant an end to all of this pain and suffering.

Maddie stood near Bubba, looking through Veronica Ebb's *Book of Revelation*. 'This was Ebb's mother.'

'I didn't know monsters like him had mothers,' Emily said.

Maddie leafed through a few pages and then stopped. She read for a few minutes, and then said, 'He beat her to death with a shovel.'

'And there was m-me thinking he was n-normal.'

Maddie closed the book. 'He was only sixteen when he did it.'

'That m-makes me feel a lot b-better.'

Maddie walked over to Ben with the book in her hand. 'I've had an idea.'

Ben didn't care. The time for ideas had long since vanished. He felt his father's wrist for a pulse. He was rewarded with a faint beat. 'I—'

'So what's this great idea, Madeline?' Emily said. 'I can't wait to hear it.'

'My name's Maddie.'

'Pardon me.'

Maddie held up Veronica Ebb's *Book of Revelation*. 'This book obviously means a lot to Ebb, right?'

Emily shrugged. 'So?'

'So if I destroy it, he'll get distracted. Then you and Ben can attack him and get the gun.'

'Or he might just blow your head off.'

'Have you got a better idea?'

'Yeah. Maybe you should put the wig on and pretend to be his mother. That would really mess with his head.'

'That might actually work.'

'I was joking. Bloody hell. J-O-K-E. Joke! You put that wig on, and you'll just freak him out even more. For God's sake, Maddie, do us all a favour and don't have any more ideas.'

'Emily's r-right. The best thing to d-do now is p-p-pray.'

'We can't just wait to die,' Maddie said. 'We got to do something.'

'Why don't you put the sunglasses on as well?' Emily said. 'Really throw him off the scent.'

Maddie looked away. 'I don't hear you coming up with any suggestions.'

'That's because there's nothing left to suggest.'

The key turned in the lock, putting an end to the conversation.

Ben gripped his father's hand. This was it. Crunch time. His heart felt as if it was trying to beat its way out of his chest.

Ebb opened the door and walked a few feet inside the Revelation Room. He put the petrol can on the floor and then walked back outside and retrieved the shotgun. He aimed it in the general direction of the group cowering in the corner. 'Good afternoon, bunnies.'

The bunnies didn't answer.

'Benjamin?'

Ben focussed all his attention on his father.

'If you don't want me to blow Madeline's head off her shoulders, Benjamin Bunny, you'd better pay me some respect.'

'What?'

'Stand up and move away from the Imposter. I want you to drag Bubba's body over there with the others.'

'My h-hands hurt.'

'Hurt, my eye. If you're referring to your reaction to the holy water, then I'm afraid that won't wash with me. The time for excuses is up, Pixie-pea. If you want to remember Madeline with a head, you'd better get going.'

Ben gave his father's hand a final squeeze. It was a see you in heaven squeeze. He forced himself to stand. His left leg was numb. The thought of touching Bubba's lifeless body made his blood run cold. Poor Bubba, who'd suffered so much at the hands of Ebb.

Ben hobbled to where Bubba sat propped against the wall. The top half of the big man's yellow overalls was stained red. His eyes were closed. His mouth hung open. A thin line of blood had dribbled from the corner of his mouth and down the side of his chin.

Ben tried not to look at Bubba. Tried to focus. He turned around and looked at Maddie. He wanted to tell her he loved her. Tell her he wished they'd had a chance to do the simple things most people took for granted.

Maddie smiled at him. For the briefest moment, the sunshine returned to her eyes. And then it vanished. Hidden behind a veil of tears.

You must do what's right, son, Pastor Tom said, from somewhere deep within Ben's mind.

Ben almost laughed out loud at the absurdity of it. How the hell did you do what's right when everything was so damned wrong? He stood more chance of giving Bubba the kiss of life. He grabbed Bubba's hands. Still warm. Something thick and noxious filled his throat.

'What have you got there, Pixie-pea?'

'N-nothing.'

'Not you, Stutter-bunny. I'm talking to Madeline.'

Maddie put the book behind her back, 'I—'

'Don't play games with me. I know you've got my mother's book. A little bunny told me. Now, you go and get the other two books from Brother Cyril and Brother Gerald. Bring them to me.'

Maddie looked at Ben.

'D-do it.'

Ebb grinned. 'You'll listen to the stutter-bunny if you know what's good for you.'

Ben stared at Ebb. Maybe he could rush him, knock him off balance.

In your dreams, Stutter-buck.

Ben watched Maddie gather the books from the breastbones of the other two skeletons. He wanted to push his fingers into Ebb's eyes and gouge them from their sockets. Rip out the pages of those books and stuff them right down Ebb's throat. Make him eat his words. But poor old Stutter-buck could only look down from the conker tree as the other kids hurled sticks and insults at him.

Ebb levelled the gun at Maddie's head. 'Put the books on the floor and then get over there with the Fallen Angel and the Imposter.'

Go on, Stutter-buck, j-j-jump!

Maddie placed the books on the floor in front of Ebb. 'You'll go to Hell for this.'

'Evil always licks its finger to test an ill wind.'

Maddie stood up straight and tall. 'I don't have a clue what you're talking about. You'll have to answer to God one day. I hope I'm there to see it.'

'You'll see nothing when you're engulfed in the flames of Hell. Now get over there with the bunnies.'

Maddie walked to the corner of the room and took Emily's hand.

Ebb turned his attention back to Ben. 'Drag Bubba to the pyre.'

You're going to die, anyway. Ben thought. *Rush him. What have you got to lose?*

Ebb pointed the shotgun at Ben's head. 'Do it. Now!'

Ben pulled Bubba away from the wall. As he applied more pressure, he felt Bubba grip his hand. He then noticed the shallow rise and fall of Bubba's chest. Confused, he looked over his shoulder at Ebb.

'What's wrong, Stutter-bunny?'

Bubba squeezed his hand.

Inch by painful inch, he dragged Bubba into the middle of the room. His lungs felt like two punctured tyres.

'Right, Benjamin, I want you to put the bodies into two separate piles. Maxine is to be laid to rest beneath Sister Alice, with brother Bubba on top. That's the good pile. And then I want you to put Brother Tweezer on top of Sister Dixie, with Brother Marcus on top of him. That's the bad pile. Have you got that?'

Ben didn't answer. He bent over and rested his hands on his knees.

Ebb looked along the barrel of the gun. 'I think it's fitting that the whore should lay beneath the rapist.'

'God will be so pleased with you,' Maddie said.

Ebb ignored her. 'I wanted to bury poor Maxine in the North Field, but with Bubba out of action, and my leg gnawed to the bone, I'm afraid she must perish in the flames along with the rest of you. But this is no time for recriminations. Get going, Stutter-bunny.'

'I c-can't do it.'

'Don't be such a baby. I'm only asking you to move two bodies.'

'He's exhausted,' Maddie said.

'So was Jesus of Nazareth, but I don't recall him complaining he couldn't carry his own cross because he had a splinter in his finger.'

'Ben isn't Jesus.'

'It's all right. I'll d-do it.'

Ebb slapped the stock of the gun twice. 'Chop chop, then.'

As Ben bent close to Bubba, the big man winked at him. Just a slight flicker of an eyelid. This one small movement gave Ben strength. He rolled Alice on top of Max. The dog emitted an awful belch of gas as Alice's weight expelled air from its corpse. Both of Alice's eyes were open, staring at the ceiling as if seeking salvation. The skin around her neck hung in loose folds. Her hands rested on the filthy concrete floor, left index finger pointing at the skeletons. A faint smile played upon her lips as if she had some secret knowledge only obtainable through death.

'Look what that swine Marcus did to Alice,' Ebb said. 'The Lord will toast his head on a pitchfork for this.'

Ben tried to shut Ebb's words out of his head. They buzzed around his brain like a swarm of angry bees seeking a hive. He dragged Bubba over to the good pile. Bubba helped Ben by taking some of the weight as he hauled him on top of Alice and the dog.

'Well done, Benjamin. Jesus has asked me to spare you from the flames. You will be shot before the bunnies burn.'

'You're going to kill us all? Just like that?' Emily shouted.

'I'd be careful about pointing the finger of blame in my direction. It's *you* that's got everyone into this mess by fornicating with Brother Marcus. If you'd kept your knickers on, Tweezer would be pinned to a cross by now, and The Sons and Daughters of Salvation would be breaking bread around the dinner table.'

'Marcus loved me.'

Ebb scoffed. 'You wouldn't know what love was if it bit you on the buttock.'

'We loved each other.'

'Very touching. Perhaps you can remind yourself of this delusion whilst you burn.'

'Why are you doing this?' Maddie asked. 'What have we done to you?'

'Done to me? Oh, heavens, Madeline, nothing. It's the Lord Jesus Christ that you've insulted and betrayed.'

'You murdered Marcus,' Emily shouted.

'And Brother Marcus murdered my faithful dog, Maxine. He also murdered Brother Tweezer in cold blood, so stick that on your abacus and add it to the sum total of his miserable existence. Anyway, I've had enough of this nonsense. There's an apple pie in the oven and petrol evaporating on the stairs. Arrange Brother Tweezer, Brother Marcus and Sister Dixie as requested, Pixie-pea.'

Ben could see the faintest rise and fall of Bubba's chest. He was amazed Ebb couldn't see it. He arranged the other three bodies in their hideous union beside Bubba, Alice and Maxine.

'You may or may not want to join me in prayer,' Ebb said. 'I accept that The Sons and Daughters of Salvation is now defunct, so the choice is yours.'

'I'll pray that you go to Hell,' Maddie promised.

Ebb ignored her and bowed his head. 'Dear Father, I ask that you find it in your heart to forgive these wretched misguided souls.'

Ben stared at Bubba. Apart from the obvious fact that the big man was still alive, there was something else that offered a possible lifeline. But what?

Ebb droned on. 'I have done all you have asked of me, Lord. My time is finished here. I trust you will find it in your heart to offer salvation to those who have earned it, and forgiveness for those who seek it.'

I might only have one eye, but I can see that dog clear enough, Old Joe piped up in Ben's head.

'Bless this house, Lord, and bless all the bunnies that burn in her. Amen.'

Ben took a step forward. *The dog. The bloody dog! Ebb cared about that dog more than anything else in the world.*

Ebb thrust the gun at him. 'Stand still, Pixie-pea.'

Ben pointed at the bodies.

'What?'

Ben took another step. 'M-Maxine.'

Ebb glanced at the dog. 'What about her?'

Ben whined in the back of his throat. He threw his voice so as it sounded as if the noise was coming from beneath Bubba and Alice.

Ebb moved towards the bodies. 'Maxine?'

Ben whined again. A long pitiful sound in the back of his throat.

Ebb waved the gun at Ben. 'Get over there with the other bunnies, Pixie-pea. You so much as move or twitch, and I'll blow your head clean off your shoulders.'

Ben did as he was told. He waited for Ebb to get close to the bodies before he whined again.

'Maxine? Is that you, girl?'

Ben hiccupped a tiny bark and threw it right out there in front of Ebb. Old Joe would have been proud.

Ebb lowered the gun and reached down to grab hold of the dog's tail.

Bubba struck with the speed and accuracy of a rattle snake. He twisted around and grabbed the shotgun halfway along the barrel. He yanked it hard enough to tip Ebb off balance. Ebb pulled the trigger as he fell forwards, blasting a hole in the concrete floor. Bubba let go of the gun as Ebb hit the deck. The gun landed a few feet away from them.

Go on, Stutter-buck, j-j-j-jump!

Ben jumped. He rushed forwards and threw himself onto Ebb's back. Ebb twisted his head from side to side and howled like a wolf at a full moon.

What you gonna do now, Stutter-buck? Piggyback him to death?

Ebb thrashed and bucked. 'My dog.'

Ben wrapped his arm around Ebb's throat and squeezed with every ounce of strength left in his body. Ebb made an awful hissing noise. Ben squeezed harder. He could hear someone screaming in the background.

Something crawled on Ben's face. For one wild moment, he thought it was a giant spider. And then he realised it was Ebb's hand. Too late. Ebb pushed his index finger into Ben's right eye. White hot pain erupted in Ben's eye socket. He screamed and relaxed his grip on Ebb's throat.

Ebb threw Ben off his back and crawled towards the shotgun. 'Maxine?'

Maxine didn't respond.

Ben tried to force himself to act, but the searing pain in his eye rendered him useless.

A low guttural growl. Ben thought the dog had actually come back to life. And then Ebb's rasping voice: 'Put the gun down, Bubba. Put the gun down. Right now!'

Bubba stood over Ebb, the shotgun aimed at his tormentor's head.

'Just you remember that the Lord Jesus Christ is watching you.'

Bubba growled and thrust the gun at Ebb.

'If you do as I say, you can come with me, Bubba. I'll spare you.'

Bubba shook his head.

Ebb kneeled in front of Bubba with his hands clasped before him. 'It's your only chance of salvation.'

Bubba pumped the gun and expelled a spent cartridge.

'Think about it, Bubba. We've been together for a long time. We're practically brothers. You can come to Thailand with me and start a new life. We'll buy a proper working farm. I'll even let you have full control of the land. How does that sound?'

Bubba shook his head and spat on the ground.

Ben turned to Maddie and Emily. 'We need to call the cops.'

'He's got a phone in his living quarters,' Emily said. 'Along with all his other luxuries.'

'Call an ambulance, Maddie,' Ben said. 'Tell them there are five dead bodies as well as the injured. And then call the cops.'

Ebb pointed at Ben. 'I'm not having those agents of the Devil—'

'It doesn't matter what you think anymore,' Ben said. 'You're finished.'

'So you *can* speak after all, Stutter-bunny. It's amazing what you can do when you put your tongue to it.'

Ben ignored him. 'Go, Maddie. Now!'

Maddie walked to the door. She turned back to face Ben. 'Please be careful.'

Ebb looked up at Bubba. 'You can have whatever you want, Bubba. Women. Slaves. Wealth beyond your wildest dreams.'

Bubba spat on the ground again.

Ebb reached out and made a grab for Bubba's ankle.

The gun roared just as Maddie walked into the Cannabis Room. She didn't see Ebb's head explode in a kaleidoscope of blood and bone and brain matter. She didn't see him fall forward and land with his right hand almost touching Max's tail.

And for that, Ben thanked Pastor Tom's God from the bottom of his heart.

Chapter Forty

Ben stood beside his father's hospital bed. It was weird viewing the world through one eye. The patch covering his injured eye meant he had to twist his head sideways to see anything on his blind side. At least the eye was going to be all right. Ebb hadn't inflicted any permanent damage.

Geoff Whittle was asleep. Ben thought sleep was the best place for him. There were tubes all over his body. Two were taped to his hand, one of which connected to a bag of saline hanging from a portable trolley. Most of his facial wounds looked a lot better now they'd been cleaned.

The consensus among hospital staff was that his father was lucky to be alive. Geoff didn't seem to agree. He considered himself bloody well unlucky to have been captured by Edward Ebb in the first place.

Maddie added another bunch of grapes to the overflowing fruit bowl. 'Do you think I should get rid of some of this stuff? Those bananas look rank.'

'Wouldn't be a bad idea.'

'He told me he doesn't even like fruit.'

'Try telling that to Mum. She thinks that fruit and fruit alone will get him on his feet again. Never mind he's got a cracked vertebra.'

Maddie dropped a rotten banana into the empty bag. 'She means well.'

After a slight pause, Ben said, 'I don't reckon he'll walk again.'

'You don't know that.'

'He's broken his spine, Maddie. Not to mention what Ebb did to him. I'm just trying to be realistic.'

'One day at a time.'

'Do you remember that doctor who told him to take "one step at a time"?'

'I thought your dad was going to get out of the bed and hit him.'

'He had a good go.'

Geoff's broken legs were encased in a cast and hoisted up at a forty-five-degree angle. His shattered shoulder was bandaged and his arm set in a sling. He'd lost a lot of weight, mostly down to his refusal to eat anything other than mashed potato and an occasional banana. The nutrients dripping into his veins did little to replace home-cooked meals, even ones of the culinary calibre of Anne Whittle. At the moment, Geoff was surviving mainly on a diet of retribution and threats.

He opened one eye and peered at his son. 'What time is it?'

Ben jumped. His father always seemed to catch him off guard. Ben glanced at his watch. 'Nearly midday.'

Geoff coughed and hacked something into his mouth which he swallowed with a grimace. 'Give me some water. I'm parched.'

Maddie picked up a glass of water and a straw from the nightstand. She held the straw to Geoff's lips. He took a mouthful and then spat out the straw. 'It's bloody warm.'

'Shall I get you some fresh?' Maddie offered.

'No. Let them do it. I pay enough taxes. Press that red button on the side of the bed.'

Ben wished his father would keep his thoughts to himself. He pressed the button.

'Sit down, boy. You look like you need the toilet.' And then to Maddie. 'You, too, love. Take a pew.'

They sat down. After a brief altercation concerning the level of care, a nurse brought Geoff a fresh glass of water. He let Maddie help him with the drink. Finished, he looked at Ben. 'How's mother?'

Flapping, fretting and worrying, Ben thought. 'She's all right. She's gone to Aunt Mary's for lunch.'

'Lunch? She'll be lucky to get a slice of cucumber on a Ryvita with that one.'

Ben smiled. Aunt Mary was going through what his mother called a *skinny phase*. Ever since Ben could remember, Aunt Mary had been going through a *skinny phase* or a *fat phase*. Ben didn't care. He liked Aunt Mary, fat or thin.

'Is she coming in to see me today?'

Ben nodded. 'Tonight.'

'Tell her no more fruit. I'll turn into a bloody gibbon if I eat another banana.'

Ben smiled. It was pointless telling his mother anything once she'd set her mind. 'I'll try.'

Geoff sighed. 'I want to go home. I'll never get better in here. I can't even get a decent night's sleep with that old bugger over there snoring like a train.'

Ben didn't want to think about the logistics of accommodating his father at home. Where would they put him? He wasn't in any fit state to get up the stairs to his bedroom. The thought of trying to cater for his father's bathroom needs filled Ben with a dread matched only by memories of Penghilly's Farm. He was better off here until they could adapt the house. In the long run, they would need to an extension built so his father could have a downstairs bedroom and en-suite shower.

Geoff asked Maddie how Bubba was.

'Bubba's fine. He loves the spare room. I suppose after Penghilly's Farm, it seems like a luxury hotel. Dad's going to give him a job when he's well enough to work.'

'At the church?'

Maddie nodded. 'Dad's teaching him sign language at the moment.'

Ben remembered the countless hours Pastor Tom had spent teaching him how to use Old Joe to overcome his stammer. He was sure Bubba and Pastor Tom would get on great together.

'And what about you? How are you coping?'

'I'm okay, Mr Whittle.'

'You saved my life. I won't ever forget that.'

'I didn't do—'

'What you did was brilliant. I hope that bloody girl's grateful.'

'We went to see her last night, but she's gone to stay with her Gran. Just while she gets back on her feet.'

'She looked quite capable of standing last time I saw her.'

Maddie helped herself to a grape. 'She lost the baby.'

'What baby?'

'She was pregnant.'

'Who the hell got her pregnant? Not that ranting lunatic, Ebb?'

'One of the cult members,' Ben said. 'Marcus. He died.'

'Stupid girl. Whatever was she thinking of?'

Ben didn't want to be drawn on the rights and wrongs of Emily Hunt's behaviour. 'Emily's dad says if we need anything, just let him know.'

'Has he coughed up yet?'

'In full. And he's given us a five grand bonus.'

'That should go a long way to curing me.'

Ben understood his father's frustration. 'We just need to take it one day at a time. Like we did in that basement.'

'Cellar,' Geoff corrected. 'We're in England, not America.' And then to Maddie, 'Could you give us a moment, love?'

'Sure. I'll go grab a coffee.'

When she left, Geoff looked at Ben and smiled. The smile was shaky around the edges. 'You did well, son. I'm proud of you. You put yourself on the line for me, and that makes you a man in my book.'

Ben struggled with the praise. 'Thanks.'

'And I'll tell you this for nowt: if you had called the cops, and they'd shown up at the farm, Ebb would have killed us all. He thought I was a cop.'

'He got that half right; you used to be.'

'And then he thought I was Satan. Then a cop again. And then an agent of the Devil. He used to come down the cellar every day trying to get me to confess. One day he'd act all nice, bringing me soup and water, the next he'd threaten me with a shovel and pour acid on me.'

Ben wanted to tell his father what Ebb had done to him on the cross, but it seemed irrelevant at the moment. 'It must have been terrible for you.'

'And he talked to those bloody skeletons. Full blown conversations. Particularly the one in the hideous pink wig.'

'That was his mother.'

'Jesus Christ.'

'He beat her to death with a shovel.'

'It doesn't bear thinking about.' And then after a few moments, 'What gave you the idea to mimic the dog?'

Ben wanted to tell his father about Old Joe and Pastor Tom. How Tom had taught him to throw his voice, but he didn't want to talk about his childhood. Not now. Perhaps never. 'I don't know. It was just a spur of the moment thing. I knew how much that dog meant to him, so I thought it might distract him.'

'Nothing short of heroic, son. Bloody heroic.'

'Thanks.'

Geoff changed the subject. 'You look like a pirate with that patch. How long do you have to wear it?'

'Just until the swelling goes down.'

'Thank God he didn't blind you.'

Ben looked at his hands. The hands that had attacked Edward Ebb. He still couldn't believe that he'd found the courage to do it.

'Look, son, I won't beat about the bush. We've got to face facts. I might never walk again.'

'You don't know that, Dad.'

'Whatever happens, I won't be fit enough to go out on operations anymore. My days of climbing trees are behind me. I'm in my mid-fifties as it is. To tell you the truth, I've been wanting to hand over the reins for a long time, but I didn't think you were up to it.'

'I know.'

'But I was wrong. I never gave you the chance to prove yourself. Ever since you could talk, I was telling you to shut up. I thought I could mould you into a man, just like my father did to me. But I was wrong. You're different to me and Granddad. We both thrived on discipline. You seem to have more of your mother's genes in you.'

Ben grinned. 'You saying I'm a girl?'

'I'm just saying you're sensitive. But that doesn't make you any less of a man. Maybe it makes you more of a man. Anyway, you've shown me you're more than capable of stepping into the breach. The job's yours if you want it.'

'But what are you going to do?'

'I'll run the office and do what I can once I'm in better shape.'

Ben's mind was caught in a no-man's-land between elation and doubt.

'Take your time and have a think about it. I'm not pressurising you into doing anything. I've done enough of that up to now.'

'I don't need to think about it. It would be an honour to work as a private investigator for Whittle Investigations.'

'You sure?'

'Yes.'

'Good. Now bugger off. I need to rest. And take that young lady out for a meal. On me.'

'Are you sure?'

'Of course I'm bloody sure. Why else would I have said it?'

Ben didn't walk out of ward 5C. He floated on legs filled with helium. He took a lift down to level two and found Maddie in the League of Friends canteen. Maddie waved. At him! How cool was that?

Ben grinned. 'Do you fancy going out for a meal?'

'I'm skint.'

'Don't worry about that. It's on the old man.'

'Then I'd love to.'

'Italian?'

'Italian would be great.'

266

They left the canteen and took the stairs down to ground level. They walked out of the hospital into a beautiful, warm summer afternoon. Ben stopped and turned to Maddie. 'How do you fancy working with me?'

'Doing what?'

'My dad's put me in charge of investigations. I wondered if you wanted to help? Be my assistant? You don't have to if you don't want to.'

Maddie smiled and poured sunshine into those beautiful green eyes. 'I'd love to, Ben.'

Ben wanted to kiss her. He wanted to hug her tight and declare his undying love from the rooftops. 'Cool,' he said, before almost walking into a bollard and stubbing his toe on the kerb.

The End

A Note from Bloodhound Books

Thanks for reading The Revelation Room We hope you enjoyed it as much as we did. Please consider leaving a review on Amazon or Goodreads to help others find and enjoy this book too.

We make every effort to ensure that books are carefully edited and proofread, however occasionally mistakes do slip through. If you spot something, please do send details to info@ bloodhoundbooks.com and we can amend it.

Bloodhound Books specialize in crime and thriller fiction. We regularly have special offers including free and discounted eBooks. To be the first to hear about these special offers, why not join our mailing list here? We won't send you more than two emails per month and we'll never pass your details on to anybody else.

Readers who enjoyed The Revelation Room will also enjoy *The Abbatoir of Dreams also by Mark Tilbury.*
Ice Cold Alice by CP Wilson.

Acknowledgements

I'd like to say a huge thank you to all those who have helped with the creation and promotion of The Revelation Room, especially Fred and Betsy and all at Bloodhound Books

Thanks to Lesley Jones who edited the first draft, and helped me to see how the story could be improved, and to Maggie James who gave her time to beta read the book.

Also, a huge thank you to my girlfriend, Cassie, who helps with all aspects of social media.

Printed in Great Britain
by Amazon